THE CRIMSON DIMENSION

D.A. VandenBrink

LAMPREY PUBLISHING LTD.

The Crimson Dimension
D.A. VandenBrink

This is a work of fiction. Names, characters, businesses, places, events, locales, and incidents are either the products of the author's imagination or used in a fictitious manner. Any resemblance to actual persons, living or dead, events, locals, or business establishments is purely coincidental.

Published by Lamprey Publishing Ltd.
www.lampreypublishing.com
Copyright © 2020, D.A. VandenBrink
Edited by Danielle Fine
Cover by Danielle Fine

All Rights Reserved. This book may not be reproduced, transmitted, or stored in whole or part in any means, including graphic, electronic, or mechanical without the express written consent of the publisher except in the case of brief quotations embodied in critical articles and reviews.

For information: d.a.vandenbrink@outlook.com
ISBN: 978-1-7770470-0-9

THE
CRIMSON
DIMENSION

To Janis

ACKNOWLEDGMENTS

While sorting through an old box of memorabilia, my wife to be, Janis, pulled out a folded piece of paper. "What's this?" she asked, as the pencil scribbling had faded so badly it was practically illegible.

"Oh, that..." I dismissed. "I once had an idea for a story."

After a brief narration, she placed the paper in the "keep" pile.

"You have to write it."

Thank you for all your encouragement, love, and support.

This story would not have been possible without my wonderful editor, Danielle Fine. Thank you for your incredible patience through this process. I have learned so much from you as we slogged through my manuscript.

PROLOGUE

Germany, 1933

William knelt before his two adversaries, hands bound behind his back. Sweat and blood dripped from his bowed head onto the floor as he fought to remain conscious. He glanced up at the pistol pressed to the back of Robert's head. What in the Hell were they going to do?

The Warrior, bloodied and leaning heavily on his flaming two-handed sword, was unable to help. William knew the rules all too well. The angel couldn't act until he or Robert did their part, and that clearly wasn't going to happen.

"Goodbye, my friend." Robert closed his eyes and swallowed. "It's been—"

The gun went off without warning, spraying blood and brains all over the carpet. William retched and squeezed his eyes shut. Any thought of escape vanished as Robert's body hit the floor with a wet thud.

Despite the inevitable, he refused to give them the satisfaction of taking his dignity along with his life. He gathered his last shred of composure, straightened, and stared into the Shakath's haunting red eyes.

"Go ahead, demon. Get it over with." He turned to the one who now held the gun to his head. "What are you waiting for?"

"Dmoltech wants the honor," Athamm replied. "I would love to finish you off, but I have my orders."

"What's the difference? Dead is dead."

"You don't understand." Nazkiel gripped William's chin and smiled. "You're the last Torren, and all the blood sources have been destroyed."

"You lie." This battle was lost, but he refused to believe God would allow their extinction. Hans and Alexander had the sources well hidden.

William gasped when Nazkiel tossed their signet rings to the floor. There was no denying the truth. The rope cut into his wrists as he tried to break free. He couldn't give up now; he couldn't die. He had to find a way out...but how? He looked to the Warrior for any sign of hope. The angel could barely stand, blood flowing over his snow-white skin from the gaping wound above his right eye. His alarmed gaze was fixed on something behind William, who turned to see Dmoltech's horrific form filling the doorway.

"Always a slave to your master's rules," Dmoltech said to the Warrior. A molten sphere appeared in his hand. "If He only considered how easy they made it to destroy you all."

The battered angel lifted the sword and deflected the fireball as it raced toward him, but he lacked the strength to fend off the second. The sword hit the ground as he exploded in a blinding flash.

A tear ran down William's cheek. He was mankind's last hope, the only one who could prevent the demons from establishing their dominion, and he was helpless. Dmoltech crossed the room, gripped William's neck, and squeezed.

The Torren were no more.

CHAPTER 1

Present Day

"I'll raise you twenty," Matt announced, pushing his chips toward the pot. His challenging look never wavered as he stared down his friend.

"Damn you." Justin studied his cards then Matt's face. "That'll put me all in."

"I know." Matt ran his fingers through his mess of sand-colored hair. "Do ya have the guts to call?" Matt knew he wouldn't risk being knocked out of the game.

"Bastard." Justin tossed his cards down. "I fold."

Matt grinned as he turned his hand over. "I had absolutely nothing."

"I knew it!" Justin threw his hands up in surrender. "I should've just given you my money when I walked in the door and gone right to watching the hockey game."

Matt pulled the chips toward his ever-increasing stack. "That's right, boys. You're all goin' down. Now you know how my broke ass can afford my share of the rent in this lovely abode."

Matt surveyed his opponents' chips. Justin was almost done, Chris was holding his own, like always, but his girlfriend, Megan, would soon be out. Eric currently had the largest stack, but not for long.

"I'm comin' for you, big guy. Enjoy your lead while you have it."

"You're always such a lucky fucker," Eric answered.

"God must've blessed you with horseshoes up your ass."

Matt raised an eyebrow. "There is no God. It's science, boys, pure science. I win because of probabilities, strategy, and the simple fact that you suck." Matt launched a pretzel at Eric.

Justin intercepted the pretzel and stuffed it in his mouth. "God, science, whatever. I wouldn't mind losing my money to you as long as I ended up with Rob's. I hate being the worst player in the room." He counted his remaining chips. "Where the hell is he, anyway?"

Matt's smile faded. "Where else? Out with Kathy."

"What's the matter with him?" Chris asked. "He's really wussing out on us lately. He's missed the last three games."

"It's Kathy," Justin said.

"Cut them some slack," Megan interjected. "They're planning their wedding, for God's sake."

"I know they have a lot of shit to do," Justin said. "But he promised he'd be here tonight. This is the last time some of us will see him before he's married. Our last chance to clean him out before she gets her hands on his money."

Matt wanted to join in on the rant, but held back. Rob was like a brother to him. They always had each other's backs, no matter what. "I reminded him about tonight. There's not much more I can do." He dealt the next hand. "Things will go back to normal after the wedding."

"Are you delusional?" Justin mocked. "She's got him by the short and curlies. He won't play another hand of poker in his life."

Okay, so that was a little exaggerated, but in many ways, Justin was bang on. Kathy had a way of dominating Rob, and she made no secret of the fact that she didn't approve of her fiancé spending time with his single friends. But no matter how hard she might try, Matt refused to allow her to squeeze him out of Rob's life.

"He should never have let her start ordering him around," Justin went on. "Women need to be put in their place."

"What do you know about women?" Megan challenged Justin. "The only romance you'll ever know is with a tub of hand cream and a box of Kleenex."

"That's right." Matt kept the conversation moving away from Rob. "Have you ever had a girlfriend?" He grinned wickedly and held up a hand. "Sheep don't count."

"Not so fast, Casanova." Megan turned her attention to Matt. "Why are you still single? You're good-looking, a lot of fun, driven—"

"Hey! I'm right here." Chris poked her in the ribs. "Remember me?"

Ignoring her boyfriend, Megan tapped her finger on the table a few times then pointed at Matt. "I know. I have the perfect person for you. My cousin's friend...she has a thing for blue-eyed jocks—"

"Thanks, but no." The last thing Matt wanted was to be part of another disastrous relationship. His parents' marriage was a drunken, abusive nightmare, and his last relationship had ended in heartbreak. His string of one- or two-night stands was working just fine for him.

"She's really nice."

The door opened, saving Matt from the brewing inquisition. Rob's laughter filled the room as he helped Kathy out of her coat. What did he see in her? Sure, she was pretty enough—blond hair, nice smile, maybe a little too thin, but there was no denying that her ass looked good in those jeans. The problem was that she was so wound up. If she would only let loose once in a while, she might actually be a little fun.

"Rob!" Eric hollered. "Get out your cash, big guy!"

"Hey, guys. Who's winning?" Rob reached for his back pocket.

"Oh no, you don't." Kathy placed her hand on Rob's forearm. "We have a ton of wedding errands to run in the morning, and you'll never fit in your suit if you stay up all night pigging out on chips."

Rob looked down at his gut and sighed. "You heard the lady. Sorry, guys."

"Are you kidding me?" Matt said. "He's been working out and looks great. One night with his friends isn't gonna kill him."

"I said no." Kathy stared Matt down. "Stop trying to get him in trouble all the time."

"How is asking him to play poker with friends causing trouble? Let the guy breathe a little. He deserves this."

Kathy's face reddened. "That's the problem with you, Matt. You're irresponsible. Rob is about to become my husband. He's moving on with his life. He won't be here forever to bail you out."

Matt stood up, accidentally knocking his chips over. "He's not married yet. He has two weeks. You're not even supposed to have moved in until the wedding." He motioned to the room. "This is still my place. Mine and Rob's."

"Come on, guys." Rob rubbed his forehead. "Don't fight."

Matt exhaled and lowered his head. Rob was right. The situation was getting out of control, especially in front of everyone. "Okay, I'm sorry." He sat down and started restacking his chips.

"No way. You're not getting off that easy." Kathy motioned to his friends. "I'm sure they all agree. You're stuck in the past. It's time to get a life." Her eyes locked on Megan. "He hasn't even had a steady girlfriend since knocking up a girl in his little hick town."

The blood rushed to his face as his friends stared at him, their gazes burning right through him—all except Rob, who couldn't even make eye contact.

"I can't believe you told her that."

"Matt, I'm sorry." Rob's face was riddled with guilt. "I never thought she'd mention it."

Kathy took a few steps toward Matt, a smug look all over her face. "Of course he told me. We talk about everything. He even told me about the abortion."

Matt leaped up from the poker table, fists clenched. "Fuck you! Fuck both of you." He had to escape before he did anything he'd regret. He grabbed his jacket and stormed out of the apartment.

What a fucking bitch. She'd gone for the jugular, and in front of all his friends. Matt kicked over a garbage can as he stormed down the street. Sure, the pregnancy had been a stupid move, but he'd been willing to step up and take responsibility. When Jodie's father made her have the abortion, Matt had been devastated.

Why did Kathy always have to run him down? He'd learned his lesson, his juvenile record had been closed, and he'd thought he'd left that all behind. He turned into a corner store and bought a pack of smokes. Three years since he'd quit cold turkey. He sat on the curb and stared at the package. Kathy had him all wrong. It was easy to judge when you grew up with Mommy and Daddy always holding your hand. She had no idea what it was like to stay out on the street until you were sure the old man had drunk himself to sleep. He'd done the best he could with the cards he was dealt...but that wasn't him anymore. He'd changed. Proved them all wrong. He stood up, crumpled the cigarettes, and tossed them aside.

Matt headed to the neighborhood park and stopped

next to a small pond. He wasn't going to risk going home before everyone cleared out. Rob could deal with the awkward goodbyes; after all, he was partly to blame. He inhaled the cool evening air and gazed at the water. A pair of ducks swam by, apparently without a care in the world. If only his life could be so simple.

Now what? He rubbed a knot out of his neck. He'd have to patch things up with Kathy; that was a given. She wasn't going anywhere, and Rob's friendship was too important to jeopardize. Matt sighed. Rob's love for Kathy had become stronger than their bond. It made sense, but hurt just the same.

Matt picked up a stone and skipped it five times—not too bad considering its shape.

What would it feel like to be someone's number one? A real relationship, mind you, not some watered-down version where you settled because nothing better came along. But even if that ever happened, would he just fuck it up? He'd sworn he'd never be like his father, but some of his reactions scared him. Why had he clenched his fists during the argument? He would never hit a woman, that was for damn sure, but he had no idea what a healthy disagreement looked like. Matt tucked his hands into his pockets and stared across the water.

He hated to admit it, but Kathy was right about one thing: he was stuck, just not in the past. Matt, about to graduate, had achieved his goal and was free to pursue his dreams. The only problem was he hadn't a clue what those dreams were. Matt pressed his hands against his temples. Getting his master's would be awesome, but the money wasn't there, especially now that he'd agreed to get his own apartment. Finding a job was the obvious move, considering his student loans were coming due, but doing what? And where? He would never set foot back home, and the idea of living in New York on his own was losing its appeal.

Nothing felt right. Everyone was moving on, and there was no denying the ever-increasing void in his life—one he wasn't sure he could fill.

CHAPTER 2

Mitchell Bromley, Manhattan's most notorious businessman, sat next to his defense attorney. The courtroom was abuzz with reporters, at what was already known as the news event of the decade. The case had it all: money laundering, the mafia, corrupt politicians, and murder.

Erica Shaw's hands trembled as she thumbed through her opening statement while the judge read the charges to the jury. She was a seasoned prosecutor, as tough as any, but working this case scared the hell out of her. Two of her witnesses had already committed suicide. She glared at Bromley, sitting in his chair with his perpetual smug look. He'd gotten to them, likely threatened to kill their families if they didn't go through with it. Chills ran up her spine when he made eye contact, forcing her to look back at her notes. The page shook so much she could barely read it, and she took a few breaths to calm her nerves. She'd make sure he got what was coming.

Still, she needed to be careful. Evidence she planned to present during this trial implicated two politicians and multiple city administrators. Whether she won or lost, her career could be at stake. How deep did Bromley's influence go? How he'd been granted bail was another mystery. Was the judge in his back pocket? Water sloshed over the rim of the cup as she tried to moisten her mouth enough to speak.

"Ladies and gentlemen of the jury." She stared each one in the eye with a solemn expression. "Mitchell Bromley is a monster. He has no regard for the law, human life, or the values we—"

The double doors to the courtroom burst open, and a man stumbled into the room. His dripping hair and sodden overcoat suggested that he'd come in from the rain; however, there wasn't a cloud in the sky. Damn it. He'd completely killed her delivery. She looked to the judge to control the situation.

"Out of my courtroom!" Judge Simmons ordered.

Murmurs swept through the courtroom when the man ignored the order and shuffled down the aisle. Erica retreated to her table. Who did he think he was? She glanced up as he passed her—

"Mr. Carlson?" What in the hell was he doing? He wasn't due to testify for days.

"Stop right there!" Simmons yelled. "Bailiff!"

Blood draining from her face, Erica spun to address the judge. "I must apologize, Your Honor. He's the state's chief witness."

What a clusterfuck. The judge would hold her completely responsible. She rushed to intercept Mr. Carlson but froze when the smell of gasoline filled her nostrils. "Oh shit!" She tripped on a table leg as she scrambled backward, falling to the floor and casting her notes into the air.

The bailiff rushed past her, his revolver in hand. "Not another step!"

The witness stopped within a few feet of the judge, raised a cigarette lighter, and rolled his thumb over the igniter.

With a resounding *whoosh*, a blast of heat engulfed Erica, and she curled up, covering her head. *No.* This had to be a dream. A gray flake of ash drifted slowly to the floor, landing in front of her nose. For a moment, the world slowed and grew silent as she stared at it, a dark smudge that shouldn't have existed. When she looked up, Carlson casually lowered his hand as pieces of his burning clothing fell from his body. He just stood there, as if waiting for a bus. How could he still be standing? This couldn't be real.

Carlson suddenly came to life, thrashing in agony, dislodging chunks of blackened flesh. His screams pierced her soul. Each time he paused to take a breath, the sizzling and popping of cooking meat filled the void. Erica went numb. She couldn't think. Couldn't run. The screams turned to moans as Carlson went to one knee. He toppled over just as a man with a fire extinguisher arrived.

The flames were out, but it hardly mattered. The damage had been done. She couldn't take her eyes off his lifeless body. Blood oozed from cracks in his charred, blistered skin, and the heat radiating from his corpse continued to cook his flesh. The smoke carried the smell of burnt hair and barbequed meat. She swallowed hard as nausea roiled in her gut, and, finally, she looked away.

The room was empty, except for three others. Everyone exchanged glances, no one spoke. The sound of sobbing said everything that needed to be said.

Carlson moaned.

"Oh God, he's alive." Every muscle in her body tensed, but instinct forced her to his side.

His lipless mouth opened and closed. Was he trying to speak?

What did you say to a dying man? "Try to hang on. Help is on the way." She regretted the words as they left her mouth. What he needed was the swift relief of death. And justice. "I promise you, Bromley will pay."

CHAPTER 3

Victoria Brooks walked home along the leaf-scattered street. Fall had come early in Manhattan, and the trees had begun to cast off their canopies of amber and scarlet. She couldn't keep herself from stopping to admire their beauty and draw in the earthy autumn aroma. The scent took her back to the woods of her grandfather's estate in upstate New York. Although she'd come to love everything the city had to offer, nothing could ever replace the beauty and tranquility of her childhood home. The rumble of a passing truck stirred her from her reverie and set her feet in motion again.

After arriving at her building, she paused to collect her mail from the lobby. As she dropped the junk mail into the recycle bin, an envelope caught her eye. She tore it open and unfolded the letter.

Victoria, thank you for...blah blah blah...show a lot of promise... She braced herself for the expected 'thanks but no thanks.' *We are pleased to offer you the opportunity to show your work at the Richardson Gallery.*

"Yes!" She clutched the letter to her chest and closed her eyes. Claire Richardson. She'd only applied because her prof had encouraged her, never dreaming she'd even be considered, and now it was actually happening. She jammed the rest of the mail into her handbag and bounded up the stairs to her second-floor apartment.

She loved her loft, especially the way sunlight streamed through the floor-to-ceiling windows of the old textile factory. The twelve-foot ceilings were supported by huge wooden beams, and the original brick walls were left exposed. The perfect environment for her and her muse.

The majority of the expansive square footage was littered with easels, canvases, and carvings. Her living space was modest: the kitchen, living room, and bedroom were out in the open. Only her bathroom in the far corner was enclosed.

Victoria tossed her bag and keys onto the entry table and threw her coat on the couch. Sitting down, she reread the letter just to make sure she hadn't imagined it. As a young artist, it was nearly impossible to get your work shown anywhere, but this was like winning the lottery. What pieces would she show? With the exhibit in less than three weeks, she might be able to finish her latest piece, but it would be a stretch...

Victoria's thoughts were interrupted by a knock on her door. "Coming!" she shouted as she leaped up and crossed the room to check her peephole.

Her grandpa stood on the other side of the door, dressed in a fashionable overcoat with a Panama hat on his head. He'd always fancied himself the Indiana Jones type.

"Can you spare a moment for an old fart?" His voice projected through the door.

"I'm sorry," she teased, "not with that hat. I don't want the fashion police raiding my place." She opened the door and greeted him with a warm hug. "It's great to see you. C'mon in."

Lawrence leaned his cane against the entry table. She hated the sight of it—a constant reminder of the accident that had almost taken his life along with her parents. He removed his overcoat and placed it in Victoria's outstretched hand. "Thank you." He smiled mischievously. "I think I'll keep my hat on. My head's a bit cold."

Touché. She'd asked for it. He took up his cane and headed for a chair at the kitchen table.

Victoria opened her cupboard and grabbed two wine glasses. "I was just about to pour myself a glass of wine. Would you like one?"

"No, thank you, but I'd love a cup of tea."

Perhaps he'd go for a glass once he heard the news. She could barely keep herself from blurting it out. This was big, though, and she wanted her announcement to be just right.

"What brings you to the city today?" She put the kettle on.

"I had a board meeting."

"Guggenheim or Metropolitan?" She could never keep track. He was involved in so many causes.

"The Met. I've decided to make another donation."

Victoria raised an eyebrow. "Another one? Didn't you give them a shitload in the spring?"

"Victoria!" His stern look said it all, but he continued. "I raised you better than that."

Victoria blushed. "Sorry, Grandpa." She was normally more controlled around him. She smiled. "Would *mucho grande* bag of cash have been more appropriate?"

Lawrence rolled his eyes. "To answer your question, yes, I did make a *sizable donation* in March, but you know what they say: you can't take it with you. Besides, it will be satisfying to see it put to use while I'm alive."

Victoria's heart skipped a beat. "You're not going anywhere for a long time." Was he hinting at some bad news? She couldn't imagine going through the heart-wrenching pain of losing a loved one again. Not now; not ever. "You're okay, aren't you?" She put her hand on his shoulder and braced herself for the answer. He was her rock, her biggest fan, and her dearest friend.

"Don't you worry. I'm only seventy-two. I plan to live to

one hundred."

She exhaled. *Thank God.* "Well then. I'd better stock up on more tea."

Lawrence smiled. "And more of those little ginger cookies you usually serve."

"Shi— I mean, crap!" She ran to the cupboard and grabbed the box. "Why didn't you say anything sooner?" Victoria placed a dozen on a serving plate and returned to the table. "Well, now that you're done scaring the bejesus out of me, I have some great news."

Lawrence's eyes widened. "What is it?"

She leaned forward. "Guess."

"Boyfriend?"

"No...something awesome..."

Lawrence shrugged. "I don't know. Just tell me."

Victoria grabbed the letter and waved it excitedly. "My sculptures are going to be in a show!"

Lawrence beamed. "How wonderful. I'm so proud of you." He stood up and gave her a huge hug. "You must be thrilled."

"I am, but I'm also nervous. It's at the Richardson."

"Look at you." He tipped his head. "You have nothing to be nervous about. Claire is lucky to have you."

Victoria removed the kettle from the stove. She was the lucky one. How could she, of all the local talent in New York, have been chosen to show her work there? She froze. "You didn't have anything to do—"

"Never!" His answer was firm, almost angry. "You know that would go against everything I stand for."

He was right. "Sorry. That was a dumb thing to ask."

Lawrence smiled. "You're just going to have to admit to yourself that you're good—great, in fact. Humility is a noble trait, but you need to own your successes too."

Sure, she worked hard to perfect her craft, but her

talent was a gift. Accepting compliments always felt like stealing someone else's credit. Success was going to take some getting used to. When she returned to the table, a tear was trickling down her grandfather's cheek.

Victoria took her grandpa's hand. "What's wrong?'

"I wish your mother were here to share this moment."

"I do too. Both of them." They'd already missed so many moments, and there were so many more to come. Would it ever get easier?

Lawrence wiped his tears then gently squeezed her hand. "Speaking of which, October twenty-fifth is coming soon. I'd love it if you'd come with me to the cemetery this year."

Victoria nodded. "I'll think about it. You know how hard it is for me." She finished preparing the tea and poured a cup for both of them.

Lawrence paused then tapped his fingers on the table and cleared his throat. "I know you hate talking about this, but have you at least met anyone lately?"

Here we go again. "Grandpa. I've told you a hundred times. I'm too busy for a boyfriend."

"I know we just joked about it, but I'm not getting any younger. You'll need someone when I'm gone." He pursed his lips. "I worry for you."

"I'm very capable of taking care of myself."

"That you are. But loneliness is a terrible thing. Losing your grandma was devastating enough, and losing your parents even harder. If I hadn't had you, I don't know what I would've done."

That was exactly her point, except that loneliness was much easier to take than the crippling pain of losing those you loved. Why put yourself in that situation?

"I have time. I'm only twenty." She patted his hand. "Mom was thirty when she had me. You should be telling me to wait."

Lawrence nodded. "Maybe you're right. I was married and had your mom by your age, but I know those were different times."

Victoria patted his hand. "Don't worry about me. I'm sure I'll meet somebody, someday."

Lawrence smiled. "Okay, but don't wait too long. I'd like to give you away at the wedding."

Victoria made her way back to the fridge. "Are you sure you don't want some wine?" She needed a glass after that exchange.

"No, the tea is wonderful." He topped up his cup. "How are your studies?"

"My art history classes are so interesting." He likely knew ten times what her prof did, so she wouldn't bore him with the details.

"Is your favorite era still High Renaissance?"

"Absolutely." The answer rolled off her tongue. "I love— Oh!" She straightened in her chair. "You won't believe this."

Lawrence stared at her intently. "You're full of surprises today. What now?"

"Remember my internship at the church?"

"Cataloging early South-American Roman Catholic art?"

"Right. Well, Father Perry made an interesting discovery and wants me to follow it up." This topic was sure to grab her grandpa's full attention. "A Jesuit priest who was a distinguished sculptor was commissioned by the Pope himself. He traveled from Portugal to Brazil in the mid-sixteenth century and founded a church in a small village near Rio. Father Perry thinks he may have continued sculpting after his move."

Lawrence perked up. "That *is* interesting. Tell me

more."

"Father Perry located a church that hasn't been altered since it was built in 1560, and it's reported to contain a number of sculptures. He thinks this might be the Jesuit's church and wants me to arrange to have its art photographed. I'm supposed to compare the works to some of the priest's work in the Vatican to see if we can determine if they're his."

"That is amazing. What a find." Lawrence's brow creased. "Wait. He wants you to photograph it? In Brazil? Isn't that asking a little much from an intern?"

Great. Here comes lecture number two. "Well, I kind of offered to go."

"Kind of?" Lawrence prodded.

Victoria let out a breath. "Okay, I pretty much begged him to let me."

"Now that sounds more like the Victoria I know." He chuckled. "Once you get an idea in your head, you jump in with both feet. I admire that about you, but I'm worried it will get you in trouble one day."

Her face flushed. "It's just that the work is so interesting. I wanted to be the one to photograph it— Oh, dammit..."

"What?"

"With this exhibition coming up, I won't be able to go before my internship is done. I was going to go over Thanksgiving."

"Thanksgiving?" Lawrence sagged. "You always spend the holidays with me."

She didn't think her face could turn any redder. "This just came up... I was going to tell you."

Lawrence sighed. "It's all right, dear. I understand."

She bit her lip. "Well, it's all moot now, anyway. I'll have to cancel."

"I'm sure the priest will understand." His face lit up. "And if you still want to go, we could arrange a trip at Christmas or during your spring break."

What a mess. She'd obviously hurt her grandpa, and now had to let down Father Perry. "I suppose. I hate leaving things undone. I really wanted to finish that assignment."

"Why not hire a photographer?"

"That was the original plan, but Father Perry only has a budget of five hundred dollars, and there's no way he could hire it out for that. That's when I offered to go." She bit her lip. "I could always add a few bucks to make the job more attractive. I wonder how much it would cost."

"You'll figure something out, I'm sure. Once you get a bug in your bed, you don't rest until you find it."

"Oh, Grandpa." She shook her head, her mind already hard at work.

CHAPTER 4

Dmoltech sat at Mitchell Bromley's desk and took a Cuban from the cigar box. He leaned back in the businessman's leather chair and looked around the office. It was decorated exactly to his taste. The desk and chairs were made from the rarest of woods, and the couches from the finest leather. The artwork decorating the shelves and walls were all collectors' pieces, some priceless. He flicked his ashes onto the silk Isfahan rug. He didn't give a shit about any of it. It was only an illusion of power, and he hungered for the real thing.

Soon.

He drew in the cigar's sweet aroma and put his feet up on the desk. The last fourteen years had been quite a ride. Possessing Bromley's body had proven to be a great decision. Bromley's expertise and political connections had multiplied his investments exponentially, making Dmoltech the envy of Lucifer's other five Nagiyd. As generals in their Lord's war against mankind, their current orders were to amass a fortune, and Dmoltech had succeeded more than the others combined.

Bromley's polished image and charismatic nature had made for the perfect cloak. He'd had all of New York State eating out of the palm of his hand, and rarely needed to reveal his true identity to get the job done. Dmoltech sighed. It was a shame he'd have to replace him. His latest scheme—laundering money through local charities—had been discovered by the FBI, and the publicity surrounding his arrest and ensuing trial had turned him into a pariah. Bromley's empire was collapsing around him.

Starting over would be a bitch, but what else could he do?

The decision made, there was one detail left to be addressed. He needed Lucifer's permission, and summoning him wasn't a minor matter. Lucifer was the one who decided when and where he would hold audience, and calling upon him was always a risky proposition. Dmoltech rubbed his temples. Pissing off the Prince of Darkness could result in a one-way ticket to Hell—a fate that terrified every being of the spiritual realm. But it had to be done.

Dmoltech got to his feet, turned to an empty area of his office, and called out, "Lucifer! I summon you and beg your audience."

A vertical line materialized just above the floor and expanded into an azure oval. Would he come? How long would Dmoltech have to wait? The gateway turned black immediately. Dmoltech swallowed. Was that a good sign, or bad?

Lucifer's face filled the portal. "What is the meaning of this?"

Realizing he still held the cigar, Dmoltech tossed it into the ashtray and bent to one knee. "Forgive me for disturbing you, Master—"

"I didn't ask you to grovel. What do you want?"

Beads of sweat formed on Dmoltech's forehead. He was off to a bad start. "I summoned you for two reasons. I request a new Shakath, as one of mine was banished."

"Banished?" Lucifer's eyebrows rose. "How is that possible when the Torren are dead?"

Dmoltech swallowed. The loss of a Shakath was a complete embarrassment. His throat went dry, and his collar seemed to tighten around his neck. "Um...the trial..." *Think, dammit*. "They're under a lot of stress. They've started fighting amongst themselves."

An unseen force struck Dmoltech, knocking him backward. His head slammed against his desk, and the room spun around him.

"Get them under control, or I'll find someone who will."

Whoever had killed Nazkiel was going to pay. "Yes, Master. I will. It won't happen again."

"Like I said, I'll replace you if it does. What's your other request?"

Lucifer hadn't agreed to replace Nazkiel, but Dmoltech wasn't going to push it any further. He'd have to manage with the five.

Dmoltech struggled to his feet, his vision foggy. He had to appear strong. He needed to spin this so he wouldn't be seen as a failure.

"I'm sure you'll agree that this one is much more reasonable. I want to change cloaks. I thought—"

"I don't care what you think. Permission denied."

Dmoltech winced. That was it? No chance to explain? He had to leave Bromley. Lucifer had to at least consider it. Dmoltech took a deep breath. "Please, Master, hear me out."

Lucifer's gaze burned right through him, but nothing more. No attack, no answer.

Dmoltech seized the opportunity. "My cloak has been rendered useless. I'll never be able to carry out your orders with him. The FBI is watching me like a hawk, and no one with half a brain will risk doing business with me again. I need to start over. I'll serve you better as another."

Lucifer took forever to respond. "You fail to understand that your orders are only a small piece of a much bigger picture. I am about to move into the next phase."

Dmoltech exhaled, and his muscles relaxed.

Finally, he thought. *I'll be rewarded for my efforts.*

It had been difficult to walk away from the prestige of his last major assignment—the leader of one of the most powerful countries the world had ever known. He'd gone from crushing nations to inhabiting a series of lowly businessmen. Only his promised position had kept him going all these years.

Wait a minute. This made no sense. How could he change roles without leaving Bromley behind? "Master, I'm confused. You want this cloak to become the president?" Wasn't he listening? Bromley wouldn't stand a chance. Even if he was found not guilty, his political chances were nonexistent.

"No. I've changed my mind about you. You can't even lead your six. They're killing each other, for fuck's sake."

"But, Master—" The news hit him like a punch in the gut. "That wasn't my fault. I'm continually plagued by incompetent Shakath. I tell them to do one thing, and they do another."

"That's exactly my point. You've gotten so caught up in human pleasures that you've allowed your Shakath to run wild. I haven't seen such incompetence in a thousand years. Look at yourself!"

He may have let things slide, just a little, but his success spoke for itself. Lucifer himself couldn't have done a better job. "I'll set everything right immediately. I'll prove to you that I'm still worthy to lead."

"Your Shakath aren't the only reason I'm not giving you the presidency. Your aggressive style will only cause problems. Look at the mess you made in Germany. You're better suited to overseeing my terrorism operations. I need someone more controlled to handle the presidency."

The Crimson Dimension

Everything he'd worked for was slipping away. How could he have gotten so careless? He wanted this. Needed it. "I beg you: if you give me the chance, I will not fail you."

"No. I'm giving the presidency to Vorych."

Dmoltech's blood boiled. Not only was Lucifer ripping away his reward, but he was giving it to his arch-rival. Vorych had nothing on him. He was half the servant Dmoltech was. There was no way he'd ever watch that little weasel take *his* position. "Vorych is a fucking idiot!"

Lucifer's blast launched Dmoltech across the room. His glass-top coffee table exploded under his weight. Shards of glass drove through his suit and into his back. He raised his hands in a feeble to attempt to block another attack. A stabbing pain in his side told him he'd broken some ribs.

"Please," he begged.

"You'll do as I say or you'll burn in Hell."

Dmoltech seethed. Following this prick into the rebellion was the biggest mistake he'd ever made. "Yes, Master," Dmoltech conceded. "I will obey."

Lucifer's face relaxed. "Then the matter is settled. I will grant your first request. Your new Shakath, Lokad, awaits you." Lucifer's face vanished, and the portal returned to its original state.

Dmoltech stared at it until he was sure Lucifer had moved on then forced his muscles to relax. He'd survived the conversation—barely—but everything was completely messed up. "Fuck!" Dmoltech got to his knees. His ribs ached, and his shirt was soaked with blood. He struggled to his feet then limped to his desk. He needed to be patched up, but the portal wouldn't stay open much longer.

"Lokad!" he called into the abyss. "By the authority of the Dark One, I summon you forth and bind you to my service."

Dmoltech winced as the spiritual flesh on his back tore

open, allowing a three-clawed talon to emerge. The talon, connected to him by a translucent tentacle, shot out of his back and streaked into the portal.

Doing his best to ignore the pain, he felt his talon hit something solid. He dug his claws in and reeled his servant through the barrier between the spiritual and physical worlds. The Shakath's fetal form spilled out onto the floor before him just as the portal vanished.

Lokad gathered himself up and faced his master. The same size and shape as an adult male, he had blistered leathery skin as black as night. His hairless head was void of all facial features, except for his oversized eyes, which shone like fire through perfectly cut rubies and were filled with panic.

His servant's gaze shot back and forth over the room as he searched for a body to possess. The Shakath was already feeling the pull of Hell, and if he didn't take a human within five minutes, he would share his predecessor's fate.

"Wait by the door, but make sure it's closed before you take him. I don't want you attracting unnecessary attention."

Lokad hurried to obey his new master.

Dmoltech groaned. The pain wasn't letting off. He pressed the intercom and paged his bodyguard. "Come into my office. I'd like a word with you."

When the door opened, a large muscular man in black jeans and a tight black t-shirt walked in. As instructed, Lokad waited for the door to close before he leaped into the unsuspecting employee.

The bodyguard toppled over as he heaved the contents of his stomach onto the carpet. He thrashed violently then lay panting in the puddle of his vomit.

Dmoltech waited impatiently during the few minutes it took his new Shakath to orient himself and gain full control of his cloak. Finally, Lokad picked himself off the floor and knelt before his master. Dmoltech looked down at his new servant and wondered how he would fare. Like humans, demons varied in intelligence and resourcefulness. One of their greatest talents was the ability to gain all the knowledge, memories, and skills of their cloak, which transferred over time from host to host. Lokad was new to the game, had no history, and needed to start from scratch.

"I'm going to warn you this one time." Dmoltech pointed his finger for effect. "If you fuck up even once, I'll release you from my bond for Hell to claim you."

"I won't fail you," Lokad answered.

"Good. Pick your ass up off the floor, grab a mop, and clean that shit up."

He needed to get to a doctor. He needed to get his shit together.

No matter what it took, he *would* regain Lucifer's favor and take back what was rightfully his.

CHAPTER 5

"Only three more reps," Matt encouraged Rob to push through his last set on the bench press.

"There!" Rob panted. "You'd think this would get easier after a while."

"It's not supposed to be easy. Just think how much Kathy will appreciate those pecs."

Rob sat up, his expression sincere. "Hey, thanks for patching things up with her."

"No problem," he lied. The woman could've at least met him halfway. Not a chance. She'd made it clear that Rob was now hers, and that Matt needed to stop womanizing and being a bad influence on him. At least her apology for mentioning Jodie had seemed genuine. "I'm not sure we're ever going to be buddy-buddy, though."

Rob sighed. "I know, but I'm really happy when I'm with her."

"I can see that, and I'm happy for you. I just have to get used to her...directness."

Rob nodded. "Yeah, she doesn't pull her punches. I'm sorry she got into all that in front of the guys."

"Well, I've been thinking a lot about what she said, and...she's kind of right." Matt grabbed Rob's arm. "If you tell her I said that, I'll kick your ass."

Rob's face flushed, and he raised his hands in surrender. "I've learned my lesson. Our stuff will stay between us."

Matt shrugged. "Anyway, I know it's time to make

some decisions about where my life is heading, but I'm drawing a blank."

Rob looked surprised. "What do you mean? You'll have your degree in May, and you'll be set."

"Yeah...I'm not so sure about that." He moved to the free weights and grabbed a pair of dumbbells. "I've been looking, and there aren't any interesting jobs I can get with just my bachelor's."

Rob nodded. "I was wondering about that. You've got the marks. Why not get your master's?"

"I keep flipping between physiotherapy and psychology, but I can't afford another three years—even with the student loans. That leaves me no choice but to get a job."

Rob finished his set and put his weights down. "Look at the big picture. You've got this. Work for a year and save then go back to school."

Rob was onto something. Matt had been stuck on the notion that he needed to lock in his future this year. This would take a few more years to pull off, but he had nothing better to do.

"You might be right."

"Of course I'm right." He shoved Matt. "Doctor Matt has a nice ring to it." Rob wiped his forehead with his towel. "Speaking of psychology, how's your big assignment going?"

Matt looked up at the clock. "Oh shit."

Rob spun around. "What?"

Matt threw his weights on the rack and started for the locker room. "It's almost six. I have to meet someone."

Rob raced behind him. "Who?"

Matt opened his locker, stuffed his street clothes into his backpack, and grabbed his coat. "I posted an ad on the research website for some test subjects to interview. I'm supposed to meet her right now."

The previous day, while he was checking his ad, a new post titled "*Anyone going to Rio?*" had jumped off the screen at him. He was booked to fly there that weekend for Rob and Kathy's wedding.

An art student researching artifacts near Rio de Janeiro wanted someone to take photos, and the assignment paid a thousand dollars. With the cost of the wedding trip, and first and last month's rent on his new apartment, he was tapped out. He had to get the job. That was some serious coin.

He sprinted across the campus to the coffee shop then paused at the door, panting. While catching his breath, he noticed his reflection in the glass. His long sandy hair was glued to his head with sweat, and his face was red from a combination of the run and the cold air. Not his best look, but what the hell. It wasn't like this was a date.

Matt stood just inside the entrance and scanned the room until he spotted the woman he'd agreed to meet. Her black tweed overcoat didn't exactly stand out, but it was impossible to miss the canary yellow knitted hat and matching scarf. She was seated, facing away from him, in a comfortable-looking leather chair near the back of the café.

This is gonna be the easiest grand I'll ever make.

"Victoria?"

"Yes." She rose from the chair and turned, holding out her hand. "You must be Matt."

Wow.

A surge of electricity coursed through him. She was hot. Beautiful face, radiant smile, and the most gorgeous emerald eyes he'd ever seen. His gaze moved quickly down her body. The overcoat hid most of her, but it was obvious she had the figure to match those looks. She had it all, and he wanted every bit of it. The photo job wasn't his priority

The Crimson Dimension

anymore, but luckily, she and it were a package deal.

"It's so nice to meet you." Matt took her offered hand and shook it enthusiastically. "I see you grabbed a coffee already. I hope I'm not too late."

"Not at all. I just got here a few minutes ago." Her gaze passed over him. "It looks like you were in a bit of a rush."

Matt lifted a hand to his unshaven face then pushed his sweaty hair aside. Maybe he should've taken some time to straighten up after all. "Yeah. Sorry. I don't usually dress like this. I was at the gym and lost track of time."

"No problem. I saved you a spot." She moved a large handbag off the neighboring chair.

"Thanks." Matt tossed his backpack down. "If you don't mind, I'll grab something to drink."

"Sure. You know where to find me."

Matt headed to the counter and ordered an ice tea. He snuck another look at Victoria while waiting for his drink. He'd had his share of good-looking women, but she was different—in a class of her own. Everything from the way she sipped her coffee, to how she brushed her hair out of her face was mesmerizing. God. If only he'd paid attention to the time and showed up showered and well-dressed. But you can't change the cards you're dealt. He'd just have to rely on his charm, wit, and self-confidence to make an impression.

Matt took his seat beside her. "Sorry to keep you waiting."

"No worries." She smiled at him.

A shiver ran down Matt's spine. What was it about her? Was it her delicate nose, or those high cheekbones? Every feature was amazing, and all fit together perfectly.

Her eyes narrowed slightly. Crap. He was staring. She'd think he was some stalker freak if he didn't pull himself together. He leaned back in his chair and wiped the stupid grin off his face. "So, your post said you're getting a BA?"

"Yeah." She seemed to relax. "Art history major with a studio art minor."

"No kidding." Whatever that meant.

"And you?"

"Science—psychology major." He took a sip of his drink. "I'm in my last year."

She smiled. "Good for you. That must feel nice."

Matt wished it did. "Absolutely, but I'm planning to take my master's, so I'll be around for a while yet."

Victoria nodded.

Matt's mind went blank. He struggled for a new topic… Nothing. What in the hell was the matter with him?

"You don't have the accent," she said, breaking the silence. Thank God. "Not from around here?"

"New Hampshire. A small town called Bennington. Rob and I moved here for college."

"Rob? Your brother?"

Matt chuckled. "You could say that. I practically lived at his place during high school." It probably wasn't appropriate to tell her that his father was an abusive, alcoholic, religious hypocrite, and that Rob's home had been his refuge. That detail had yet to impress a woman. "What about you?"

"I'm from upstate, but I have a loft in Greenwich. I'm only a few blocks from here."

"How do you afford a place like that?" Matt blurted. He was twenty-three-years old and up to his eyeballs in student financing. How could a younger student be living in such a prime location?

Victoria's eyebrows rose.

Crap. *Smooth, Matt*. "Sorry. None of my business."

She took another sip then exhaled. "It's okay. I get asked that a lot." She shifted in her seat. "I'm an only child, and my parents died when I was twelve. I inherited enough to see me through comfortably."

Matt cringed. He'd wanted to keep the conversation light, but there was no ignoring it now. "I'm really sorry to hear that. You must miss them very much."

Victoria looked down. "I really do. There isn't a day I don't think about them."

Matt rarely thought about his folks, and when he did, the memories weren't fond. He'd completely written his father off, and his mom—well, she was a different story. She was trapped in the same hell, but at times he hated her too, for not having the courage to leave.

He needed to reset the conversion.

"What do you do in your free time?" Maybe—fingers crossed—they had some interests in common.

"I love going to exhibits, but I spend the vast majority of my time at home sculpting." She shrugged uncomfortably. "I'm actually quite a homebody."

Okay, so definitely not the kind of girl he'd ever considered hooking up with—the artsy, cultured type wasn't his thing—but, god, she was gorgeous. And way out of his league. He should probably just get the details for the photo job and walk away...but then he'd have to tear up his man-card. You didn't let an opportunity like this slip away without trying. They might not be a match, but even a one-night stand would be a victory...and what a night that would be.

"Seen any good bands lately?"

Victoria leaned back and glanced at her watch. "Oh crap! I didn't realize how late it is. I have to study for an exam tomorrow. We'd better get down to business."

Shit. He was losing her. He had to reel her back in. "We can get together again tomorrow if you'd like."

Victoria paused. "Thanks, but the rest of my week is

crazy. Let's see what we can get through before I have to run." She leaned forward. "Your email said that you're leaving for Rio soon. When exactly?"

"Saturday morning." He couldn't wait. His first tropical vacation. "I'm going for Rob's wedding."

"Cool. I'm assuming you're in the party?"

"Best man," Matt said with a smile.

"Sorry. Off topic." She swept her hair behind her ear. "The pictures I need are in a village just outside Rio..."

Matt did his best to pay attention but found himself distracted by her warm voice and the way she pursed her lips every time she paused to collect her thoughts. And he couldn't stop staring at those eyes.

"...what do you think?"

"Yeah. Sure." He had no idea what she'd asked.

"Really?" Victoria beamed at him. "Thank you!"

God, she was beautiful. He would do anything to make her smile like that.

"I have all the instructions written out for you." She reached into her handbag and retrieved a large envelope. "My email address is there in case you have any questions."

Their hands brushed when Matt took the envelope. Goosebumps broke out over his skin, but vanished when he felt the weight of the package. It was really heavy. He swallowed hard. He might've underestimated the effort involved in this thing. "Um—"

"Thanks again," she interrupted. "Gotta run!" With another heartbreaking smile, she gathered her belongings. "Email me when you get back in town. We can meet here again, and I'll have your cash."

"Whoa, there." Matt held his hands up. He didn't want her to go so soon. He was just getting started.

"What's the matter?"

Judging by the worried look in her eyes, she was afraid

he'd changed his mind. He felt horrible for ruining that smile, but it was the perfect opportunity to turn on the charm. "This doesn't seem fair."

"What do you mean?"

"I'm agreeing to travel to some tropical village for you, and all I'm getting is a grand? That will barely cover the flight and all the malaria shots I'm going to need."

"Is that not enough? I'll cover all your expenses."

"No—that's not what I meant." He fought the urge to ask for more. One thousand was more than enough, and it wasn't her money he was after.

"Well," she said, now looking confused, "you got the privilege of meeting me."

He laughed. "I have to admit it's been quite a treat, but it's still not enough. You have to even the score."

She shifted back in her seat. "How?"

Matt had a long list of ideas in mind, but wasn't going there. Not yet. "Go out with me Friday night."

Victoria's eyes widened, and she paused. "You'll sleep in and miss your plane."

Not the response he'd hoped for, but not a no. "You don't know Rob's fiancée. She'd never let that happen."

Victoria looked as if she were desperately trying to think of more excuses.

Matt's heart sank. Perhaps he wasn't as charming as he thought. But he couldn't give up that easily. She was a ten, and he'd regret not giving it another try.

"It won't be anything special. We'll just grab a bite and go over the photo safari in more detail. I'm sure I'll have a ton of questions after I read the epic novel you just handed me."

Victoria blushed. "It's not a novel, you ass. There's just a lot of information."

"Exactly." He smiled. "I want to make sure you get your money's worth."

Victoria bit her lower lip. "Well..." She was finally

warming up, and he needed to keep it going.

"Say yes..."

"Okay, fine. I have to eat anyway, so I'll let you buy me dinner."

"Perfect. How about Randall's Grill at five?" He'd been there for Rob and Kathy's engagement dinner. It was sure to impress.

"Make it six, and don't be late." Victoria pointed at Matt. "To be clear, we're just going over the details. We're not hitting the clubs or anything after. I really can only spare a couple of hours."

"You have my word." He'd convince her to change her mind.

Victoria stood and offered Matt her hand. "Thanks again for taking the job."

He cupped her hand in both of his. "My pleasure." Matt watched her walk out. It was a shame her coat was so long. If the rest of her was any indication, her ass would be perfect.

Mission accomplished. He had a date. Not the biggest endorsement he'd ever received, but a girl like that could afford to be incredibly picky. He really needed to step it up if he stood any chance of hooking up with her.

He jammed the envelope into his backpack and headed for home.

CHAPTER 6

"How far is this guy? We've been driving for hours." Radok shifted in his seat as the Cadillac sped north away from Manhattan. He ashed his cigarette out the partly opened window.

"I told you," Zaralen replied. "He's holed up in a cabin near Lake Ontario. They hid him in the middle of nowhere." He braced the steering wheel with his knees, leaving his hands free to open his whiskey flask.

"And how did you find this out?"

"For fuck sakes!" Zaralen snapped. "My contact in the DA's office. Where'd ya think I got it?"

Radok took his last drag and tossed the butt. "I don't know. This just doesn't feel right."

Zaralen's heart skipped a beat. He stared at Radok's face as long as he dared before turning back to the road. The headlights illuminated the dashed lines as they raced by on the dark highway. Satisfied that Radok had nothing concrete to add, he put the flask to his lips for another shot.

The two Shakath were en route to pay a visit to Roger Peterson, an accountant hired by the DA to investigate Bromley. Peterson was the last of four witnesses whose testimony could put him behind bars.

"You haven't told me shit. What's the layout of the cabin? How many cops do we have to avoid?"

"There's nothing to tell. He's sitting on his ass in a fucking cabin. No one's watching him."

"Give me a break. He's their star witness and they're not watching him?"

"Don't worry. My friend at the DA has taken care of everything."

Zaralen turned off the main road onto a gravel drive. After a few miles, an old ramshackle cabin came into view, barely visible in the black night. "Let's go." He got out of the car and stretched his legs.

"Are you kidding me? They have him in that Hellhole?"

"Stop your fuckin' whining. Let's go." Zaralen snuck along the edge of the bush, with Radok following close behind. He pulled his nine-millimeter pistol out from under his coat.

Radok crouched behind Zaralen as they approached the porch. "What's the gun for?" he whispered. "Dmoltech said not to hurt him. We're only supposed to take control of the little fucker."

Shakath didn't have many powers, but what they did have made them far superior to humans. Controlling a person was an easy task with the use of a Shakath's six Qaton. The imp-like creatures could be summoned and directed to attach themselves to a human. Depending on the number attached, the amount of control varied. A single Qaton acted like a tracking device. All six would allow the Shakath to completely control that person's speech and movement.

"Come on," Zaralen urged. He motioned to Radok with his gun.

"Are you sure—"

"Shut up and try the door."

Muttering, Radok grabbed the doorknob with his right hand. Zaralen made his move. He jammed the gun into his partner's wrist and pulled the trigger.

Radok screeched as he grasped the bloody stump with

his other hand. His nearly severed appendage dangled to the side, held on by a small piece of skin. Each heartbeat made blood squirt out between his fingers. "Holy shit! Get something to wrap it. Quick!"

Zaralen didn't move. He stared into Radok's pleading eyes with no hint of remorse or sympathy.

"Oh no!" Radok let go of his mangled wrist and reached for his own gun.

Zaralen watched with amusement as Radok struggled to pull his pistol from under his left lapel. "It's tough to grab it with your left, isn't it?" He fired another shot. This bullet tore through the back of Radok's undamaged hand, and continued through his upper arm.

Radok screamed in pain as that arm fell limp to his side. "Please don't kill me!" He dropped to his knees on the wooden veranda.

With both Radok's hands disabled, Zaralen returned his gun to its holster. "You've probably guessed by now that Peterson isn't here. In fact, there isn't a soul within miles of this place. You're finished."

"Why? What did I do to deserve this?" Radok's face turned ashen. He was losing a lot of blood.

"I told you to stop trying to figure out who killed Nazkiel."

Radok's eyes widened. "You?"

"You couldn't leave well enough alone, could you? Nazkiel is rotting in Hell, and now you'll be joining that son-of-a-bitch."

"I won't tell." He jammed his stumps into his body in an effort to stop the bleeding. "Bandage me up and get me to a fresh cloak before it's too late. I promise I won't say a word."

"I never trust an ass-kisser. This is your own fucking fault."

Radok's face hardened. "Then do it, you prick! Finish me off." He pointed his stump at Zaralen, spraying him with blood as his heart pumped out another measure of his cloak's life.

"Now that was just plain rude." He wiped the splattered blood from his face. "Why would I want to end your suffering? That wouldn't be any fun at all. It's not often I get to see a life slowly slip away like this. It's actually quite fascinating."

Radok spat. "I'll be waiting for you in Hell. This isn't over."

"Spare me the theatrics."

Radok's cloak toppled over face-first onto the blood-soaked planks. The pulsing blood slowed then stopped altogether.

The spirit of the dead man rose out of his body then floated about three feet off the ground. It rotated, slowly at first but picked up speed until it was a blur. Beams of light burst in every direction before fading away as the man's spirit was received into heaven.

"Now for the real entertainment."

Zaralen turned back to the dead body just as Radok separated from his expired cloak. The faceless black figure jumped to its feet and bolted through the locked cabin door.

"You're wasting your time!" Zaralen yelled after him. "I wasn't lying when I told you no one's in there." Not that he could blame him for trying.

After a few minutes, Radok bounded through the cabin wall back into the yard, searching frantically for a new cloak as he raced around the limits of the property.

"You're history." Zaralen took another swig from his flask.

Radok raised his hands in defiance as dozens of tiny

flames ignited on his oily skin. They multiplied, spreading over his body until he was completely covered. Following a blood curdling scream, the flames vanished.

Zaralen shuddered. "Better him than me." Radok was now burning in the eternal lake of fire—a fate that awaited him too, but not yet. Perhaps never, if they could win this war.

After fetching supplies from the car, he got himself cleaned up, changed his clothes, and emptied two jerry cans of gasoline over the body and any possible evidence.

Following a celebratory swig of whiskey, he touched his lighter to the fuel. The flames lit the yard, licking hungrily at the soaked wood. It was an amazing sight, but one too dangerous to stay and enjoy.

Zaralen's headlights illuminated the end of the gravel road, and the wheels of his car found pavement once again.

Damn, I'm good.

He finished the last of his whiskey, turned on the radio, and accelerated toward home.

CHAPTER 7

Victoria stared at her reflection in the full-length mirror. She held her black evening dress against her body and sighed. Was it too revealing? It showed a lot of leg, and the plunging neckline was sure to get Matt's attention. Her face flushed, and she immediately put the dress down. Perhaps something more conservative.

The search continued. The blue one she'd worn on her last date was nice. Over a year ago, she'd agreed to attend a charity event with a blind date, thinking it would be better than going solo. Big mistake. They were supposed to go as friends, but he'd kept pushing for more. Same old story. Victoria took out the dress and looked it over—way too formal. She jammed it back on the rack. Why couldn't Matt have suggested somewhere more casual? She had nothing that fit Randall's dress code that also said "hands off."

What statement was she trying to make? She'd mostly agreed to go out with him because of the photo assignment, but she'd also thought it might get her grandpa off her back. It wasn't like she was interested in him...although he was pretty hot. She smiled. The poor guy hadn't stood a chance. As soon as they'd met and his jaw had practically hit the floor, she'd known he would agree. She *hadn't* anticipated getting roped into dinner, but a couple of hours plus matching Father Perry's five hundred dollars was fair enough.

She looked back at the black dress. Screw it. She'd never gone out anywhere without looking her very best.

After all, she wasn't dressing up for him; she just wasn't about to dress down for anyone. She slid it on, checked her hair and makeup one last time, and stepped into her heels.

Victoria looked at the clock in her car. Traffic was heavier than usual, and she was sure to be late. At least Matt wouldn't get the impression that she was too eager. She nervously bit her lower lip. What was she thinking? This was a mistake. She was clearly attracted to him, and that made going on this date a really dumb move.

"Shit," she mumbled under her breath. This was so confusing. What if she developed feelings for him? Real feelings.

No. She wasn't ready for a serious relationship, and no guy was going to change her mind—no matter how good looking he was. She'd be nice, have a few drinks, hopefully a few laughs, and maybe make a friend. That was as far as she would go.

When Victoria entered the restaurant, Matt was waiting near the hostess. "Hey there!" He motioned for her to join him at the front of the line. "Our table's ready."

He looked good in black dress pants, a light blue shirt, and gray sports coat. Despite making a valiant effort to spruce himself up, his hair was still a mess. But somehow it worked for him.

"Hey. You clean up nice."

Matt grinned. "Only for special occasions."

"Is it?"

"Well, yeah, it's our first date."

Here it goes. Not even one minute in and he's started. Perhaps she should make an excuse and just leave.

Before she could answer, he brought his hand out from behind his back and offered her a single red rose.

"Aw. Thank you." His gesture melted her heart. She brought it to her nose. "I love roses." What a sweetheart.

No one had ever done anything like that for her before.

Matt smiled. "You're welcome. Can I take your coat?"

Victoria turned and let Matt slide off her jacket. He took a step back, eyes wide, and gestured at her. "You look...beautiful."

Goosebumps pebbled her body, and her heart fluttered... Wait a minute. Was she out of her mind? This wasn't supposed to be a date. She absolutely should've picked a different dress.

"I'll just be a minute." She almost ran to the ladies room.

Victoria stared at herself in the mirror. She was such an idiot. What did she expect? She'd known how this was going to play out before she'd even arrived. He would be charming, and she would be swept off her feet. She opened her purse and grabbed her lipstick. What was wrong with her? Why did this have to be so difficult? She needed to stick to her guns and not get caught up with him. Otherwise it would end up the way it always did. She would fall for him, and then her inability to risk letting herself love completely would eventually drive him away. It was inevitable—so why go there?

She gave herself a reassuring nod then headed back to the lobby.

The hostess led them to their table, explained the evening's specials, and left them alone to look over the menu.

"What would you like to drink?" Matt asked.

He had that enamored look on his face again. She needed to cool his jets.

"I'd love some wine. What about you?"

"I'd normally order a beer, but I might just try something a little more refined tonight."

Victoria grabbed her phone and texted her friend. *"Call*

me in 30. Need a bailout. Tx." She stuffed it back in her purse and smiled. "Sorry about that. Where were we?"

"Beer, wine."

"Oh yeah, Just have a beer. Be yourself, like you're out with your friends. What's your brand? I like a honey brown myself."

Matt looked up from the liquor menu. "Wow. You're a beer drinker?"

It didn't look like he'd picked up on the friend reference. Probably too subtle. "Of course. Why?" She needed to be more obvious.

"I just thought that with your upbringing—"

"Why can't a girl like me enjoy a beer?" Victoria didn't need to manufacture her annoyance.

His face flushed. "That came out all wrong. It's not that drinking beer would be— I just thought—"

He kept digging his hole, which wasn't a bad thing, but it bothered her nonetheless. "Why do people always make assumptions about me? I'm just like everyone else. I'm not some stereotypical little rich girl."

Matt looked horrified. "I'm sorry. I didn't mean it that way."

Shit. She was being way too hard on him. He'd done everything right, and that was clearly a problem...but not his problem. "I'm the one who should be sorry. That wasn't fair of me."

"Good evening," their waitress interrupted. "I'm Cara, your server for this evening. Would you like a drink?"

"Yes, we would." Matt smiled gratefully up at her. "I'll have a Bud, and I believe she would like some wine."

Finally. She needed a drink, and fast. A little alcohol should calm her nerves and stop her from being so bitchy. The plan was to discourage his advances, not crucify the poor bastard.

"Yes," Victoria agreed. "I'd like a Gewürztraminer. What do you suggest?"

"I recommend the Hermann J. Wiemer. It's an excellent choice."

"That sounds good."

"Just a glass for you?"

"Let's make it a bottle." Cara's judging stare burned through her. "He wanted some as well."

Matt was scanning the menu, likely noting the price of the wine. Ordering a full bottle probably hadn't been the best move, considering his past comments about being strapped for cash.

"As a thank you for taking the photos, I'd like to pay for dinner. Consider it compensation for your upcoming case of malaria."

Matt laughed, and his posture relaxed. "That's nice of you, but no thanks. I asked you out, so I insist on paying."

"Are you sure? We can go Dutch."

"I'm sure." He looked a little disappointed.

Good. Maybe he's getting the point that this isn't going anywhere.

Matt cleared his throat. "I think we got off to a bad start. I admit I made some assumptions—wrong ones, obviously. Let's clean the slate. Tell me what you're all about. Start with your childhood and work your way up."

That was pretty probing, but she'd kind of asked for it, and his request was safe enough. At least this topic wouldn't leave any room for his advances. "I was quite a tomboy. I used to climb trees and build forts out in the woods. I even have a strong right hook. Just ask Brian Spenser."

Matt laughed. "I think I feel bad for Brian Spenser."

"Oh, don't. He had it coming. He looked up my skirt at recess during fourth grade and had a black eye for two weeks for his troubles."

"I'll keep that in mind. I don't think I'd like to be on the receiving end of one of those lethal weapons."

"Sarcasm?" Victoria imagined Matt trying to sneak a peek and blushed. "I took six years of Kung Fu. I'm not a black belt, but I'm sure I could give you a shiner if you asked for one."

Matt put his hands up in surrender. "My bad. So... I've learned that you could probably kick my ass and that when you climb a tree, I'd better not look up."

Was he mocking her? "Now you're getting the picture."

"Do you come with a rule book?" A stupid grin covered his face. "I'd hate to cross the line."

What an asshole. "You just did."

Matt's grin evaporated. "I was joking..."

Fuck, this guy was arrogant. She leaned slightly forward. "I'm not laughing."

Matt's face turned red. He leaned back in his chair and sighed. Finally. He got it. Matt nodded. "You're right. I'm sorry. But you can't blame a guy for trying, can you?"

What do you say to that? Thank God she had that bail-out call coming.

The waitress arrived with their drinks. As soon as the wine was poured, Victoria grabbed her glass and downed it in one gulp.

"Thirsty?" Cara asked, as she poured another.

Victoria blushed. "Very. Matt, you should have some."

Matt shook his head. "Thanks, maybe later." He sounded completely checked out.

Cara set the bottle down. "Have you decided on the menu?"

This was going to be the longest dinner ever. She wanted to walk out right then, but she didn't want him bailing on the photos. What a mess.

"Yes, I think so." Victoria chose the blackened salmon with chipotle squash puree and mango rice, and Matt ordered the sirloin, medium rare, with a baked potato.

Victoria stared at Matt's blank expression. She'd completely killed him. How could she salvage this? She reached over and touched his arm. "I'm sorry. I'm under a ton of stress, and I took it out on you."

Matt perked up. Perhaps the touch wasn't a bright move. Victoria topped up her wine glass.

"I get it." Matt nodded. "The last ten minutes didn't happen. Let's start over...as friends."

A ton of bricks lifted off Victoria. She smiled. "I'd like that."

The conversation became effortless. No awkward silences, no manufactured topics. Despite actually enjoying herself, it was getting late, and they hadn't touched on the trip. Victoria sipped her wine. "So, did you have any questions about the photos?"

"I was hoping I could learn a bit more about your exploits, but yeah, I do have a few. I read through the package you gave me. You didn't say the statues are in a church."

"Yeah. Is that a problem? Avoiding the big guy?"

"No." Matt laughed. "If he were real, he'd be avoiding me."

What did he mean by that? "So you don't believe?"

Cara stopped at their table. "Your meal will be a moment. May I top up your wine?"

"Please," Victoria replied, and turned her attention back to Matt. "Where were we?"

"You were about to tell me your views on God."

Victoria cocked her head. Wasn't he about to tell her his views? Whatever. "Well, I believe in a god, but not in the conventional way. I think God is the energy that holds everything together. I believe in life after death, and I believe in spirits. I would imagine that there's a heaven, sort of, but not a hell. I'm not sure. And you?"

"Nah. I was brought up religious, and nothing about it ever rang true to me. I doubt it, but even if there *is* someone out there, he doesn't give a rat's ass about us. And if there's a heaven or a hell, I'll find out when I get there."

That definitely sounded a little bitter. What had happened to him to put that darkness in his voice? "I don't know. I struggled with that when my parents died, but it's impossible to believe that all of this is just an accident of some kind. It's too beautiful a world not to be planned. Sometimes things go sideways, I have no idea why, but I still believe."

Victoria studied Matt, waiting for a response. He just sat there, apparently in deep thought. She took a few more gulps of wine, and put her empty glass down, feeling a little lightheaded. Better slow down.

"Any more questions about Rio?" It looked like a good time to get back on topic.

Matt's attention returned. "Yeah. What about the sculptures you mentioned? The package is full of maps, bus schedules, and stuff like that. There's nothing explaining what they look like or anything." He poured her another glass of wine.

"That's because I don't know what they look like, or how many you'll find. That's why you're going—so I can catalog what's there."

"So let me get this straight. I'm taking two days out of my vacation just so you can make a list." He shook his head. "Something doesn't add up."

"What's not to add?" That had come out wrong. She couldn't be drunk, could she? She hadn't eaten yet today, but she'd only had two glasses. Or was it three? Victoria scanned the bottle to see how empty it was. Crap. Three, for sure. Where was the food? A little something in her stomach should set her head straight.

Matt grinned. Apparently, he thought this was funny. "I guess it doesn't matter to me. I just got the impression that it's important to you."

"Oh, it is! It's more than just a list. This could be an important find—if the sculptures are by who I think they are."

Matt perked up. "Like, it will be worth a lot of money?"

"No, not at all. How can I explain this?" She paused. "To me, art inspired by religion is so powerful compared to other works. I've always felt there's so much more to life than what we can see and feel. That energy is what inspires great work. I have a muse." She giggled.

Matt leaned in. "A muse?"

"She's my inspiration. I've named her Rossi, after Properzia de' Rossi."

Matt slid back in his chair and brought his napkin to his mouth, unsuccessfully hiding his smirk. "So you believe that spirits influence artists, and you have one named Rossi?"

"Sort of. Don't laugh." She must've sounded stupid to him, but who cared at this point? She was feeling good and having fun. "And I believe that I've felt the spirits of my parents on occasion. I can't explain it, but my art makes me feel closer to them."

"Sorry to interrupt." Cara arrived with their dinners.

The aroma made Victoria's stomach growl. Perfect timing. She needed to sober up. She dug in, happy for the lull in conversation.

"Damn, this is good!" Matt pointed at his steak. "What about your art? Are you any good?" He cringed. "I'm sure you are. Sorry—dumb question."

The Crimson Dimension

"You're pretty cute when you put your foot in your mouth."

Matt's mischievous grin shocked her back to reality. What was she doing? Flirting with him was the last thing she needed to be doing.

"You look just like my cousin's baby brother. He's a cute little kid." That should right the ship. "And for the record, I am pretty good. As a matter of fact, my sculptures are going to be shown in a gallery beginning next week."

"Wow! You must be *really* good. And pretty excited."

"I am, but I'm also nervous. This could either make or break me."

Victoria's cellphone buzzed. "Hey, Jen. Sorry, can't talk right now. Yup. Nope. Yup." She slid her phone into her purse.

"Bail-out call?"

Victoria cringed. "That obvious?"

Matt smiled. "I assume I passed."

How was she supposed to answer that? A yes would only encourage him, but the truth was that once he'd stopped trying to impress her, he'd passed with flying colors. "The jury's still out." She bit her lip. "Where were we?"

"You were worried this show might break you. Don't worry. I'm sure you'll be fine. What do you sculpt? Do you make those head things, or vases, or plates?"

"Those head things are called busts," she said. "And before you open your mouth and say something perverted, they're called busts, not breasts."

"I wasn't going to—" His gaze dropped slightly.

"Yeah, right." Was he staring at her chest? She blushed and adjusted her necklace. "That's what every guy says."

Matt laughed. "So, do you make busts?"

Finally, her head started to clear. "I've done a few, but

I've since moved on to full body. I'm working on a classical contrapposto right now."

Matt shrugged. "Classical what?"

"Human figure in a position where... Sorry. Too much info. Michelangelo's David is the best known example."

"That blows my mind. I can't even draw a stick figure."

"Well, then I'll just have to teach you." She blinked at him stupidly for a moment. Yikes. She stared at the empty bottle. Had Matt drunk any of it?

Matt smiled. "I'd love a lesson." He leaned forward and touched her hand. "You know what? You've got to be the most interesting and genuine person I've ever met."

Butterflies fluttered in her stomach, but not from the wine. That had to be the sweetest compliment she'd received from a man. Nothing about her looks or her artistic talent. Those were things she had no control over. He'd given a sincere compliment on her character, and that meant a lot.

She closed her fingers over his hand then, catching herself, pulled back. If she stayed any longer, she'd lose herself. "I had fun tonight." She leaned back slightly. "But your time is up."

Matt flinched. "Ouch!" He mimed stabbing himself in the heart.

"Don't be a baby. I promised you two hours, and you got three."

"It looks like you owe me an hour then."

Victoria laughed. "I don't think your math is right."

"It is by my calculations. You can make good with my first art class. You did promise."

"Maybe some other time. I really have to run." She dug her keys out of her purse.

"No way, lady." Matt grabbed her keys.

How dare he? She tried to snatch them back, but he

pulled his hand away. "Give them back."

"No judgment, but you shouldn't be driving. I'm going to drive you home and make sure you're tucked in."

Fuming, she squinted at him, trying to aim a withering glare at his...blurry outline. *Damn.* He was right. She was in no shape to drive, but she didn't want him at her place. She was feeling too good and might just do something she'd regret. She couldn't risk that. "Thanks, but I'll take a cab and pick my car up in the morning."

Matt waved his hands. "I'm sorry, Victoria, but I can't give you your keys until you're safe at home." He grinned. "And I'd like to meet Rossi."

She was going to regret telling him that for the rest of her life. "You really are an ass, aren't you?"

Matt laughed. "I have my moments. And I'm not backing down either."

She was stuck. She had no option but to accept. "Okay, you can drive me home, but no funny business."

When Victoria stood, the room started to spin. How could she have let herself drink that much? Matt put his arm around her and escorted her out of the restaurant. She felt safe in his strong arms. He was such a gentleman.

"Where did you park?" Matt asked, looking up and down the street.

"I used valet." She handed the slip to the attendant and watched him run off. The cold air was helping, but she still felt a bit wobbly. She held on to Matt's waist for support. "I'm sorry I drank so much. I hope I didn't embarrass myself too badly."

Matt placed a kiss on the top of her head. "I'm having a great time. I've enjoyed seeing the real you."

The kiss was sweet, but again, she couldn't let it go without comment. "Thanks for taking care of me, but I need to make it clear. Nothing's going to happen at my place, okay?"

Matt looked uncomfortable. "Hey, take a look at that Beemer." Was he avoiding answering? "Probably owned by some high-class snob." When she didn't answer, he closed his eyes and sighed. "It's yours, isn't it?"

She fought the urge to kick him in the junk. "Yeah, it's mine. Just shut up and get in."

Δ Δ Δ

Matt glanced over at Victoria, half asleep in the passenger seat. Her legs were amazing, especially with that dress riding up her slender thighs. He smiled. This had to be the most bizarre date he'd ever been on. When she'd finally relaxed, it seemed clear she was into him, but she was all over the place. Hot to trot one minute, cold as ice the next. She hadn't said anything about a boyfriend. So then what? He'd been a perfect gentleman and more than understanding during the roller coaster of her emotions. And he hadn't mentioned anything about his past, so it couldn't be that either.

Despite it all, she was amazing. He never would've guessed she was a tomboy, and their senses of humor matched perfectly. Maybe it was that he'd never had to work so hard to impress a girl before, but he wanted her more than ever. He still dreamed of a roll in the hay, but that might not be enough now. How long could he keep this one going before he fucked it up?

"Thanks again, Matt." She sat up, looking more alert.

"No problem. Feeling a bit better?"

"A lot. The cold air feels good." She reached over and patted his leg.

Matt's pulse quickened. There were so many mixed signals, he didn't know what to think.

"Hey," Victoria pointed out the window, "that's the

The Crimson Dimension

church I'm interning at."

Huh. Maybe she was more religious than she'd let on. Maybe *that* was the explanation he'd been looking for. "Really?"

"It's amazing, isn't it?"

"What?" He slowed the car to get a good look.

"The architecture. There aren't many buildings left like this one."

He didn't see anything more than an old church. "Well, at least I know where to go if the check bounces."

It seemed like a matter of minutes from when they'd left Randall's until she was turning the key in her door. The moment of truth. The entire evening came down to this one second.

"I had a great time, Matt." Her words were still slightly slurred. She opened the door a crack and blocked the view, almost as if she were guarding a secret in there.

Shit. He'd read way too much into her actions. It clearly wasn't going to happen. "I really enjoyed getting to know you. I'd like to see you again."

"You will, silly. When you come back with the pictures."

"How about your cell number? I only have your email."

Victoria giggled. "For sure. Let me set my purse down and grab my cell." She opened the door and took a few steps to her entry table.

Matt followed. "Nice place." Nothing over the top.

"Hey," she scolded. "Who said you could come in?"

Matt looked to the right. "Holy shit! This looks like a workshop."

"That's exactly what it is. I warned you. This is where I spend all my time."

Matt scanned the room. "This is all your work? Can I see it?"

Victoria sighed. "Well, considering you already weaseled your way in here, I guess I'll show you around." She crossed from the living area into her work space.

Matt followed her through the maze of paintings, sculptures, and supplies. There had to be fifty pieces at least. They looked incredible, but still nothing compared to her in that dress.

"So, what do you think?"

Matt nodded. "I've seen better." He couldn't hide his smile.

"Asshole." She punched him in the arm. "Seriously."

He took another look around, really taking it all in. "I never imagined— I thought you'd be okay, but these are amazing. You really did all this yourself?"

There was that smile again. "Yes. This is my escape. It's like all the world's problems just fade away when I'm in here." She stared at a painting of a wooded landscape. "Do you have a place like that?"

"Yeah. My secret fishing hole. That's where I'd go when things got bad."

She turned to him with a look of genuine concern. "You didn't have a very good childhood, did you?"

Matt looked down. "No." He shouldn't have let that slip out.

"Do you want to talk about it?"

"Not really. Let's just say that my dad and I don't get along very well. But none of that matters anymore. I moved away, and I won't be going back."

Victoria nodded. "You're right. It doesn't matter anymore. You've got your whole life ahead of you."

Matt took a step toward her living area and spotted a bottle of wine on the counter. "I think I'll take you up on that glass of wine now." If he could get her on the couch, he could work his magic.

"Sorry, buddy." Was she on to him? "You made me drink that bottle all by myself. You had your chance." She walked toward her door.

Dammit. "It's still early. I won't stay long."

"I need to get to bed." Victoria grabbed a notepad from her table. "Heads up." She tossed it to him.

Matt caught it and pulled the pen out of the coil. "Is my art lesson starting?"

"Nope. I want all your vitals."

"Gonna run a background check on me?" Matt jotted down his number, email, and apartment address.

"I just might."

"Oh, I'm moving out at the end of the month. I haven't memorized my new address yet, so I'll give it to you later. You'll have to come to my housewarming party—"

"Hey," Victoria interrupted, "I don't even know your last name."

"Reynolds."

Victoria offered her hand to Matt. "Well, Mr. Matt Reynolds, it's been a lot of fun."

Matt stood up, and placed a soft kiss on the back of her hand. Their gazes locked. This was it. He leaned in for a kiss.

Victoria leaned back. "I think we should call it a night."

Matt looked down. "I'm sorry. I thought you wanted—"

She took a step away from him, shaking her head. "No."

This was nuts. "I don't get it. You look amazingly hot in that dress. We had a great time. You invited me into your apartment—"

Victoria's face reddened. "Seriously? What happened to 'let's be friends?' And you forced me to let you drive me here."

"What are you talk—" *Shit*. She was right. And he *had*

worked his way into her apartment rather cleverly...but that didn't change the fact that she was sending a ton of signals. Maybe he was a little on the eager side, but he couldn't have imagined all of it. He took a deep breath. *Here goes nothing.* "I don't know how to say this, so I'm just going to blurt it out."

Victoria's eyes widened. "What?"

"I've really enjoyed spending time with you tonight. You're a lot of fun..."

"Uh-huh?" She took another step back.

He had to force himself to look her in the eye. "I'm not sure where I stand. I think you're into me, but truthfully, I'm a bit confused."

"Holy shit." Victoria's eyes widened. "A little forward, don't you think?"

Matt cringed. What was he doing? Would he ever learn? "I'm sorry." Why hadn't he just thanked her for the night and left on good note? "I shouldn't have said that. I have a habit of blurting things..."

After a long pause, she shifted to face him. "Look, I had a lot of fun too. You're a really nice guy..."

Those words always spelled doom. Next, she would say something along the lines of just wanting to stay friends. He'd spare her the effort.

"I understand." His heart sank. "Sorry to have put you on the spot."

She took a step toward him. "No—"

"Really. No need to say anything more. It's okay."

"I mean yes."

Matt rubbed his forehead. "Huh?" Was she capable of making sense?

Victoria bit her lower lip. "I'm just not sure about getting into a relationship right now. I've got my hands full with my sculpting and school, and I don't want any of it to suffer."

No more bullshit. "All due respect, but I'm not buying it."

"You're really not making this easy." Victoria blushed and fidgeted with her hands. "I actually find you attractive, and I enjoyed dinner with you—"

"Yes." Matt's heart raced.

"Not so fast." She held up her hand. "I can't believe I'm telling you this... I've been hurt before, and I'm not ready for a relationship. I'm very happy with my life the way it is."

Okay, so all hope was not lost. He could work with this. "That's actually good news."

Victoria looked at him suspiciously. "I can't wait to hear how you'll spin this one."

"I'll be honest. I've been struggling with this whole thing too."

She raised her eyebrows. "If we're being honest then it's my turn to call bullshit. I'm not stupid. You've been drooling over me since we met."

Drooling was pushing it...a little. "Not that. I'm working on some relationship shit of my own." He might as well put all his cards on the table now. "I like you—a lot. And that's not good because I'll probably fuck it up. Looks like I've already fucked it up."

Victoria just stared.

Matt exhaled. "On that note, I'd better get going." He put on his coat.

Victoria grabbed his hand. "Hey. I had a great time tonight. I'm really glad we met."

"Me too." Perhaps he hadn't blown it after all. "I'm back on Sunday, the fifteenth. Why don't we get together the following Wednesday at the café?"

Victoria nodded. "I'd like that. It will be interesting to

get a look at your photography skills."

"I'm not promising anything great."

"Just as long as your thumb isn't in all of them." She grinned.

"Deal." He gave her a quick hug and walked through the door.

"Goodnight, Mr. Matt Reynolds."

CHAPTER 8

Dmoltech leaned forward over his desk and held the rolled-up hundred-dollar bill above the line of cocaine. He snorted a line off the glass then passed it to Mandy. The pretty blond waitress took her turn then stepped back for her friend Denise to take hers.

The tremors from the bass speakers on the dance floor took on a whole new dimension. Drugs were a pleasure he could only enjoy through his cloak. That, and getting off. "Let's get more comfortable," he suggested. He dropped onto his leather couch and held his arms out for the coked-up beauties. Women were a dime a dozen, and he couldn't care less if they were coke addicts or worse, as long as they spread their legs.

Just as Denise removed his belt, a stabbing pain ripped through his body. He jerked upright. The women jumped back as he shot to his feet. "Fuck! Not again!"

"What's the matter, Mitch?" Mandy asked.

For the second time in one week, one of his Shakath's cords had been cut.

"Get out of my office!"

Denise stood and put her hands on his shoulders. "Come on, Mitchie, you'll soon forget whatever's buggin ya."

Dmoltech shoved her, and she tumbled to the floor. "I told you to get the Hell out! Go!"

Mandy rushed over and helped her friend up, and the pair made a quick exit.

Now that he was alone, Dmoltech searched his bonds. Radok had been ripped away from his service. He picked up a jade carving and hurled it across the room. Not only had he just lost another valuable servant, but he didn't dare summon Lucifer to replace him. After taking a minute to slow his breathing, he grabbed his cellphone and called Bayeth.

Of his six Shakath, Bayeth was the one he could count on the most. Unlike the others, who'd always operated on the premise that a male cloak was a more effective choice because of their stronger bodies and better opportunities, she'd demonstrated that using women, particularly strikingly beautiful ones, got the job done quicker and easier.

Her current cloak was a stunning brunette with luscious lips, long, sexy legs, and a perfect, toned body. She dressed in short skirts and high heels, and her low-cut tops showed off deep cleavage. With her keen mind added to the mix, there were few situations she couldn't control. If she ever did get in over her head, she had Toal, her partner and bodyguard, to get her out of trouble.

"Hello." The sultry voice answered his call.

"It's me," he barked.

"What's wrong?"

"Radok was just banished! What the Hell is going on here?"

"I don't have a clue."

"Well, I do. One of you is obviously out of control."

"Are you suggesting I had anything to do with it?" Her tone was harsh, yet somehow still calming. "You know you can trust me."

"Trust? There's no such thing. Call the others. I want everyone in my office tomorrow morning at ten. Things are going to change around here." He snapped the phone shut.

The Crimson Dimension

△ △ △

Dmoltech arrived at his office at nine thirty and found all his Shakath already present. He sat down behind the desk and lit a Cuban. The room was silent as he made deliberate eye contact with each one in turn.

Athamm sat on the far left with the rookie, Lokad, at his side. Having suspected that Athamm was responsible for Nazkiel's disappearance, he'd asked Radok to find him proof. Now Radok was also gone. Dmoltech watched Athamm for signs of guilt, but his cloak, the Gambino family mob boss, showed none.

Bayeth was seated next in line. Despite his rant, he did trust her. Her partner, Toal, was too stupid to be able to kill off Nazkiel and Radok. Toal's musclebound body filled his chair. Strength and intimidation were the only tools he knew how to use.

Zaralen was the most relaxed looking of the group. Wearing blue jeans, a leather jacket, and running shoes, he stood out from his well-dressed associates.

"As I'm sure you all know," Dmoltech began, "Radok is gone. Does anyone know what happened to him?"

As expected, no one spoke up.

"Two Shakath in one week is no coincidence. One of you is up to something, and I'm ninety-nine percent sure who you are. Once I get my proof, Hell will be nothing compared to what I'll do to you.

"I had a long conversation with Lucifer about you all. I told him about your infighting, your lack of respect, and your incompetence. He has given me full permission to purge every one of you if things don't improve around here."

His lies had the Shakath's full attention.

"That's insane!" Zaralen's face flushed with anger. "I've

served you well, and you know it. You can't banish us all for the fuck-ups of one."

"This is exactly what I'm talking about." He was seething under his calm veneer. "If you ever speak to me like that again, you're finished. I don't care how good you think you are."

Dmoltech was walking a fine line. He needed his Shakath, now more than ever, and couldn't afford to lose their experience. On the other hand, he had to assert his authority in order to impress Lucifer.

"I've decided not to replace Radok at this time." His statement drew puzzled looks. "I'm also moving Lokad to work with Zaralen. Athamm will have to pick up the slack by himself. As a matter of fact," he pointed at Athamm, "I want a twenty percent increase from you by New Year's."

The vast majority of Dmoltech's income came from the mob's gambling operations. Bringing the money in was the easy part. The real challenge was handling it afterward.

"That's impossible." Athamm jumped up.

"That's your problem! Complain again, and I'll make it fifty percent. Now sit the fuck down."

He took a step back and motioned to the others. "I want the rest of you to get in touch with all your contacts affected by this damn trial. Make it clear that it's business as usual. You'll have to get creative in finding new ways to keep the money moving." The cash flow wasn't his priority right now, but his orders would occupy Athamm so he couldn't cause any more problems. He walked back to his desk and sat down. "And finally, we have to end this bullshit trial once and for all. How many more witnesses are there?"

"Just the accountant," Zaralen replied. "The rest are either scared shitless or dead."

"I still can't believe he connected me with the charities.

That should've been impossible."

"He's a smart fucker. My friend at the DA's office says that without him, they'll have a lot of trouble explaining it all to the judge."

"Well then, find him, and do it fast."

"Yes, sir."

"And tone down the theatrics. The suicides are attracting too much attention, so leave him alive. Take him with your Qaton and control his testimony during the trial. I want an acquittal. I don't want any doubts about my innocence."

Dmoltech paused a moment to make sure he hadn't forgotten anything. "Oh. One more thing before I'm done. I won't tolerate losing any more of you. If anyone's partner is banished, they will be too. I suggest you start watching each other's backs."

His five sat in silence. Their fearful stares told him he'd succeeded in reining them in.

"Now get the Hell out of my office!"

CHAPTER 9

The sun reflected off the wake of the catamaran as it cut through the waters of the South Atlantic. Kathy sat on deck, drink in hand, trying in vain to enjoy the sights and smell of the salty air. Linda, her maid of honor, looked like she was having an equally difficult time. The guys were driving Kathy crazy. Since they'd left shore, Matt and her husband of four days had been debating what they claimed was the most important issue in life: alcoholic beverages.

"Caipirinhas taste okay, but nothing in the world beats an ice cold beer on a hot day." Matt raised his drink. "My vote goes to this Brahma."

"We're talking about real drinks, not beer," Rob countered. "Every place in the world has their own brand, and they all taste pretty much the same. Caipirinhas are Brazil's specialty. It's time you concede. I've clearly got you beat on this one." He motioned to Kathy for support. "Right, babes?"

Kathy threw up her hands and glared at him. She was staying out of the argument. The ladies had made the mistake of joining in on the first discussion regarding the best local dish, but they'd soon learned that the boys were only interested in hearing themselves talk. From that point on, Matt and Rob had debated everything. The last episode had included a round of rock-paper-scissors to decide that thong bikinis were not the bathing suit of choice over the traditional bikini. After all, Matt had insisted, not every woman could get away with wearing a thong.

She'd had enough. They'd had their fun, and it was getting old really fast. "I'm not getting sucked into another one of your stupid debates. Give it a rest." She rolled over onto her front to even out her tan.

Despite her irritation, she had to admit that Matt was right about the thongs. Not everyone could pull that off, and she was definitely not one of them. High metabolism ran in her family, and no matter what she ate, she just couldn't put on the pounds. It had taken a lot of courage to wear the modest bikini on this trip. The top barely stayed in place over her non-existent chest, and she'd had a hell of time finding a bottom that hugged her tiny butt. But Rob's reaction in the store had left her little choice but to step out of her comfort zone. Knowing how much it turned him on, she couldn't deny him. The stress of planning the wedding had really brought out her bitchy side, and she owed it to him to make this trip perfect, even if that meant cutting Matt some slack.

He was all over the place, never sticking to a plan—if he even made one at all. She was organized, a real planner, and it had served her well, making her the top salesperson for her pharmaceutical company in only eight months. It was through her sales to Linda's employer, a large independent medical laboratory, that they'd first met. Kathy had just moved to New York from Canada and didn't know a soul. When Linda heard, she'd reached out to Kathy, and they soon became the best of friends.

Linda sat up and grabbed the tube of sunscreen. "I agree. You guys are a pain in the ass. The next one of you to make a comment walks the plank."

As Matt opened his mouth, the catamaran hit a wave, completely drenching him. He sat there looking dumbfounded with his long hair glued to his head, struggling to catch his breath because the salt water had filled his open mouth.

"Poetic justice!" Kathy could barely get the words out she was laughing so hard.

"It looks like the guy upstairs agrees wholeheartedly." Linda threw a towel at him.

"You can't argue with God." Rob laughed. "The Caipirinhas win."

"I don't disagree that you can't argue with something that's not real."

Oh no. They were definitely not going there.

"It's over, boys." Kathy gave Rob the look he knew all too well.

Rob patted Matt on the arm and shook his head.

"Exactly," Linda added. "We just want to enjoy the day."

Matt's stupid grin vanished. "Okay, fine. I'll call a truce, but only since it's your honeymoon. As a wedding gift to you, the debates will end." Matt raised his beer in a toast to Rob and Kathy. "To the newlyweds."

With the matter put to rest, Kathy lay back down on her blanket. "It doesn't get any better than this: sun, surf, cold drinks, and Matt soaked to the bone. That alone was worth the price of admission."

"I hoped you enjoyed that water as much as we did, Matt," Rob said with a hint of disappointment in his voice. "That's the last of the ocean you're getting this week. Your trip into the jungle starts tomorrow."

Personally, Kathy wouldn't have cared about him leaving early, at all, except that it hurt Rob. Did Matt have any idea the effect his impulsiveness had on others? This was their special week, and Matt and Linda were supposed to be there to celebrate with them. How he would even consider going traipsing through the jungle for some girl blew her mind. Not that it was the first time Matt had made decisions which made no sense to anyone with even a shred of good judgment.

Would he ever grow up enough for a woman to take him seriously? Sure, he was good-looking, charming, and exciting, but he wasn't husband material. His impulsive, carefree nature didn't exactly scream *ready to settle down*. He had a lot of maturing to do.

"I'm sorry." Matt's gaze shot between Rob and Kathy. "I just couldn't turn down the thousand bucks. I could barely afford this trip."

"Nice try. We offered to help pay," Kathy challenged.

"You know how I feel about taking handouts."

"I won't miss the debates." Linda rubbed her neck. "But with you gone, I'm going to be a third wheel. They won't be able to sneak off without worrying about me."

"It's time they stopped sneaking off and started seeing a bit more of the night life. I thought consummating a marriage was a one-time event. You don't travel all the way to Rio just to stay in bed and fu—"

Kathy shot Matt a look that told him he was about to cross the line.

He raised his hands in surrender. "I'm sorry, guys. I know it's a bad idea, but I gave her my word."

"She must be really hot," Linda teased.

"Well, now that you mention it—" He grinned.

Kathy picked up on Linda's subtle attempt to lighten the conversation and decided to let the issue go. "Don't worry, Matt. Go take your pictures. Just make sure you're at the airport on Sunday so you don't miss the flight home."

"Pictures?" Linda cocked her head. "I'm really lost now. I thought Matt was meeting some lady here. And what's the money all about?"

Kathy sat up. "He agreed to help this random woman with a project she's doing. She needs some photos taken of a church near Petropolis."

"Yeah." Matt shrugged. "Since I'm in the area, I thought I'd help her out."

"You're heading to Petropolis?" Linda asked. "Cool! Did you know that's where the Emperors of Brazil spent their summers? The travel guide says it's up in the hills and it's supposed to be a very beautiful and romantic place."

"I'm not actually going there. I'm heading to a small village in the vicinity."

"Well," Linda's enthusiasm faded, "it's very kind of you to help her out."

Kindness had nothing to do with it. He was in it for the cash and probably some tail. In any case, the balance of trip would be a lot quieter, and the break from him welcome.

The catamaran came about as the skipper steered back toward the next group of tourists waiting on the beach.

Matt looked over at Rob, who'd gone silent. "Hey, I'm really sorry. I didn't think this side trip would take so much time."

"I told you it's okay." Rob took a drink and lay back. "Go take the pictures, but just stay out of trouble. I don't think you'd like the prison system here."

Matt grinned. "Thanks, buddy. You're the best, even though you know nothing about drinks. All beer does not taste the same."

CHAPTER 10

Matt opened his eyes to the sound of his cellphone alarm on the nightstand. Stale air filled his nostrils, and he debated rolling over and getting a few more hours of sleep. This part of the trip was supposed to be his vacation. He wished he could spend the day back on the beach playing volleyball and inspecting bikinis, but his promise to Victoria had brought him into the hills. His sense of responsibility, combined with the hard and uncomfortable bed, left him little chance of falling back asleep. This whole photo trip was likely a huge waste of time. The end of their date had gone sideways, and seeing her again was going to be really awkward. Hopefully, her excitement would erase it all. If not, at least he'd be heading home with a thousand bucks.

"Let's get this over with," he told himself as he swung his legs out of bed and stood.

The cockroaches scattered into their hiding places as he collected his clothes. Compared to the five-star-resort he'd enjoyed with Rob and Kathy, this place was a dump. It had eight rooms on the second floor, and a communal washroom at the end of a dark, narrow hallway. The main floor housed a small restaurant and check-in desk, which doubled as the local bus terminal. Matt didn't mind—the place suited his needs...and his budget.

He got dressed and stuffed his belongings into his backpack with room to spare—he'd left most of his luggage with Rob. He threw it over his shoulder and headed for the washbasin. The splash of cool water on his unshaven face was refreshing, and for the first time since waking, he felt vaguely human. He ran his fingers through his wet, muddled hair, and went down the stairs.

As he entered the lobby, the smell of fresh-baked bread caught his attention. His stomach growled and, knowing it would be a long day, he decided to fill up before leaving. He found an empty table and ordered the breakfast special. The coffee was just as he liked it, steaming hot and strong. As he ate, he looked over the map. There was no bus service past this point, but if he was lucky—very lucky, considering how far they were off the beaten path—he could hitch a ride. The worst-case scenario would be an hour-and-a-half walk.

He'd only been walking for fifteen minutes when the road, which had been wide enough for two-way traffic, narrowed as it rose out of the valley. What would happen if two vehicles met? With inches to pass one another, and no guard rails to prevent a plunge down the steep embankment...he was glad to be on foot. The further he ventured, the thicker the vegetation became, until the trail was covered by a dense canopy of rainforest. Birds of every size and color filled the branches, and the barks of a troop of howler monkeys echoed through the pass. Occasionally, the trees thinned enough to offer a view of the breathtaking mountain peaks and crystal-clear waterfalls. Although the setting was different from the woods back home in Bennington, it brought back fond memories of his fishing hole.

The bray of a donkey, accompanied by the sound of conversation, announced an approaching peddler and his two sons. The native Brazilians greeted Matt and stopped to show him their wares. Their cart was filled with wood carvings, jewelry, and an assortment of roots and herbs.

The Crimson Dimension

Matt had seen similar carvings in the tourist shops with hefty price tags, but judging by their dress, these peddlers didn't see much of the money.

He recognized that they spoke Spanish, but, only knowing the key phrases of "Where's the restroom?" and "I'd like a beer," he didn't understand a word. Assuming they were trying to sell him something, he shook his head before continuing his trek.

As he rounded the next bend, the village came into view. He soon left the shade of the forest and felt the heat rising off the dusty earth. Appearing unaffected by the temperature, a group of children were playing soccer on the unpaved street. It was as if he'd stepped back in time. The church, undoubtedly the center of the village's existence, stood at the end of the main street. There was an arched entranceway set between a pair of whitewashed two-story bell towers. Each tower held three small bells that hung in their own arched alcoves. Above the entrance and between the towers was a beautiful stained-glass window: a white cross centered in a collage of blue shapes. It was surely at least a couple hundred years old, yet somehow in perfect shape.

The children abandoned their game and gathered around him as he stopped to take a few pictures. He'd never been in a situation like this before. There was no way he was the only American who'd ever been there, but visitors must be rare.

"*Fotografiarme*," a young boy urged.

"Do you speak any English?" Matt asked. The boy looked blankly at him, but Matt guessed he wanted his picture taken. He aimed his phone and took a few shots.

The boy squealed with delight when Matt showed him his cell display. Instantly, the others repeated the phrase. This was nuts. Who'd never seen a cellphone before? As remote as this place was, nobody was *that* removed from the world. As he shared more pictures with the kids, though, he started to change his opinion. Maybe this wasn't so crazy—maybe this was how life was meant to be. The kids were free from all the pressures, demands, and day-to-day bullshit he had to endure. They looked happy, healthy, and no one had to post any of it on social media. What would it be like to live here? Maybe a life off the grid was the answer.

The kids seemed to multiply, and some began to tug at his shirt for attention. Matt took a few steps, hoping they'd get the message and move on.

"That's all," he said. "No more. No *gracias*."

A stern word from an old woman sweeping the doorway of her home sent the children back to their games. Thank God she was there. He gave her an appreciative nod. She smiled at him and went back to her work.

Remembering his assignment, he strolled across the village, past the large stone well, and stopped before the church. While taking a few shots of the bell tower, he noticed dark clouds forming to the east. Not wanting to get caught in the threatening storm, he headed inside to finish his task and be on his way.

In the foyer, he looked around for someone in charge, so that, as Victoria had suggested, he could get permission before snapping any shots inside. The last thing they wanted was for him to have come all this way only to be asked to leave for disturbing someone's religious experience. Finding no one in the entranceway, he looked through the second doorway into the sanctuary. Two rows of wooden pews, enough for about forty parishioners, faced the wooden pulpit in the front.

"Hello?"

No answer. With no one to interrupt, he took some pictures.

The Crimson Dimension

As Matt stepped over the threshold, the sanctuary came into full view, revealing an awe-inspiring sight. Dust motes sparkled and danced along a beam of sunlight shining through the stained-glass window. As if by design, the light shone directly on three statues. Positioned in a stone alcove, an image of the Savior stood majestically between two winged angels. Despite Matt's beliefs, the sight brought goosebumps to his skin. The rest of the place ceased to exist.

He made his way past a set of candelabras and almost tripped over a wooden bench as he approached the sculptures. Although smaller than they'd first appeared, they were amazing works of art even Matt could appreciate. The three-foot marble figures were perched on a much larger block of stone. They were incredibly detailed, and so lifelike. How could anyone possess the skills needed to turn chunks of rock into something so beautiful?

Although the statue of Jesus was a masterpiece in its own right, it was the pair of angels that stole Matt's attention. Their large, muscular frames supported powerful wings that towered above their heads and extended down to the ground. They appeared ready for battle with their massive two-handed swords. The beings were a complete paradox of weakness and power. Their naked forms made them totally vulnerable, but their weapons argued otherwise. He'd never seen anything so amazing. Maybe this was what Victoria meant when she talked about art inspired by religion. Despite his views on God, chills ran up his spine.

Matt envisioned the angels in an epic battle against the forces of evil. Demons screaming as the warrior's blade sliced through flesh. Severed limbs flying and the stench of their vile blood filling the air as it painted the landscape.

He laughed at the thought.

Matt often wished he'd grown up in a different time, a simpler time, when scores were settled with steel and the spoils went to the victor, but *his* damsel would have to be won over with photos and dinners. He readied his mighty cellphone.

He photographed the statues from as many angles as he could manage. While taking close-ups of Jesus's face, he noticed some dark debris on the right eye. Wanting the photos to be perfect for Victoria, he decided to clean it off and retake the spoiled pictures. As he brushed the dirt with his index finger, the mark smudged.

"What the hell?" he muttered.

Matt gulped. You didn't swear in a church. He took a quick look around to make sure no one had come in and heard him. Thankfully, the sanctuary was still unoccupied except for the furniture and afternoon sunlight. When he refocused on the statue and the annoying spot, it glinted through the lens. It wasn't dirt but something wet, perhaps a liquid used to keep the marble clean. The bright sunlight made it difficult to know for sure, but whatever it was, it had to go. He reached into his backpack and pulled out his spare shirt to use as a rag.

The majority of it came off on his shirt, but there was still a smear left behind. He stared at the stain on the shirt. It was hard to see against the printed pattern, but it was definitely red.

"Why would anyone use red soap to clean a white statue?"

Matt took a step back as another red droplet formed. "Blood?"

Had it come from him? Shit. He checked his fingers for a cut, but there wasn't one. He had to get the statue cleaned up before someone thought he was vandalizing it.

The Crimson Dimension

When he looked up again, the red liquid was trickling down the statue's cheeks as if Jesus were crying. He stood utterly still in disbelief. "This isn't happening."

There was only one explanation...

"Very funny!" he called out to the empty room. "Where are the cameras?" He looked around but saw none. "You guys can come out now."

He was being pranked. Right? He walked around the small church, looking for Rob, the likely culprit. No one appeared, and his throat tightened.

"The joke's over!" he said, louder this time.

He searched the statue for wires, hoses, or any other way the tears could've been staged but found nothing. A shiver ran up his spine. A solid chunk of marble shaped like Jesus was bleeding.

"Victoria?" he called out. Again, nobody. "This is impossible."

Of course, he'd seen news reports of shit like this—images of the Virgin Mary in pieces of toast, crying statues, and all the other *miracles*—but he'd dismissed them as wishful thinking or, in some cases, the church's desperate attempt to strengthen its numbers.

Well, whether it was Rob or a hoax staged by the church, he wasn't going to be played any more. He grabbed his water bottle from his backpack, gulped down the last of his water, and held it under the flow of liquid. The sound of approaching footsteps announced that he had company. Finally. Time for the punchline. Just in case the charade was going to continue, he jammed the bottle and his shirt into his backpack, and spun around.

"Pardon me," an old priest said as he approached. "I was told we had a visitor. I came as fast as I could. I am Father Alonso Devante."

"Hello. I'm Matt. I was just taking a few photographs

and admiring the architecture."

"Is something the matter?" Father Devante asked. "You look troubled." His gray eyes seemed concerned. He was in his seventies, if not older. His hair was white with traces of the black it had once been, and his thin face showed evidence of a hard life. The cross hanging from his neck swung like a pendulum as he walked to Matt.

How had a priest in this backwater village come to speak such good English? Nobody else he'd met so far had even bothered to try. He was clearly part of the prank.

"Umm, no, everything is fine." He'd play along a bit longer, perhaps find a way to turn the joke back on the old man. "Interesting statue you have over there."

The priest focused on the statue. "*¡Dios santo!*" Devante stumbled and grabbed the pew for support. He spun to look into Matt's eyes. "What have you done?" he demanded, as his face paled.

Matt's stomach dropped. The fear in the priest's eyes was real. Nobody was that good an actor. Which meant...this wasn't a TV show. It was really happening. And he was in trouble. Maybe deep trouble.

"I didn't do anything." Matt pointed at the statue. "It was like that when I got here."

The priest stared at his outstretched finger. It was still red from when he'd first touched the liquid.

"You must not leave!" Devante ordered. "You do not understand the significance of what has happened. You must remain here!"

Matt took a step back. No one was going to tell him what he could or couldn't do. Especially not some old priest. Too many times, his father had used scriptures and religious arguments to manipulate Matt. His face flushed.

"Not a chance." He started toward the exit.

Father Devante grabbed his t-shirt. "Please! Don't go!"

The Crimson Dimension

"Get your fucking hands off me!" Breaking free from Devante's grip, he started for the door.

"Wait. Son. Please wait."

Wrong choice of words. "I'm not your son." Matt reached the door.

"You have the blood on you. You can't take it. You do not know what you are doing!" The voice of the pleading priest faded as Matt ran out of the church, down the street, and past the well to the edge of the village. The priest's shouts, now in Spanish, were accompanied by the voices of the villagers.

He looked over his shoulder as he ran. A couple of men had taken up the chase. Matt's dash became a sprint, and he soon left the men in his dust. He spun around, now running backward, and held up both middle fingers. "Fuck you!"

He ran full out as far and fast as his legs could carry him before his lungs demanded that he slow down. Even at this slower pace, he would be back in town soon and could put this fiasco behind him. His mission was done. He had the photos for Victoria. He'd grab the first bus out of there and meet up with his friends at the airp—

A vehicle rounded the corner, and he turned to see an old rusted pickup closing the gap. The driver honked the horn as he pulled up beside him. Three men were squished into the cab along with Devante.

"*¡Detener!*" the man shouted at him through the open window.

Whatever he wanted, Matt was done. He turned toward the thick jungle, but his feet tangled in the underbrush, and he went down hard. The impact winded him, and by the time he got his breath back, the men were on him.

Matt fought, but their combined strength was too much. They forced him to his feet and walked him to the truck.

This was fucked up beyond belief. What had he gotten himself caught up in? His heart pounded, and his hands shook uncontrollably. When they reached the road, Father Devante was waiting. "You are very lucky we caught up with you. You don't understand what kind of trouble you could have gotten yourself into."

He couldn't let them sense his fear. He'd sworn he'd never be at someone's mercy ever again. Controlling his nerves, he relaxed his stance and stared Devante down. "I've done nothing. Let me go, or I'll report you."

Devante shook his head. "You have things all wrong. I mean you no harm. I am here to help you."

"You have a pretty fucked up way of helping people." Matt tried to break free, but the men were too strong.

Devante said something to Matt's captors in Spanish. Two of the men tightened their holds while the third released him and walked back to the truck.

The man returned with a first aid kit.

"Let me see your hands," Devante ordered. He opened the kit and took out a bottle of rubbing alcohol and a rag.

"What are you doing?" Matt tried to pull his hand away. "Look, I have some money. I'll give it to you if you let me go."

"I'm not interested in your money, and I'm not going to hurt you." Father Devante looked sincere, and there was an honest appeal in his voice.

Was the fake blood toxic or something? Matt extended his hands. There was no hiding that the statue's blood was still on his finger.

"Good." Devante looked satisfied. "You are lucky you are not cut." The priest poured the rubbing alcohol over the stain and scrubbed with the rag. He studied Matt's fingers again, nodded, and then inspected Matt's clothing.

"I need to look through your bag."

"No. You can't take it. Everything I have is in there. My passport, my plane ticket. I fly home tomorrow."

"I do not wish to cause you grief. I only want to search your belongings to be sure none of the blood got on them. I will return your things when I let you go."

There was a way out of this. "Fine." He handed it over. The old man would take the water bottle, but so what? He could have it, and then Matt could get the hell out of there.

Father Devante rummaged through the bag and laid out all its contents on the hood of the truck. He put Matt's clothing, plane ticket, and passport back in the knapsack. "What have we here?" The old priest's face hardened when he found the water bottle containing the blood. "What did you think you were going to do with this?" He spun to his assistant and shouted some instructions. "How did you learn about the statue? Who do you work for?"

Fuck. This wasn't going as planned. He needed to play it off like he didn't have any idea. What was he thinking? He *didn't* have any idea. "I don't know what you're talking about. I'm just a tourist. While I was looking at the statue, the blood started coming out of it."

"You expect me to believe that?" he accused, just as the man arrived with a rifle. "I want the truth," Devante demanded.

Matt's knees buckled. He'd never had a gun pointed at him before. This was going sideways really fast. "Okay. I'll tell you. Just put the fucking gun down!"

Devante pushed the barrel down.

"I know a girl who's studying art in college. She thinks the sculptures might be done by some famous priest and asked me to photograph them. It's some kind of assignment to pass a course. When I was taking the pictures, the statue started to drip. I thought it was a prank."

Devante studied Matt's face for what felt like an hour before he appeared to relax. "Your eyes suggest that you speak the truth."

"I am! I do! Check out those papers. They'll prove I'm not lying."

Devante spent considerable time going over Victoria's instructions. Finally, he nodded and stuffed the papers back into their envelope. "The documents satisfy me. You have no idea how lucky you are that we caught you. What you have done could have had very grave consequences." He pointed at the water bottle. "This belongs in Rome, not in your possession."

This was the second time Devante had mentioned that there could be trouble. Wasn't this trouble enough? He couldn't imagine what this guy's definition of real trouble was. All he wanted was to get out of there with Victoria's pictures, and get back home.

Unfortunately, as he'd feared, the priest went straight for his phone.

"What's your passcode?"

"Go to hell."

Devante gave a few more instructions in Spanish, and his man pointed the rifle again. This was going to be disastrous. Assuming he even got out of there alive, what would he tell Victoria?

"Okay, okay. This isn't worth dying over." Matt gave them his passcode.

Following a thorough inspection, Devante turned to Matt. "No suspicious messages, but the pictures are concerning. Since we have no reception here, I know they were not transmitted. However, I'm afraid I must destroy your phone. I can't have them distributed."

Matt went numb. Besides losing Victoria's pictures, the

phone was worth lot of money. "Just delete them!"

"I may be an old man, but I know that nothing is ever truly deleted." Devante took the water bottle, Victoria's instructions, and Matt's phone and placed them in the truck. He handed Matt's remaining belongings back to him. "You must promise never to tell anyone what you saw, and forget that this ever happened."

Thank God. He was getting out of there alive. "I promise. No one would believe me anyway."

Without another word, Devante and his three companions returned to the truck and drove away.

When the truck disappeared the way it had come, Matt's hands started trembling again. What in the hell had just happened? One minute he was at peace with the world, and the next he was held at gunpoint for taking some fake blood. This was so fucked up he never would've believed it if he hadn't been living it. No one else would believe him either. He needed to get out of there before they changed their minds and came back. Without his phone, he couldn't even call for help.

Matt turned for town and started running.

Now what was he supposed to do? There were no pictures for Victoria. How would she take the news? Matt stopped in his tracks. What if she'd known what she was getting him into? He looked back to make sure no one was coming. He couldn't imagine Victoria risking his life, but who knew? After all, he hardly knew her. One thing was sure: she owed him some answers. No matter how hot she was.

CHAPTER 11

Father Devante breathed a sigh of relief as he finished pouring the contents of the water bottle into a small glass vial. He capped it, wrapped it in some cloth, placed it in a hollow in the wall, and then slid the loose brick back in place.

Following the procedure to the letter, he gathered up everything stained by the blood and climbed the stairs from the church's cellar. Stopping at the statue, he wiped it clean with an alcohol swab before proceeding outside. After making sure he wasn't being watched, he built a small fire and tossed in the bloodstained items and Matt's phone. He waited until the flames had consumed all evidence that the miracle had happened.

The church had gone to great lengths to ensure that the statue remained a secret. Known to a very small sect of the Roman Catholic Church, it was the last of its kind, having been chiseled by the hand of a Torren. If it fell to ruin, the ancient writings warned, the Torren would be no more. Afraid that moving it from its original location might negate its miraculous properties, the Church had decided to leave the statue in the same place where it had first bled many years ago.

Devante had been granted the responsibility of guarding the sacred statue. He'd watched faithfully and diligently for the day the tears would flow again, and he shuddered at the thought that the blood had nearly been taken. He shook his head then smiled. Mankind's only hope of freedom was now safe and sound.

Still, Devante couldn't stop thinking about Matt. He was a loose end, and that left an empty pit in the priest's stomach. Devante didn't think Matt had bad intentions, but if two college students had learned of the statue's existence, and managed to find it, it could only be a matter of time before the Dark One did as well.

Caution was vital to his mission, but he was letting negative thoughts drown out this momentous occasion—the event he'd personally been praying to witness for over forty years. The Torren would live again. Satan's unchecked influence on the earth was about to meet some serious opposition, and he was blessed to still have enough years left in him to be part of it.

Devante's joints ached as he rose from tending the fire. His role in the ensuing battle would not be as he'd imagined in his younger years. As an initiate, he'd dreamed of receiving the sight of the Torren. Those years had come and gone, and his calling had changed to guardian, advisor, and historian. He prayed the initiates were ready. The blood suggested that Satan's armies were preparing to rise against mankind. There could be no other reason for God to have begun the process. The priest made the sign of the cross.

Devante had one more important task to perform. He returned to the church's cellar, retrieved the satellite phone from its hidden location, and keyed in the number he'd committed to memory.

"I have news," he said to his contact in the Vatican. "The time is now."

There was a very long pause, followed by a new voice. "Can you repeat yourself?"

"The time is now."

"Is it safe?"

"Yes, but our secret has been discovered."

"We will send for you immediately."

Devante put away the phone, locked the door behind him, and went up to the sanctuary. He bowed before the statue and prayed.

CHAPTER 12

Victoria packed up her things as her last class of the day came to an end. The cold air stung her face when she stepped outside, and she pulled her scarf up to shield her neck from the wind as she trekked across the campus to meet Matt.

Victoria could hardly contain herself. She was about to get her first look at the statues. If Father Perry's research was right, it would be an amazing discovery. She finally understood her grandpa's passion for historical works.

And then there was Matt.

He'd been surprisingly quiet since returning. Other than contacting her on the student research blog to ask for her number again, he'd only texted her once to confirm meeting up. What was up with that? Maybe he changed his mind about her after their date. That night had been a train wreck. She couldn't believe she'd told the guy she was into him. That was what she got for drinking a whole bottle of wine. But once he'd stopped trying so hard, he was actually a really nice guy. Easy to talk to, caring, genuine. And he had secrets, some dark past. More than a little intriguing.

Ten minutes early. She grabbed a cup of coffee to warm herself and pass the time until Matt arrived. Making herself comfortable in an empty booth, she faced the busy street and sipped her cappuccino while watching the pedestrians hurry by.

"Hi there."

His voice snapped her out of her reverie. "Hi. You kind of startled me."

"Sorry." He stood there with a coffee in hand.

"No problem. I was watching for you, but I must've missed you come in. Hey! Nice tan!" It looked great contrasting his sun-bleached hair.

"Thanks." His response was unemotional. He plopped down in his seat and stared at her blankly.

That was odd. Where was his unbridled energy? Perhaps it was jet lag. "So, tell me about Rio. I want to know all about the trip, the wedding, the sights, and of course, your photo excursion."

"It was okay, I guess. Well, not bad... I mean..." He studied her intently then set down his coffee cup.

"Are you all right?" He was rigid. Not himself at all. "Is anything wrong?"

"No, I'm okay." He fidgeted as he offered a few details about the wedding and some of the sights.

She felt a twinge of jealousy when he mentioned being paired up with Linda. "Why didn't her boyfriend come along?"

"Boyfriend?" He looked confused. "No. She's single."

"Oh." Not what she wanted to hear. "Well, it was nice of you to be friendly."

Matt didn't appear to hear her. He took a sip of coffee and stared at the cup.

"What's the matter?"

"I'm afraid I have some bad news."

"What?" Had he and Linda connected during the trip? Was it possible that everything was over before it even got started? She braced herself for the announcement.

Matt put his cup down and turned it restlessly. "I lost my phone. That's why I had to contact you over the blog."

"That's your bad news?" Victoria exhaled. "You got me

all worried over that?" She leaned back in her chair. "You can always get a new one."

"I already picked one up." The handle of the cup caught Matt's thumb, and he almost spilled the coffee all over the table. "That's not the issue." He paused, appearing to be struggling for words. "The pictures were on my phone."

Victoria sat in silence for a few seconds as the news sank in. "Please tell me you backed them up?"

"I didn't have the chance. I...ran into a bit of trouble." His tone suggested it was somehow her fault.

What wasn't she understanding? Shouldn't he have been apologizing? "Trouble? I thought you said you lost your phone. You're not making any sense."

"It doesn't matter." He leaned forward, staring directly into her eyes. "Or does it?"

"Of course it matters." What in the hell did that mean? "They're important to me. What happened?"

Matt gripped the table with both hands. "Look, I told you they're gone. I wasted two days in that shithole." His voice rose. "You owe me an explanation. You owe me my thousand bucks."

Victoria recoiled. She still had no idea what was going on, but she wasn't about to take his shit. "It's one thing to screw up, but you don't have to be an asshole about it. I was really excited about the pictures. They meant a lot to me, but you obviously don't care!"

Matt hit the table, spilling his coffee. "Wait a damn minute. I risked my life to get those pictures for you. Don't go telling me I don't give a shit, you spoiled brat!"

Victoria leaped to her feet and grabbed her belongings. She couldn't hold back the tears, and everyone in the café was staring. She needed to escape.

"Shit." Matt grabbed her arm. His eyes pleaded. "Don't go. I didn't mean that."

Victoria pulled away. There was nothing he could say or do at this point. "I obviously made a big mistake." She wrapped her scarf around her neck and almost ran over a couple as she bolted out the door.

What the hell was that all about?

She crossed the street and headed for home. It just didn't make any sense that he would act like that after their last time together. Not only had he lost the pictures, he'd implied it was her fault. Had he even gone? She should've listened to her gut and not let herself feel anything for him.

"Victoria!" Matt ran behind her, closing the gap.

Victoria reached into her purse for her mace. Keeping her eyes forward, she flagged an approaching cab. Matt gripped her shoulder. She spun to face him, mace held out toward him. "Leave me alone."

Matt stopped in his tracks. "Let me explain—"

"I said, leave me alone!" She slammed the cab door.

CHAPTER 13

At least the subway wasn't crowded, and he would have a seat to himself for a change. That was about the only thing that had gone right today. His meeting with Victoria was a disaster. He'd imagined them meeting again, showing her the perfectly executed photographs, and earning himself a kiss for his efforts...or maybe—

The screeching sound of the steel wheels rubbing against the track brought him back to the painful reality: He'd missed out on that kiss, and would probably never see her again. Not to mention being out the grand and the price of a new phone.

The whole thing was just so...embarrassing. Not only had he lost her pictures, he'd also been chased down and captured. By a priest. And now that it was completely obvious that she didn't know anything about the dangers he'd faced, he would have to explain *everything*, and he wasn't ready for that.

Still, he should've handled things better. Why had he snapped at her? As soon as those harsh words had left his mouth, he'd regretted it. Why did every confrontation he got into escalate so badly? Why had that even turned into a confrontation in the first place? Rubbing his forehead, he replayed the chain of events.

His fear of being out of control was killing his relationships. He wasn't an abused kid anymore. It was time to grow up and learn to deal with shit like normal people did. Matt put his head in his hands. Easier said. There was some serious healing he needed to work through, and he'd known it for a while. Perhaps it was time to deal with everything he'd bottled up. Was he ready?

Personal shit aside, what was he going to do about Victoria? She hadn't given him any answers, and he still couldn't make sense of it. But he'd put her through enough, and she didn't deserve to be on the wrong end of his issues. He'd text her an apology and promise never to bother her again.

That drama behind him, there was still the statue and the priest. He wouldn't tell anyone about what had happened because he wasn't sure what to make of it himself. Even Rob would think he was crazy. The last thing he needed was to be labeled a nut—especially if he became a psychologist. Who would trust their mental health to a basket case?

Matt closed his eyes and sighed. He was fucked up. He didn't need to become a psychologist; he needed to see one.

Although he'd ridden the subway to and from the university countless times, this trip seemed to take forever. When he finally got home, he paused at the door and took a deep breath. Chapter closed. Time to move on. If only that empty feeling in his gut would go away. Not in the mood to chat, especially with Kathy, Matt headed straight to his room and shut the door. He stepped over his luggage, which he had yet to unpack, and flopped onto his unmade bed.

As much as he tried, he couldn't let it go. Matt's way of dealing with disappointment was purely fight or flight, and since there was no one to fight, he put on his headphones, cranked up the volume, and lost himself in some familiar tunes. He would have to come to terms with Rio, and

Victoria, but for now, he would do his best to forget about it.

Every time he glanced at his backpack, his heart raced. The shit he'd gone through was only supposed to happen in movies. Perhaps unpacking would help clear his mind. Sitting on the edge of the bed, he emptied his suitcase, tossing the dirty items into his laundry basket and placing the odd piece of clean clothing back into his chest of drawers.

In his backpack, he came across the shirt he'd used to wipe to the blood off the statue. He stared at the stain, remembering how careful Devante had been to get every bit of the blood.

"Looks like you missed some, you prick." He threw the shirt into the laundry basket. "If it weren't for you, I'd have those damn pictures and be out on another date with Victoria."

Matt finished emptying the contents of the backpack, and glanced back at the stained t-shirt. He shook his head and exhaled. "Fucking priest."

He grabbed the backpack, turned it over, and dumped out a surprisingly large amount of sand—all he'd brought back from the trip. That and a few drops of blood. He stared at the shirt again. If he could prove that the bleeding statue was a trick of some sort, it might put this whole thing to rest. Matt grabbed the shirt and examined the dried stain. He'd seen bloodied clothing before, and, superficially, this spot didn't look any different. Matt had no idea how to tell whether it was real or not, but he knew someone who could.

Matt tossed the shirt aside and headed into the living room, where Rob and Kathy were watching TV. "Kathy, do you have Linda's phone number?"

Kathy hit pause and turned to Matt. "You have it. You

exchanged on the trip. Remember?"

Matt held up his new phone. "I lost everything. *Remember?*"

"Oh yeah. Sucks to be you." She shot him a devious glance. "Why do you need her number? I thought you had a thing for the statue girl. Besides, I don't think you're Linda's type." She turned her attention back to the program.

He shook his head and tried again. "I'm not planning to ask her out. I just need to ask her a question."

She hit pause again, this time looking annoyed. "What about?"

Matt took a step toward her. "None of your business. Just give me the number."

Kathy tensed. "Just—"

"Jesus, Matt," Rob interrupted. "You've been in a crappy mood ever since we left Rio. Don't talk to her like that. You two were just starting to get along."

Rob was right. He was doing it again. "I'm sorry. I've been a little preoccupied, but this is very important to me." He turned to Kathy. "Please give me her number."

Kathy spouted off the number faster than Matt could think, and it took three more attempts before he got it keyed into his phone. He returned to his room and dialed Linda.

"Hello?"

"Oh— Hey, Linda. It's Matt." He picked up the shirt and sat on his bed.

"Hi, Matt. This is a surprise. How are you?"

"Okay. Well, all right, I guess. What I mean is...um...I have a question for you."

"Yes?" She sounded excited.

"I need your help with something. Can you meet me at your lab in an hour?"

The Crimson Dimension

"My lab?" Her voice dropped off. "What?"

"I have a sample of some kind of chemical. I need your help to find out what it is. I was thinking that, since this is what you do, you could analyze it for me."

"What are you talking about? What kind of chemical?"

"It's hard to explain. I can't tell you a lot about it, but I can tell you this much—it looks like blood, but I'm sure it isn't. I don't know if this matters, but it's dried and it's on my shirt." He was sure Linda could figure out what the stain really was. "Consider it a challenge. Some mystery CSI shit."

"Um…" The pause made him squirm. "We aren't supposed to use the lab for personal reasons."

"This is important, Linda. I wouldn't ask you otherwise."

Another pause. "I suppose I could."

Matt jumped up. "Thanks!" He stared at the stain. "So if I brought the shirt over to your place tonight, could you have a look at it tomorrow?"

"Tonight? I'm almost ready for bed."

Matt looked at his watch. It was nine. No wonder she was single. "I'll just drop it and be on my way."

"Okay." She exhaled. "Bring it over. But I'm not promising anything because I have no idea how good your sample is. I'm guessing it's probably contaminated. Put it in a plastic bag to keep it clean. I'll see what I can do tomorrow."

"Thanks, Linda! I owe you big time." Matt felt a glimmer of hope. For the first time in days, he might be able to make some sense of everything.

"Yes, you do. It had better be as important as you say."

Matt jotted down the directions to Linda's apartment, threw the shirt in a bag, and headed out the door.

He arrived at her apartment in Jersey just after ten

o'clock. She invited him in for a few minutes to warm up while she had a brief look at the shirt.

"There's not much here, and as I suspected, it's quite dirty." Her face suggested he may be out of luck.

"You'll figure it out, I'm sure." She had to make it work.

Linda shrugged. "I'll do my best. I'll call you as soon as I have any news."

CHAPTER 14

Matt looked up from the computer in the NYU student lab and stared at the wall-mounted clock. He rechecked the battery on his cellphone before putting it down on the desk.

Focus.

Leaning back in the chair, he ran both hands through his hair. This shouldn't have been so hard. He'd received enough interest from his web posting to finish his psychology assignment, and needed to work out the required controls to make his results reliable. But his mind was blank. The only thing he could think of was what Linda would say.

Hopefully, his shirt wouldn't test positive for blood, proving once and for all that the whole thing was a hoax. Then he would call Victoria and tell her everything. If he explained the bizarre events at the church, and his subsequent capture and mugging, Victoria might be sympathetic and agree to see him again.

But what if it *was* blood? If Father Devante had gone to that much trouble to set up a sham, he could've used real blood—perhaps from a chicken or some other animal. Worst case would be Devante's blood or some other villager's. If that were true, he'd be no closer to proving what had happened.

He replayed the events in the church in his mind and couldn't think of any way the statue could've been rigged. What had he missed? How had Devante pulled it off? He'd taken a hard look and could've sworn there were no pumps or hoses involved.

There had to be some explanation, though. He couldn't have witnessed a miracle. Things like that didn't happen. Not in the real world. Matt rubbed his forehead. But what if? If this were some kind of sign from above, he'd be forced to reexamine everything he'd believed in—or, more accurately, what he'd chosen *not* to believe in.

Matt cupped his hands behind his head, and allowed the ridiculous notion to play out in his mind. Why would he, of all people, have witnessed this miracle? There were countless others much more deserving. And what was he supposed to do about it? What did Father Devante's warnings mean? The questions were endless, and each answer only raised more.

His cellphone rang, startling him, and he almost knocked it to the floor. "Hello. Linda?"

"Hey there."

"What did you find out?" Matt jumped to his feet and started pacing.

"Not a lot at this point. I have some answers for you, but I'm not finished yet. It's very confusing. I've been running tests for hours and can't figure it out."

"What do you mean? Is it blood?" Matt asked.

"Yes, it's blood. But I don't know what kind yet. Can you come down to the lab?"

"Sure."

"You'll have to hurry because we're closing soon, but I should have the tests completed by the time you get here."

"Do you at least know if it's human?" This was the answer that would tip the scales one way or the other.

"I'm not sure. I need more time. I should know more when you arrive."

"I'm on my way. Thank you. I'll see you soon." He

scrambled to collect his belongings and rushed for the subway station.

He arrived at the lab just as the receptionist was putting on her coat. "I'm sorry, but we close at five o'clock on Thursdays."

"I'm here to see Linda Harris. She's expecting me. I'm Matt Reynolds."

"Ah, yes, she told me you were coming. One minute later, you'd have been out of luck. I was just about to lock up for the night. Have a seat. I'll let her know you're here."

Matt sat in an oversized burgundy leather chair while the receptionist called Linda over the intercom. She then picked up her purse, headed out the door, and locked it behind her. Matt watched her walk out of sight and continued to stare at the street, bouncing his leg as he waited.

"Things are never simple with you." Linda's voice broke the silence.

Matt stood up. "Did you figure it all out?"

"Come on back to the lab. I'll explain in there." Linda started down the hall. "I hope this is as important as you say."

"It is," he assured her.

"Good, 'cause I've spent the better part of my day trying to analyze it." She turned to Matt and gave him a weak smile. "You're lucky it's odd enough to grab my curiosity. It's not often I get challenged like this."

Matt followed Linda down a series of sterile hallways and past a number of offices. The lobby was the only part of the building that showed any signs of life. The rest of the place was cold, uninviting, and smelled of disinfectant. Linda led him into a large room filled with an assortment of equipment that identified it as her lab. She stopped at a cluttered counter, picked up a small pile of papers, and thumbed through them.

"The suspense is killing me!" Matt exclaimed. "What did you find out?"

Linda laughed. "You look more eager than my niece on Christmas morning." Her eyes shifted to the papers in her hand. "As I told you on the phone, it's definitely blood, but I can't seem to type it."

"Can you tell if it's human?"

"Yes, since we talked, I was able to determine that it is human, but it's still very strange." Linda sounded both intrigued and concerned.

"What's so odd?"

"Let me try and explain. I did a basic Hemastix test, which confirmed that it's blood. I then ran a precipitin test to see if it was human or not. And the test was positive."

"So—" A knot formed in his stomach. "It's definitely human..."

"Yes, without question. But this is where things get strange. I tried to type the blood, but it didn't test positive for any known blood type."

"What?"

"Exactly. It makes no sense at all. And there's something else. Take a look at the sample." Linda directed him to one of the nearby microscopes.

Matt studied the blood for a few seconds before realizing he had no idea what he was looking for. He glanced back at Linda with a puzzled look.

"Do you see the movement?" she asked.

Matt looked again. Tiny particles were coursing around the blood cells. "Yeah. They're moving like a school of fish. What are they?"

"Good question. Microorganisms would all move randomly. I've never seen anything like it before."

"Google it," he joked.

"Funny... I ran a series of tests and ruled out bacteria, viruses, and parasites. I'm baffled, because I can't find a trace of sodium or nitrogen in them. According to the tests, they shouldn't be alive at all."

"I don't understand." There had to be an explanation. Something other than where this might be leading. "Could it be a chemical or something?"

"No, they definitely appear to be alive." Linda tapped her finger on the counter. "I must've missed something. I'm going to rerun a test or two. Can you pass me that microscope slide?" She crossed the room to set up another piece of equipment.

Matt unclipped the slide containing the blood sample. "What's the next step?" he asked as he hurried to pass it to her.

In his haste, he caught his hip on the corner of the large stainless-steel table. Losing his balance, he threw both hands out to catch himself. The hand holding the slide slammed into the wall. Instinctively, he tightened his grip, and the glass shattered, piercing his palm.

"Fuck!" Matt yelled in agony. "Motherfucker, that hurts!" Blood filled his palm and dripped to the floor.

Linda rushed to his side and took his hand in hers. "Jesus! Are you okay?"

She guided him to the sink and ran cold water over the wound. The flow of water kept the gash clean enough to see the triangle of glass sticking out of Matt's skin. Linda pulled it free.

"Holy shit, that stings!" He squeezed his hand shut to slow the bleeding. "I can't believe I did that."

Linda removed the first aid kit from the nearby wall and wrapped Matt's hand. "You might need a stitch or two. I'd have that looked at," she advised him.

"I'll be fine, but thanks anyway. It'll heal." He turned

back to the equipment. "I guess I wrecked that sample. We'll have to get another."

Linda grimaced. "I'm afraid we can't. That was the last one I had."

"You've got to be kidding," Matt muttered. "Can't you take more from my shirt?"

"Sorry. It was challenging to get a usable sample at all, and the last of it just went down the drain."

"Damn it!" Matt was livid with himself. "There's nothing more you can do then?"

She shook her head. "Sorry."

Matt's heart sank. So much had been riding on this moment, and it was gone. *Idiot!* There was no one to blame but himself. "I guess that's it then," he admitted in defeat. He hung his head and exhaled. "Thanks for trying."

"You don't look so good."

"I'm okay," he lied. "Disappointed, that's all."

"I don't mean just now. I noticed a difference during the flight home, but thought you might've been tired from your trip into the hills. Did something happen up there? Are you in some sort of trouble?"

"I'm fine," he said, though he wasn't sure he was.

She raised a skeptical eyebrow. "I remember you wearing this shirt in Rio. Did you get into a fight or something?"

"Linda," he sighed, "I'm not in any trouble. It's something I found that I was curious about. That's all."

"You're a horrible liar."

Matt curled his hands into fists. Why couldn't everyone just leave him the hell alone? How was he supposed to answer when he couldn't even begin to understand what the truth might be? His jaw tightened...but he took a deep breath and relaxed it. Another, and he opened his hands. What in the hell was doing? Linda was only trying to help, and didn't deserve his anger. He wouldn't blow up at her. He'd already fucked things up with Victoria, and his chances of seeing her again were slim to none. She'd be nuts to give him another chance, but for some reason, he couldn't accept that. Something about Victoria made it impossible to give up hope.

"Matt?"

"Oh... Look...don't take this the wrong way. I appreciate your help, but I can't explain how I got it or where it came from."

Linda's stare pierced him, but he managed to keep his cool. "All right...but you sure you're okay?"

"Yeah." Matt sighed. "Thanks for your concern, but this is something I need to deal with on my own."

They barely spoke as she led him back through the maze of hallways to the front door. She stayed behind to finish the jobs she'd neglected while doing the research for him, and he started down the street toward the subway terminal with his head hung low. Could anything else go wrong for him this week? So far he'd alienated the woman of his dreams, sliced his hand open, and screwed up any chance of uncovering the truth about the blood.

He struggled with his reunion with this helpless feeling.

"No fucking way."

Matt wasn't about to allow this to bring him down. He'd proved he wasn't a loser, so he wouldn't behave like one. He refused to allow his father to have the last laugh.

CHAPTER 15

Matt adjusted the collar of his coat to keep the cold wind from blowing inside his shirt. The sting in his palm intensified each time he lifted his hand and gripped the material.

Ignoring the pain, he thought about the results. The substance from the statue wasn't just blood, it was human blood. Could it be possible that a crying statue of Jesus in a remote church in Brazil wasn't a hoax, after all?

"No way," he told himself. "It can't be true. It can't."

There had to be some other explanation. The only two possibilities he could see were that a simple priest in a remote village had somehow set up a hoax with real human blood, or that the statue had actually bled.

The problem with scenario A—aside from the lack of pipes or hoses in the statue—was that while the blood was human, it didn't have all the characteristics of normal blood. The likelihood of the priest creating some living substance that modern science couldn't explain was almost as hard to believe as a sign from above. Matt tried to swallow, but his mouth had gone bone dry.

The freezing wind bit at his ears—he'd been in too much of a hurry to get to Linda's office to remember a hat and gloves—and he lifted his hands to warm them, bracing for the expected surge of pain. It didn't come. When he pressed his thumb against the wound, trying to see if he could awaken the pain beneath the bandaging, there was nothing but a light burning sensation. He clenched and unclenched his hand a few times, hoping the burning would settle as well, but it only made the sensation spread into his wrist.

Tucking his hands into his pockets, he continued down the street, trying to block the burning feeling from his mind and think about other things.

He descended the stairwell to the subway platform and took his place among the other commuters awaiting the next train. When it arrived and emptied some of its passengers, he filed through the door and walked along the aisle until he found a seat. He gave a polite nod to an Asian woman seated beside him. She offered an uncomfortable smile and shifted over. Given how he looked—tired, unshaven, bandaged up—she might've mistaken him for a vagrant.

The subway jerked forward toward Hoboken. Matt sighed and slouched in his seat. What a fucked-up day. He shut it out and made himself relax. The familiar sounds of the train's wheels clicking on the tracks almost lulled him to sleep, but the burning in his palm wouldn't let him go. With every minute that passed, the sensation grew stronger, until he was gripping his wrist and grimacing in pain. Linda must've missed a fragment of the microscope slide. He unwrapped the dressing to examine the wound.

Shock squeezed his chest, and the hair on the back of his neck stood up. The gaping wound was disturbingly deep, but to his amazement, there was no sign of blood. The worst of it was that his hand had turned a pale gray, a skin tone popular in zombie movies.

He lifted his hand to get a closer look, and the wound began to pulse with his heartbeat. While he stared at the strange cut, the veins around it bulged, almost popping through his skin.

"What the hell?" he gasped.

"You need to have that looked at," the Asian woman offered. "It looks badly infected."

Matt wasn't in the mood to discuss it with a stranger. He nodded brusquely. "Yeah. Thanks."

He'd never seen a cut behave like this, and he'd seen plenty in his lifetime.

Every heartbeat forced the throbbing pain further up his arm. He tore off his coat. The inflated veins were moving up his arm. He let out a panicked cry.

"Damn junkie!" the lady cursed. She stood up and headed down the aisle.

The attack advanced past his shoulder and into the base of his neck. A crowd was forming, but none of that mattered anymore. Fear paralyzed him.

As the engorged veins made their way up his neck, his throat constricted, and he struggled for air. The pain progressed up over his jaw, across his cheek, and toward his eyes. The harder he fought, the more intense the pain became. His screams reverberated through the subway as the searing pain exploded into his eyes.

Then darkness.

△ △ △

Matt opened his eyes, his vision blurred. Thank God he could still see. And the pain—it was gone. The attack must've ended when he passed out. He blinked away tears to find himself looking down on a crowd of people gathered around an unconscious man. They were trying to rouse him with no success. Matt moved in for a closer look.

What the fuck?

This was impossible. The man was him.

"I'm dead," he said in a surprisingly calm voice. "Holy shit, I'm actually dead."

The people below were trying to revive him, but they

were doing everything wrong. Someone needed to give him CPR. At least mouth to mouth.

The scene started glowing, and his ability to watch himself faded away. This was it. He wasn't going to wake up. The light became brighter until it swallowed him. His questions about God were about to be answered. The moment of truth was upon him.

△ △ △

"Buddy, are you okay?"

Matt jerked upright at the sound of the young man's voice.

His head cleared, and his vision returned. "What happened?"

"I think you overdosed, man. Just stay down. We'll get you help."

"I'm alive?" What in the hell was going on? He couldn't think straight.

The guy laughed. "Yeah. As far I can tell."

He lay on the subway floor with a crowd of concerned onlookers surrounding him. The pain hadn't returned. Amazingly, he felt fine. After sitting up, he examined his arm. No bulging veins. His skin looked normal. He turned his hand to look at his palm. The cut was gone.

"My hand— What's going on?"

"What are you on?" a girl asked in an amused tone. "You were totally freaking. You were thrashing and clawing at yourself."

"I'm not on anything," Matt objected. "I'm fine. I feel okay. How long was I out?"

"Only for a few seconds."

He expected to be dizzy when he stood up, but wasn't.

"You should sit down," a woman offered. "We'll get you some help at the next station."

"I'd rather stand, thank you." Nothing made sense. Why wouldn't everyone just leave him alone?

He avoided eye contact with the crowd. How embarrassing. Nothing like that had ever happened to him before. He didn't want their pity, or their help. As soon as the door opened, he bolted.

Emerging at ground level, he breathed the cold into his lungs. The fresh air felt fantastic. He stood for a moment, trying to piece together what had just happened.

His hand looked perfect. No sign of the cut, or the engorged veins, or the gray color. Was he going crazy? No. Even though there was no visible evidence, he had definitely cut his hand—Linda and the Asian woman had both seen it—and the people on the subway had witnessed him pass out. It *had* happened.

It had to be the blood. Despite his attempts to flush and clean the wound at Linda's lab, the microscopic entities in the blood sample must've gotten into his bloodstream and caused the seizure and blackout.

Matt swallowed. Was this what the priest had meant when he'd warned Matt about getting in trouble?

CHAPTER 16

Father Devante followed the two Swiss Guards down a marble hallway. His escorts stopped in front of a handcrafted door displaying the image of the All-Seeing Eye.

"We can take you no further. You must enter alone."

The sixty-eight-year-old priest took a moment to catch his breath. The trip to the Vatican had taken a lot out of him. Twenty-three hours of nonstop travel had been hard enough when he was young. But now, finally, he was home.

"Thank you," he told the guards as he pushed the door open.

The room was decorated magnificently. Crimson tapestries hung from the ceiling, embroidered with battle scenes—mighty angels with flaming swords fought beside men against jet-black demons. Although it had been over forty years since his last visit to this room, nothing had changed. Devante walked along the crimson rug running from the doorway to the altar at the far end, where Cardinal Nicholaus Sergius stood waiting.

Cardinal Sergius was the leader of the secret sect of the Torren, unknown to most who served at the Vatican. Standing to his right were two men dressed in priest's vestments. These men, Devante assumed, were the initiates chosen to receive the sight. Ingesting the blood would transform them into members of the Torren. The first to walk the earth in over half a century.

"Welcome home, Alonso. You look well, my friend."

"Thank you, Nicholaus. I am thrilled to have arrived, but the trip has been quite taxing."

"I am afraid rest will have to wait a little longer. We have work to do. May I have the sacred blood?"

"Of course."

Devante reached into the pouch hanging from his side and produced a small wooden box containing the vial. He carefully set the box down on the altar beside two silver chalices. Both initiates would drink simultaneously to ensure that the Torren would view each other as equals.

He unfastened the latch and opened the box.

"*¡Dios santo!*" Devante gasped. He stared at the vial in disbelief. "I do not understand."

"What is the matter?" Cardinal Sergius rushed to his side.

"The blood! It has turned to water."

"Are you sure you handled it correctly?"

"I am certain. No one has even touched it since I took—" He grabbed the altar for support as his heart stuttered in his chest. "There was a young man."

"Devante!" Sergius shouted. "What are you saying? Out with it!"

The cardinal's fierce outburst was justified. The blood, in the wrong hands, was disastrous to their cause. How had this happened?

"On that day, I was told I had a visitor. I came upon a young man. He was there when the blood flowed and had collected it in a bottle."

"God help us!" Sergius bellowed. "One of the Shakath?"

"No! I am certain he was mortal. It was a coincidence." Or was it? "I took the blood from him, cleansed him, and sent him on his way. If he'd been infused, the blood would have turned to water at that time."

"You couldn't have taken it all then! How thoroughly

The Crimson Dimension

did you search him?"

He had to have missed some. Devante hung his head in shame. He'd failed the church, failed mankind, and failed the God he'd vowed to serve. How had the young man escaped with the sacred blood, and more importantly, how had he come to be infused?

"We need to find this impostor...this *thief*," Sergius ordered. "What do you know of him?"

"I'm afraid I only remember his name, Matt, and that he carried an American passport. But he was connected to a woman. Her name and email address is on some papers I brought."

Cardinal Sergius slammed his fist on the altar then paced in a circle. "Then all is not lost. The initiates will travel to America and contact her. You must return to Brazil in case the boy is trying to find you."

"Yes. Of course. I will leave first thing in the morning."

"We must correct this mistake by bringing him here to be trained."

Mistake? Devante considered. *Perhaps not... God does not make mistakes.*

CHAPTER 17

The chill that ran up Matt's spine had nothing to do with the near-freezing temperature. He wasn't the type to be afraid. And when backed into a corner, he generally knew how to handle himself. This was different.

The mysterious wound and blackout had to have been caused by the blood, but what was he supposed to do about it? And what if that wasn't the end of it? He could see a doctor, but there was a bigger chance he'd be committed to a mental institution than that anyone would believe him. Besides, what would they know that Linda didn't? She was an expert in her field, and she had no clue what the substance was. A doctor would only send a sample of his blood to someone with less expertise.

He could have Linda take a blood sample directly from him, but if he did that, he would have to tell her where the blood had come from. Then he'd be back to the sanity issue.

Matt took another look at his hand and shook his head in bewilderment. There had to be an explanation for how the gash had healed itself in less than an hour, but he couldn't think of one.

"Look out!"

He only managed to look up before he slammed into a teenage girl, knocking her to the concrete.

"Screw you!" she shouted as she hit the frozen sidewalk. She was about seventeen, and as goth as they came. Why would such a pretty girl do that to herself?

"Watch where you're going, asshole!"

"Sorry." Matt helped her pick herself off the sidewalk. "I didn't see you—"

A dark spot appeared in his vision. Shit. Was he going to black out again? He blinked rapidly, but instead of fading away, the black formation took on a definite shape. As the image cleared, he found himself staring at a hideous translucent being.

"Jesus!" He recoiled.

"Asshole!" she yelled. "First you knock me on my ass and now you're judging me?"

Matt stared in disbelief at the creature perched on the girl's shoulder. The impish being stood about one-foot high. Its face somewhat resembled a bat's, but with a much larger mouth, full of small, razor-sharp teeth. Its hairless, gray-black, leathery skin was stretched over its grotesque, bony body.

The creature appeared to be aware of him. It scrambled behind her, displaying its two leathery wings and a foot-long sinewy tail as it went. It peeked out from its hiding spot and hissed at him like a tomcat.

Matt shot his gaze back and forth between the imp and the young woman. She was still ranting about his closed-minded and prejudicial views, seemingly completely unaware of the disgusting being. Apparently finished with her verbal assault, she turned and stomped away. The demon creature kept its hold on her as she headed down the street.

His first instinct was to follow her, but he paused when his hair stood on end. He had an odd feeling he was being watched. Expecting to see more of the creatures, he spun around to face them.

"What the..." Matt lost all sense of danger as he gazed up at the majestic being. It had to have been at least ten feet tall, and its skin gave off its own light. It looked identical to the statues in Devante's church. Most amazing was the massive, flaming two-handed sword. There was no doubt in his mind that he was looking into the eyes of an angel.

Holy shit. While he marveled at it, a group of pedestrians walked right through it without the slightest idea that they had. Clearly no one else could see or sense it.

"Hello?" Matt said to the heavenly visitor.

The angel didn't answer, but looked earnestly from Matt to the woman with the imp. Matt felt an overwhelming urge to follow them and turned just in time to see them round the corner and disappear from sight. When he looked back at the angel, it was gone.

What the hell *was* that? All of that couldn't have just happened...but it had seemed so real. Matt tried to shake it off, but he couldn't let it go. He needed to prove it was a figment of his imagination or it would eat at him forever. Matt rushed to find the girl.

As soon as he spotted her, the angel reappeared at his side. "No fucking way." Matt stared at it. "Are you for real?"

The angel remained silent.

"Well, if you're not gonna say anything, maybe she'll have some explanations."

He tailed her until she entered a shop, the angel keeping pace the entire time.

Matt followed her in and took a quick look around. She was near the back of the store, thumbing through some merchandise. He walked over to the nearest display that gave him a clear view of her and pretended to shop. The imp was still on her. Each time it crawled across her head, the woman rubbed her temples and grimaced.

To Matt's alarm, she turned and gazed in his direction.

He dropped his head and acted like he was reading the package he was holding. Shit. She was coming his way.

"Are you stalking me?" she accused.

He tried to act surprised. "Chill out. I'm just buying this."

"I have trouble believing you're looking for a pink cell cover." She pointed to the item in Matt's hand.

"I—" There was no use continuing the act. "Okay, the truth is, I did follow you here."

The woman's eyebrow rose.

"Don't worry. I'm not a freak or anything. I just have to ask you something." The angel moved in behind her.

"What?" She eyed him suspiciously.

Matt had to strain to keep his attention off the imp. "Do you see anything strange?" How was he supposed to ask her this without sounding crazy?

"Besides you?" She tilted her head and scowled. "What in the hell are you talking about?"

"I mean, do you see...demons and angels and stuff like that?"

Her face instantly reddened, and she crossed her arms. "Asshole. Just because I dress different, I'm not a freak." She placed her hands on her hips and got right in his face. "Newsflash, you're the fucking freak!"

Guess not.

Matt took a step back, but he still needed to find out what the imp was doing. "I'm sorry. I didn't mean—"

"Fuck off and leave me alone!" Her raised voice was attracting a lot of attention.

Matt tossed the cell cover onto the rack and headed for the door. As soon as his feet hit the pavement, the angel disappeared. "This is crazy," he mumbled under his breath.

There had to be a rational explanation.

Maybe the blood contained some sort of hallucinogen,

and this was all a drug-induced trip. He laughed. He'd done his share of drugs, but never anything *this* strong. Still, the idea made more sense than anything else he'd considered.

The priest was mixing a hallucinogenic drug with blood. The drug was part of some living organism native to that area, which was why Linda couldn't identify it. Devante was faking the miracles and performing some kind of religious ceremony to get the villagers to ingest it. Matt wasn't sure what he meant to accomplish by drugging them, but it was probably to exercise control over them for one reason or another.

Whatever the motive, he didn't care. Nothing mattered except that he wasn't going crazy. For the first time since visiting the Brazilian church, he felt in control. Everything now made perfect sense. All he had to do was wait for the drug to wear off, and life would return to normal. If only he'd figured this out before blowing it with Victoria. Things would've turned out differently between them. They'd probably be out on a date right now, having the time of their lives. Perhaps he still stood a chance. He grabbed his cellphone, scrolled to her number, and pressed send.

"Hello?" she answered.

"Hey, it's Matt."

"What do you want?" Her tone turned as cold as the air.

"I want to apologize. I was a complete asshole."

"Yes, you were. Is that it? I'm busy."

"No! Listen, you deserve to know the truth. I'd like to explain myself."

"I can't talk right now. I'm setting up for my art show. Maybe we can talk next week or something."

He knew a brush off when he heard one, and it seemed likely that if he didn't get the chance to explain himself right then, he never would. "I really think you'll want to hear this. It's about the statues."

There was a long pause.

"I'll be done in about an hour. If you can make it here by then, we can talk."

"Thank you!" Everything was back on track. He felt recharged. "You're not going to believe what happened, but it's the God's honest truth."

The address Victoria gave him was within walking distance. "I'll be there by nine. Guaranteed."

"Well, don't be late."

"I won't."

CHAPTER 18

Damn stoplight. It was almost eight thirty.

A businessman stopped next to him. The man looked worried, glancing frequently behind him. "Come on, come on," he urged the light.

Matt scanned the street for whatever was upsetting the guy, but saw nothing unusual. The light changed, and the businessman launched off the curb. In his haste, he dropped a small parcel. Matt picked it up and went to return it, but the man was already halfway across the road. As Matt called out, his voice was stolen by a wave of nausea.

"Oh shit. Here we go again." He braced for another blackout.

He leaned over, fighting the overwhelming urge to vomit, and was almost run over by two men.

"Easy!" Matt warned the pair, who ignored him and raced across the street. The nausea left him as fast as it had come on.

"Assholes," Matt muttered. He gripped the package and chased after the businessman, who suddenly stopped and spun around.

"What do you want?" the man asked the pair who'd just bumped into Matt. "Stop following me!"

No wonder the guy was acting so strangely. Matt kept his distance.

"You're Roger Peterson, right?" the smaller one asked.
"Yes?"

"We'd like to talk to you for a minute."

"Who are you?" He held his briefcase to his chest.

"We're with the DA's office."

Matt shook his head. They didn't look like lawyers. He shifted to the side to get a better view. He was scanning the area to see if the two had any accomplices when the angelic figment of his imagination reappeared.

Not you again, he thought. *When's this stuff gonna wear off?*

Turning from his hallucinatory companion, he focused on the men.

"What are your names?" Peterson asked. "Who's your supervisor?"

"You're talking to none other than the mighty Lokad," the larger one motioned to himself, "and my esteemed colleague, Zaralen."

"Don't use our names, you dumb fuck!" Zaralen objected.

Matt had heard enough. He started toward the group, hoping that returning the package to Peterson would scare the two thugs away. At the same time, Peterson turned and ran.

Matt stopped in his tracks when a black object spewed out of Zaralen's mouth and hit Peterson in the back. The dark form uncurled, just like the one on the goth girl.

What the fuck? Matt squeezed his eyes shut and shook his head. This had to be the drugs. Right?

Zaralen opened his mouth again, and five more of the imps streamed toward the escaping man.

Instinctively, Matt spun to face the angel. "Protect him, you dumb shit!"

In a flash, the angel bounded between the imps and their intended target. The airborne demons changed direction and soared just out of range of the angel, who'd taken a combative stance with the flaming two-handed sword above his head. The two men jumped back and scanned the crowd.

Matt squeezed his eyes shut. This was crazy. The drugs had him to speaking to his imaginary friend, and it was listening to him. Were the three men also hallucinations? They looked too real. Matt opened his eyes, hoping it would all be gone, but Peterson was still there, holding his head, and moaning in pain.

Lokad opened his mouth and spewed out five imps of his own. The flying demons flocked together and rose into the air above the street. The imps circled then raced past Matt, picking up speed as they set their course toward Peterson and the angelic warrior. Shit. The angel was about to get his ass kicked. Sure, he had the sword and was built like a tank, but he was also completely naked and there were a dozen sets of claws racing toward him. The angel handled the ornate sword at an amazing speed as the pack closed the gap. Perhaps he could manage.

The imps split into two groups, extended their talons, and let out a chorus of hideous shrieks. One group went after Peterson, and the other raced toward the angel.

His blazing sword struck each of Peterson's attackers with lightning speed. As the blade cut them in half, their severed bodies ignited and incinerated.

The second group of imps swarmed the warrior's head. Blood flowed over his snow-white skin. The angel leaped out of the throng and, with amazing precision, cut them down too. One of three remaining creatures managed to slip by and reach Peterson. He now had two of the demons clinging to him.

The second imp's impact upset Peterson's balance, and he reached out to break his fall. His briefcase flew from his hand, and he landed awkwardly on the street, right in the path of an approaching bus. The angel streaked to Peterson's side and knocked him back, just inches clear of being hit.

The spiritual battle raged on. With Peterson safe, the angel continued to fight the last of the imps. The beings passed through people as if they were non-existent. No one appeared to see or feel the angel or the demons. The more intently Matt watched, the more vivid the beings became—until they seemed more real to him than his surroundings. It looked as if the crowd had become the apparitions.

The angel spun backward and sliced through the last of his opponents. The creature's severed body burst into flames and incinerated.

"Holy shit!" Matt exclaimed. "That was totally awesome."

"You call that awesome?" an enraged woman asked. "The poor man was almost run over by a bus. What kind of sick person are you?"

"No. I meant the angel!"

The lady shook her head. "The what?"

"Never mind."

Matt looked back at Peterson. The two imps were still clinging to him. Why didn't the angel slice those two in half like the others, or kill the men who'd spewed them out? The warrior stared at Matt, as if it expected him to do something.

"What?"

If the spiritual beings were just a figment of his imagination, how could Peterson and the two men have been affected by them? Or were they all hallucinations? Was anything he was seeing real?

He looked from the angel to the imps on Peterson then turned to find the two men. Lokad had disappeared, but he spotted Zaralen in the crowd, facing Matt's direction. His eyes stood out against the darkness of the night, glowing red like burning embers.

Hallucination or not, he was going to get some answers.

He headed toward the red-eyed man.

CHAPTER 19

Zaralen was pissed. What should've been a simple assignment had just turned into a total disaster. How in the Hell had the Warrior found them and fucked everything up? The meddling angel's appearance should've been impossible as there were no Torren alive to guide him.

Zaralen studied Peterson to see how many of his Qaton had gotten past the Warrior's blade. To his dismay, only two of his had survived the battle, and all of Lokad's were dead. He needed five to control Peterson's testimony. They were fucked. As it stood, all Zaralen had accomplished was a way to track Peterson. That only required one Qaton, but he couldn't recall his second because the Warrior would cut it down the moment it left the protection of its hold on the human.

Besides failing their mission, they were likely in deep shit. The crowd had witnessed the altercation that had almost led to Peterson's death, and people could identify him as a suspect. Many were staring at him, especially a messy-haired punk across the sidewalk. It would've been so much easier if Dmoltech had allowed them to snuff Peterson out, but he wasn't about to disobey his master, especially after their last meeting. Still, he might be able to salvage the situation if he could speak to Peterson without being overheard by anyone in the crowd. A verbal threat should be enough to keep the shaken man from testifying.

Even though the Warrior had made quick work of the

Qaton, Zaralen wasn't afraid. One huge advantage of having a soldier of God as your adversary was that they had no choice but to play by the rules. The Warrior couldn't strike him down as long as he was cloaked. The blade couldn't discern between him and his cloak, and killing a human was forbidden.

He stepped off the curb and walked toward Peterson. As he approached, the angel spun and pointed the sword at his chest. Zaralen stopped.

Then again...

The Warrior shouldn't have been allowed to be there without a Torren commanding it, and the Torren were extinct. Perhaps the rules had changed.

Not prepared to test that possibility, he backed off to a safe distance and raised his middle finger to the white warrior.

"Excuse me," the punk who'd been staring at him said. "Can I talk to you for a second?"

"Fuck off." He glared at the kid and pushed him aside.

"I know what just happened. I saw it all."

Zaralen spun to face him. "What did you see?"

The kid paused. "I'm pretty sure you know you what I'm talking about. The angel, the demon creatures..."

Zaralen took a step back. No fucking way. The Torren were all dead. This should've been impossible...but the angel was proof enough. Sweat beaded on his forehead. His chances of survival were slim, but he wasn't going to be banished to Hell without putting up a good fight. "I assume you want to do battle somewhere a little more private?"

"Battle? Huh? No." He held his hands up. "I just want some answers. That's all."

"The fuck you do. Let's get on with it."

"I'm serious. I need your help. I don't know what the hell is going on."

"What?" It seemed impossible, but...could this idiot be telling the truth?

"I know you're probably not real, but can you explain any of this?"

Zaralen's heart rate slowed. "How did you get this ability?"

"This is nuts, but I think it came from some blood from a statue. I accidently got infected when I cut my hand. Can you help me?"

Un-fucking-believable. It was true. He *was* Torren, but he didn't have a fucking clue. The scale had tipped in Zaralen's favor. The Shakath had obviously missed a statue, and he needed to find it. Along with the punk's second. He needed to earn his trust, and play it cool. Then he could kill him. "I'm glad we met. How did you find me?"

"Pure coincidence."

Zaralen knew better. Torren were subconsciously drawn to the Shakath and had a history of showing up at the most inopportune times.

"Look," the Torren continued, "will you please just tell me what's going on?"

"Sure. I can help you. Let's go somewhere private to talk."

"I don't think so." The kid slowly shook his head. "I don't know much, but I saw enough to know you're not one of the good guys. I have no beef with you. Just tell me what's going on, and I'll be on my way. As far as I'm concerned, none of this ever happened."

Zaralen opened his coat to show his holstered gun. "Don't even think of running. You're coming with me."

The Torren fled.

CHAPTER 20

Matt sprinted down the street with Zaralen in pursuit. The man's glowing red eyes bobbed up and down in the darkness as he gave chase. A shot rang out.

A woman collapsed in front of him, blood soaking her coat, and he skidded to a stop. Her screams ripped through Matt's soul. What had he done? He bent over to try to stop the bleeding.

Another shot rang out. People were screaming and running in every direction. He had to go. "Oh God... I'm sorry...please don't die."

Matt sprinted for blocks, screaming for people to run for cover as he darted through them. What had he gotten himself into? He was in way over his head. People were dying. *He* could die. His legs ached and his lungs burned, but he forced himself to keep going. Stopping would cost him his life. He rounded a corner and scanned the street for a possible escape. A restaurant two shops away looked promising. He had to get through the door before Zaralen caught up.

Heart pounding, panting wildly, Matt pushed past the short line of people waiting to be seated. The host, dressed in a black suit and tie, took one look at Matt and stepped out from behind his post.

"May I help you?" he asked in a tone that implied he already knew the answer.

"There's a guy after— I need to hide," he gasped, barely

able to get the words out.

"Not here." The host grabbed Matt by the arm. "This is a respectable estab—"

"Listen to me!" Matt broke free of the host's grip. "There's a man with a gun out there. Call the cops!" He was putting them in danger. "Where's the back door?"

The host froze. "I... You..."

Matt's gut roiled—the same sensation he'd felt when Zaralen first bumped into him. His time had run out. He spun to face the open door and saw the threatening red glow of Zaralen's eyes. Matt pushed the podium over to gain a few precious seconds and bolted through the restaurant. Another shot rang out, and screams, mixed with the sound of smashing dishes, filled the room.

Matt burst through the kitchen doors, scrambled past cooks, dishwashers, and crates of food, until he found the exit. He spilled out into the dark alley and hid behind a nearby dumpster. Moments later, Zaralen bounded through the door.

Matt had turned the wrong way. The street was only fifty yards away, but on the other side of Zaralen. There was no telling if the alley dead-ended behind him or not. He couldn't risk it. Hopefully, Zaralen would assume he'd sought safety in the crowded street. Matt hunkered down, struggling to control his breathing.

Zaralen strolled along the alley toward the street just as Matt had hoped. He paused along the way, searching in dumpsters, until he reached the end. He holstered his gun before looking up and down the street then turned and started back in Matt's direction. Did those glowing red eyes have night vision?

Shit! It was now or never. Matt sprang up and sprinted down the alley. He rounded the corner and ran into a solid brick wall. A dead end.

"No!" Matt yelled.

He spun around just as Zaralen knocked him off his feet.

The creature straddled him and grabbed him by the collar. "No more games," Zaralen demanded. "Who sent you?"

"Sent me?" Matt threw his weight to the side and rolled his body out from under Zaralen's. Delivering a solid knee to Zaralen's ribs, he managed to reverse their positions. Matt punched him in the face repeatedly until Zaralen started to go limp. "Who are you, you red-eyed motherfucker? What the hell is going on?"

Matt looked down the alley, hoping the cops had arrived. He froze as cold metal pressed against his temple.

"Get off me." Zaralen held the gun between Matt's eyes.

Matt stood up and backed away. Zaralen picked himself off the ground, never losing his aim. Matt wanted to run, but the hundred yards to the street looked more like a mile.

"No one hits me and lives."

Zaralen hadn't pulled the trigger. Maybe there was a way out of this. He needed to stall until help arrived. "Take it easy, man. I'm sure we can work something out." Where were the police?

Zaralen took a step toward Matt. "Who's your partner?"

"What are talking about? I'm alone."

"You're going to die if you don't start talking." Zaralen tightened his grip on the gun. "Where's your partner, and where's the statue?"

Matt had no idea what to answer. His mind went blank.

"One, two—"

"Drop the gun, and put your hands up!" Two police officers had finally arrived. "Drop the gun. Now!"

"Good riddance." Zaralen smiled and steadied his aim.

Matt squeezed his eyes shut. *This is it.*

The sound of the gun was deafening, but nothing happened. When he opened his eyes, Zaralen was lying on the ground. One of the police officers had shot him before he'd managed to pull the trigger.

Matt exhaled. Thank God he was alive. He stared at Zaralen's body. Was he dead? Did he have some power that might bring him back to life? Matt couldn't risk it. He lunged for the gun and grabbed it out of Zaralen's hand. Zaralen was still breathing—a slow, labored breath. Matt pointed the gun at the downed man. The two police officers advanced, guns readied, until they stood within twenty feet of him.

"Drop the weapon!" the female officer instructed.

"I can't. He might shoot me." Matt looked back at Zaralen's chest. It stopped moving. One last breath escaped, rising up in the cold air.

The breath of air didn't dissipate but grew and took on a transparent human form. Goosebumps covered Matt's body. The man's spirit floated three feet off the ground, hovered over its body, and appeared to examine its former home. It smiled with the most peaceful expression Matt had ever seen. Then, it rotated—slowly at first, but then faster until Matt could no longer make out any features. Thousands of beams of light shot from the blur, which faded within seconds. The spirit evaporated.

"You need to put down the gun," the female officer repeated. "He can't hurt you anymore."

"Now!" her male counterpart ordered.

The command jarred Matt out of his mesmerized state, and he bent to place the gun on the ground. He was about to release the weapon when Zaralen's hand moved.

"He's still alive!" Matt yelled. He recoiled, raising the

gun in defense.

"He hasn't moved a muscle," the male officer responded. "Now put the gun down. This is your last warning!"

Was he imagining things? Regardless, the police officers were losing their patience with him. Matt tossed the gun away from Zaralen's body. The hand moved again.

Something was wrong. He had no idea what was going on, but he was sure he'd just witnessed the man's spirit leaving his body. So how was it moving? Was it muscle reflex? His heart nearly stopped when an opaque human form separated from the dead body.

"Oh shit." Matt took a step back as the being gathered itself and stood, facing away from him. It looked like a man...or rather the shadow of a man. It turned its head in Matt's direction. Glowing red eyes filled him with fear. This was far from over.

Matt readied for the attack, but the demon turned back to the approaching police officers, who seemed unaware of its presence. The creature sprinted toward the male officer, and dove at him. The blackness vanished into the cop's torso.

The policeman dropped to his knees and heaved the contents of his stomach onto the pavement. Falling over backward, he went into severe convulsions.

"Officer down!" his partner yelled into her radio. "Hurry, he's having a seizure or something!"

The convulsions stopped as suddenly as they'd begun. The cop opened his eyes, and to Matt's horror, they were no longer human. Zaralen's penetrating red stare locked on Matt.

This was beyond fucked up. Could the demon be stopped? Matt's legs burned, and he could barely breathe, but there were no other options but to get the hell out of

The Crimson Dimension

there. Matt closed the gap before the cop could get to his feet and kicked him with every ounce of strength he had. The cop hit the ground hard. Matt sprinted toward the street, now filled with onlookers.

"Stop!" the woman cop screamed.

Matt picked his spot and broke through the crowd. He ran until his legs could no longer carry him.

CHAPTER 21

"How much longer are you going to be?" Claire, the gallery's manager, asked. "I'd like to get going."

Victoria glanced at her watch for the fourth time since nine o'clock. *Where is he?* She dusted off her sculptures yet again. "Just a few minutes, if that's okay with you. I'm expecting someone. He's running a bit late."

"Boyfriend?" Claire smiled.

Victoria laughed. "He'd like to think so."

Claire's eyebrows rose. "Oh, I see. Having troubles?"

Victoria didn't want to spill her guts to Claire—their relationship was a professional one—yet the woman was so genuine and approachable. She reminded Victoria a lot of her mother, and it was at times like this that she missed her most. Perhaps a bit of advice would be helpful.

"You could say that. The weird thing is that he's not even my boyfriend. We've met a few times, and he hasn't turned out to be who I thought he was. But for some dumb reason, I keep hoping it will work out."

Claire sighed. "I remember when I first met my Steven. I thought he was the biggest jerk alive. I wouldn't give him the time of day, but he kept persisting until I finally went on a date with him. We've been married for forty-six years now and have four children and seven beautiful grandchildren."

What would it be like to be part of a family like that?

"Well, this is the complete opposite. I met him and

thought he was wonderful. Then I found out he *was* a real jerk."

Claire patted Victoria's arm. "I'm sorry, dear."

"Yeah, but then he called me tonight and apologized, and he seemed so sincere about it. He said he was coming over...but he should've been here an hour ago."

"Maybe something came up."

"I doubt it. He's been really unreliable."

Claire shook her head. "Why don't you call him? It's obvious you care about him."

Were her feelings for Matt that transparent? She thought about calling for a few seconds, but there was no way she was going to appear desperate. "You know what?" She shook her head. "I think I'll pass. I'm happy being single, and I don't need my life turned upside down. Especially for some guy who doesn't know whether he's coming or going."

"Well, perhaps he isn't the one for you...or perhaps it's you."

Wow. That came out of nowhere. Her face flushed. "What do you mean by that?"

"Forgive me." Claire blushed. "That may have seemed rather harsh. I hardly know you, but we've chatted enough tonight for me to think that something's holding you back. I see it in your art. You're very talented, but I think you have more to give. I think you play it safe. Your work is good, but it could be exceptional. Don't be afraid to take a risk or two. Open yourself and be vulnerable. That's when you'll realize your true potential."

How had the conversation switched from Matt to realizing her potential? Claire was beginning to sound like someone else she knew. "That's what Grandpa always says."

"Well, he's right.

She hated to admit it, but it was true. "I know. I feel it too. I'm never quite happy with my work, and I can't put a finger on it. And I do want a relationship. It's just too bad we can't chisel off their faults." Victoria walked over to the coat rack and put on her coat.

"Oh, but we can." Claire giggled. "Men can be putty in the hands of a smart woman. Just look at my Steven. He turned out all right in the end."

Maybe she was right. But was Matt worth the effort? "Thanks for your encouragement, and thank you again for showing my work. It's a true honor."

"The honor's all mine. Someday I'll be bragging that I gave you your start."

Victoria wrapped her scarf around her neck. "I'm not so sure about that, but thanks all the same. I'll see you tomorrow."

"Good night, and drive safe."

CHAPTER 22

Zaralen watched through Officer Lowry's eyes as the Torren ran past him and disappeared into the crowd. He struggled to gain enough control of his new cloak to stop Matt from leaving the scene—or even tell his partner to do it.

That damn punk delivered a wicked kick, but fortunately hadn't knocked him out. He struggled to his feet. "Why in the Hell didn't you shoot him, you stupid bitch?" he barked at Officer Karen McKinney.

Karen startled. "What are you talking about? I could've hit the crowd. There was no shot. Besides, would you have preferred it if I left you to die?"

"I'm fine!"

"You sure as hell didn't look fine." She pointed at his vomit. "And where do you get off calling me a bitch? What's wrong with you?"

Zaralen had control of Lowry's body, but the fight for his mind wasn't quite over. He kept forcing his will until the man finally lost the battle. *He's mine.* All of Lowry's thoughts and memories flooded Zaralen's consciousness. It was ten times better than shooting up. Shivers ran up his spine.

"Rick."

Amazing. This guy was a gold mine. The skills. The knowledge and training. This was going to be some useful shit.

"Rick! Are you listening to me?"

"What?" It would take a few more minutes for Zaralen to be able to respond to his new name without hesitation.

"You better sit down until the medics get here. I don't know what happened to you, but I think you should rest for a while. I'll tape off the area."

Playing up the illness would give him time to plan his next move. "Yeah. Thanks. I'm not feeling too good." He sat down on a crate and spent a few minutes getting more of a feel for Lowry.

As the longest-standing member of Dmoltech's Shakath, Zaralen had served for over four hundred years. During that time, he'd only used about three dozen cloaks. Changing cloaks too often was a rookie move that made it nearly impossible to establish and maintain one's networks. Other Shakath went through cloaks like water, and never tasted the same success. Zaralen didn't care. In fact, he was glad. It enabled him to out-perform them all, which had put him at the top of the pecking order. But, as much as he'd have preferred keeping his old cloak, this cop would give him access to a lot of information and could prove very useful. If he didn't get banished for failing their mission. Fuck. They'd blown it completely, thanks to that damn Torren. Then again, a Torren was the best excuse a guy could hope for. Not that he was happy one was alive. For the last half century, they'd enjoyed an uninhibited era of corruption and decay. That was about to end.

"Let's have a look at you." The paramedic had arrived.

"I'm fine. I must've eaten some bad food or something." He stood up and walked over to Karen, who'd been joined by two other officers. She was head down, focused on her notepad. "Listen, I don't feel great, but I'm sure I'll be okay after a good night's sleep. I'm heading home."

Karen looked him over and nodded. "Yeah. You look a

lot better. What about your report?"

"I'll write it in the morning."

She nodded. "All right. What did the medic say?"

"He said I'm fine. I just need some rest." He turned away and walked to his patrol car.

Looking at his watch, he realized that he was going to be late for the follow-up meeting with Dmoltech. He flipped on the lights and siren and sped across the city.

△ △ △

Zaralen arrived at The Cathedral, New York's most popular nightclub. Aptly named, it had once been New York's largest Catholic church. Dmoltech had bought the property and transformed it into a nightclub for the sole pleasure of turning the renowned place of worship into the playhouse and office of demonic beings.

It was normal for the club to be filled to capacity, and latecomers were accustomed to long lines with the faint hope of getting in. Thursday nights were always slower than the weekends, and the night's bitter weather had kept many at home, but the club was still overflowing.

He pushed through the line, ignoring the insults and obscenities the cold and intolerant crowd directed at him. A large bouncer stepped in front of him, blocking his progress. "You're not welcome here," he said. "Unless you have a warrant, you can go fuck yourself."

Zaralen looked down at his uniform then rolled his eyes. He hadn't even thought to change clothes before arriving. Regardless, it made no difference to him that the bouncer hadn't a clue who he was. He was second-in-command, and he'd better be treated as such. He pulled his gun from his holster and jammed the barrel under the bouncer's chin.

"That's no way to talk to me."

The bouncer recoiled but then regained his composure. "No disrespect," he offered. "But my orders are that no cops are allowed in without a warrant."

Zaralen sighed. "I'm on the list, you little prick." He returned his gun to its holster, allowing the bouncer to check.

Picking up a clipboard, he asked Zaralen for his name.

"Not that list. The list. Hand me the keypad."

The bouncer's face flushed, and he unclipped a wireless keypad from his belt. He handed it to Zaralen, who typed in his six-digit code before passing the device back.

"I'm terribly sorry for inconveniencing you," the bouncer apologized after the authorization flashed green. "Mr. Bromley is in his office." He stepped aside and let Zaralen pass without further comment.

"Remember this face," Zaralen demanded. "If you ever obstruct me again, I'll blow your fucking head off."

Shit. It would take weeks, possibly months, to reestablish himself as the respected and feared associate of Mitchell Bromley.

Zaralen entered the nightclub and was engulfed by a throng of people. The heavy beat of dance music thundered through the club, and strobe lights made the crowd flicker in and out of existence. The foyer had been converted to a cashier's station, where the cover charge was collected. In keeping with the theme, the money was accepted by way of a collection plate.

Zaralen placed his hand over his holstered service pistol and forced his way through the crowded dance floor toward the back of the club. The nave, where the parishioners had once sat, and the domed transept had been converted into a multilevel dance floor. The altar was now home to the DJ. A large addition had been built onto the back of the church to house a few offices and a storage

The Crimson Dimension

area for liquor and supplies. Above the crossing was a private balcony set aside for VIPs, which had a great view of the dance floor.

Zaralen's blood pressure rose when he encountered another bouncer at the foot of the stairway. He was not in the mood to explain everything again. To his relief, his presence had been relayed ahead. The man unhooked the velvet rope and motioned for him to proceed.

Zaralen received a few curious looks and watched in amusement as a woman did her best to hide her cocaine without spilling it all over herself. He strode past her and stood before a solid iron door. The plaque above it read "God." He typed his six-digit security code into the keypad on the wall, and walked in.

CHAPTER 23

Dmoltech drew on his cigar as he paced back and forth in his office. He had called a meeting for ten o'clock and did not tolerate lateness. It was now ten fifteen. All his Shakath were present, with the exception of Zaralen. Dmoltech had just looked at his watch again when a police officer came through the door.

"Who let you in here? Get the fuck out!" Not only were the cops bad for business, but they'd been harassing him day and night. Arriving in an excessive show of force, they'd arrested him and walked him out in handcuffs in front of his patrons. The arrest was nothing more than a theatrical production for the media, who'd been waiting with cameras ready, obviously tipped off by the DA.

"Please forgive my tardiness."

Dmoltech looked through the policeman standing in front of him, and recognized Zaralen within the cloak. His temper cooled. "I see you've acquired a new skin, Zaralen. And one of New York's finest, at that. I'll forgive your lateness considering your fine choice of cloak. This one may prove very useful. Now take a seat. We have important business to conduct."

Zaralen bowed and took the empty seat next to his trainee, Lokad.

An explanation for the change of cloaks would have to wait. Dmoltech was running out of time, and needed an update on Roger Peterson.

"Have you secured the accountant?"

Zaralen looked down. "We ran into a problem."

Dmoltech slammed his hand down on his desk. "Can't you simple-minded vermin do anything right?"

Mitchell Bromley's trial was scheduled to begin on Monday. If convicted, Dmoltech would have to answer to Lucifer for this failure. The consequences were unimaginable.

"If the accountant testifies, I'll send you all down!"

His five subordinates nervously exchanged glances.

"I will not fail you, my Lord," Zaralen replied.

"You are failing me! You're all failing me!"

Athamm jumped up. "You can't possibly be serious about blaming us all for that imbecile's mistake!"

"Shut the fuck up!" Dmoltech closed his eyes for a moment before continuing. He turned to Zaralen. "Explain what happened out there tonight."

Zaralen glared at Athamm. "I'd be careful who you're calling an imbecile." He looked back to face his master. "It was no small matter. Just as I dispatched my Qaton, a Warrior appeared."

"Bullshit!" Athamm jumped to his feet again. "Everyone knows we killed the last of the Torren eighty years ago! The Warriors disappeared with them."

Athamm was right about that. Zaralen was full of shit.

Dmoltech turned to Lokad. "I know you've never seen a Torren before, so I want you to describe what happened in detail." He looked back at Zaralen. "You'd better hope I believe him."

Lokad looked at Zaralen then back at Dmoltech. He cleared his throat. "Zaralen sent his first Qaton, and it attached itself just like it should have."

"How would you know?"

"He'd just finished teaching me how to bring mine forth. I placed one on a girl for practice."

Dmoltech nodded. "Go on."

"He released his other five, but before they got to Peterson, a huge white angel swooped in with a flaming sword. I sent the rest of mine also, but the angel killed them all. Well, almost all of them. One more of Zaralen's got to Peterson. All of mine are gone except the one still on the girl."

Dmoltech felt as if he'd just been punched in the stomach. The return of the Torren was inconceivable, yet Lokad was too convincing for the story to be some pile of bullshit. He stood motionless, letting it sink in. How in the hell could the Torren have reemerged? They'd found every statue, and he'd personally killed the last of their kind. The knot in his gut tightened. Another war was on its way.

Focus.

Dmoltech had immediate issues to deal with. The return of the Torren would greatly complicate matters, but he had to press on with his plans. Those stupid fuckers had just lost most of their Qaton, and he couldn't ask Lucifer for replacements.

Dmoltech tapped his finger on his chin. How could he spin this? Of course—he could blame the Torren for this recent fuckup, and more importantly, for killing Nazkiel and Radok. Lucifer would understand and gather his forces to hunt the Torren down. Or, better yet, if Dmoltech could singlehandedly deliver the Torren to Lucifer, it would prove his worth and advance his position. It would be risky, but he was more than willing to sacrifice his Shakath to achieve success.

"Tell me about the Torren."

Zaralen interjected. "Lokad ran away before he showed himself. I faced him alone and almost killed him. That's how I lost my cloak."

"You expect us to believe you singlehandedly fought a

Torren and survived?" Athamm challenged once again.

"I told you to shut your mouth!" Dmoltech took his cigar and butted it out on the top of Athamm's head. The stench of singed hair was overshadowed by the sickening sound of sizzling flesh. Athamm cringed, but he knew better than to move. The other four shifted in their seats. Dmoltech pulled the cigar away then flicked it into Athamm's face.

"Continue."

Zaralen swallowed. "The Torren appeared to be untrained. He was confused, and I don't think he knows any of his abilities. He won't be hard to put down. I was about to kill him, but two cops showed up and ruined everything."

Dmoltech rubbed his chin. "A Torren, even untrained, is not a minor matter. And if there is one, there has to be another. That means there must be a blood source somewhere out there."

"There is. He told me he got infected from a bleeding statue."

Bayeth ended her silence. "We will find them, and the statue."

Toal, her partner, followed Bayeth's lead. "He won't get away from us."

Dmoltech always welcomed Bayeth's input, but cared little for Toal's. "I didn't ask you to speak, you stupid ape." He was useful as Bayeth's lapdog and bodyguard, nothing more.

Toal's muscular body shrank back in his chair.

Dmoltech couldn't allow the Torren time to learn, but Peterson had to be stopped before the weekend was over. They had no option but to deal with both threats at once.

"This couldn't have happened at a worse time," Dmoltech began. "But we will stop the witness, and we will kill the Torren." He walked back to his desk and sat down. "Zaralen and Lokad don't have enough Qaton left to control Peterson, so I'm assigning Bayeth to use hers."

"That's going to be impossible," Zaralen interrupted. "The Torren commanded the Warrior to protect Peterson. That white fucker will kill her Qaton as well."

"Why didn't you mention that before, you ass?" He jumped up and started pacing again. Perhaps that news wasn't as bad as it first appeared. The Torren would be much easier to kill without his Warrior to protect him, and Peterson could still be controlled. "We'll just have to use the old-fashioned method of persuasion to keep him from testifying."

"That's not going to be so easy either." Zaralen's face showed that he had more bad news.

"Now what?"

"Everyone on the street thinks we pushed Peterson in front of a bus. I'm positive he'll be under full police protection by now."

"Holy shit! What else could go wrong? Do you fuck-ups have anything else to add? I want it all on the table right now."

"Forgive me, my Lord," Lokad offered. "He lost his balance when the Qaton hit him. I panicked and ran. People thought I pushed him."

Lokad was quickly proving to be one of the worst Shakath to have surfaced in centuries. Dmoltech had hoped that placing him under Zaralen's wing would improve his performance, but he still showed no signs of competence. During the couple of days he'd been with Athamm, Lokad had made a lot of serious errors in judgment. He'd repeatedly failed to curb his lusts and had already attracted attention from two rapes and a senseless beating. There was no doubt in Dmoltech's mind what

Lokad intended to do with the woman who carried his last Qaton. He had a mind to dispose of Lokad right there and then, but he was already down to five. This wasn't the time to lose another.

He retrieved another cigar from the box on his desk and took a moment to think while lighting it. The sight of the cigar caused all eyes to turn to Athamm, who broke into a sweat and cowered in his seat. Blood, which was seeping from his burn, trickled down between his eyes and along the side of his nose.

Dmoltech turned to Zaralen. "Use your Qaton to find out where Peterson is being held. After you tell Bayeth where he is, your involvement with Peterson is over. Your next task will be finding the Torren. I want him alive. Since I can't trust any of you to do anything right, I'll personally interrogate him to get the identity of his second and the location of the blood source."

He paused to draw on the cigar before continuing. "There's the remote possibility that one of the priests we control might know of his existence. I'll call them and instruct them to let me know if they learn anything."

Having finished with Zaralen, he gave Bayeth her orders. "You will deal with Peterson. Thanks to those fuck-ups, you won't be able to get near him because of the cops, nor will you be able use your Qaton because of the Warrior. I don't care how you handle it, but I want results before the weekend is over."

"What about me?" Athamm's voice was barely audible.

Dmoltech's conviction that Athamm had killed Nazkiel and Radok faded. Could it have been the Torren? Not likely considering Zaralen's account of the guy. Regardless, it was better to keep Athamm away from the others for now. "Go back and run your operations. I'll call you if I need you."

CHAPTER 24

Matt sprinted up the flight of stairs to his apartment. He took a quick look behind him to make sure no one was following before running down the hall. Home. He slammed the door behind him, secured the deadbolt, and fastened the chain as fast as he could.

Rob and Kathy were sitting on the couch, staring at him with bewildered looks.

"What's wrong?" Rob jumped up. "Are you all right? Is someone after you?"

Matt couldn't catch his breath enough to answer, and waved his hands placatingly instead. "I'm fine," he finally managed. "It's nothing."

"Nothing? You're white as a ghost." Kathy ran over and put her hand on his shoulder. "Linda called over an hour ago. She was worried about your hand. She said you were acting really strange." She grabbed Matt's arm.

Matt shoved his hands into his pockets to hide the absence of the wound. "I just ran home, that's all. Everything's fine." He flashed a weak smile to support his lie. "I have a lot of work to do tonight. I'll be in my room."

"Buddy..." Rob called.

Matt closed his door and flopped onto his bed. He was shaking uncontrollably. Linda had told them about his hand. So, it was true. He'd been cut, and the wound had miraculously healed. There was no way he could've hallucinated the entire night. Everything had actually happened. He jumped up and ran to the window. The street was empty. No one was down there. No red eyes. He drew his blinds.

Had he escaped, or could the demon find him? Did they know shit like that? Was he safe anywhere? Was anyone?

What about that woman? Zaralen had shot her. Everything had been such a blur, but the image of her face was etched in his mind. Her expression had said it all. She'd known Matt was the target, and he was responsible. If he hadn't run, she would've been fine. And he'd left her lying there. She could've died. The guy in the alley had for sure.

His mouth went dry.

Now what? There was no denying it. The spirit world was real, and he was caught up in it. If he'd only heeded Devante's warning. But how was he supposed to have known?

He'd walked into a shitstorm and was lucky to be alive. Zaralen with his red eyes, the little imps, the angel... Where in the hell had the angel gone? It had been injured. Had it died? *Could* it die?

Matt took another look out his window. Nothing. He forced himself to relax.

The only reason *he* was still alive was that Zaralen had wanted to know the location of the statue, and who Matt's partner was. He had to have meant Father Devante. Matt took a breath. The priest had warned him. Devante had to know what was going on and could surely help...but how on earth was Matt supposed to get to him? He barely had a dime to his name after the trip, rent, and the new cellphone. It didn't matter. He had to find a way.

"Devante, you little fucker," Matt muttered under his breath. Why hadn't the priest just been straight with him?

Then again, Matt never would've believed him.

He sat on the edge of his bed.

Should he have known better? He shook his head. How could he? They were just fucking statues...although it was haunting how accurate they were. The warrior angel looked exactly like them, or rather they looked exactly like him. And what about the statue in the middle? The image of Jesus...

Matt closed his eyes and swallowed.

God is real.

He fought hard to suppress his next thoughts. Matt didn't want to go there. He couldn't. Balling his hands into fists, he drove them down into his mattress.

Tilting his head back, he looked up. "Fuck you."

It was so much easier to believe God didn't exist than deal with a supposedly loving deity who just sat back and allowed horrible things to happen. Matt leaned forward, and rubbed his forehead. *Why?* It wasn't a difficult question, but the answer had eluded him his entire life.

Why would God bother with him now, especially after his life was finally on track? What could he have possibly done to have this curse put on him? Sure, he'd done some stupid shit when he was kid—skipping school, shoplifting, and the odd fight. The worst had been the joy ride in a hotwired car. But it had all been a cry for attention, the result of being left to fend for himself. No one had cared if he lived or died—except Jodie. Was this punishment for getting her pregnant?

Matt rolled onto his back, put his hands behind his head, and stared at the ceiling.

No. Nothing he'd done could possibly warrant what was happening to him.

Everyone important to him either let him down or left him. His mom had checked out, Jodie was sent away, and now Rob was moving on with his life. But they were human and had their own shit to deal with. God was supposed to be different. He was supposed to be the one who never left your side. Did He care at all?

A woman had been shot tonight, and a guy killed right in front of him. Collateral damage? Perhaps God had a beef with Matt, but didn't their lives mean anything?

And what about the angel? Was he just a tease? Gone when he was needed most. Why had he abandoned Matt, leaving him to fight for his life?

Where was God tonight? Where had He been his entire life?

As a child, Matt had been told that God was always watching over and protecting His children, but Matt had never known that God. He'd spent so many nights kneeling at his bed, praying for the beatings to stop. They never had. Why had He stood by during all the abuse?

Matt clenched his jaw.

Why? What was so wrong with him that God would pass him by? Deep down, he knew he was a good guy. Why couldn't God see that? Why couldn't his dad?

The tears came. Matt buried his face in his pillow so Rob and Kathy couldn't hear. It all boiled to the surface. Every heartache, all the pain. He tried to push it down, but he couldn't stop it. He'd promised himself he'd never cry. That was the one thing they could never take from him, but who was he kidding? He was broken and there was no denying it. He let the tears flow and allowed himself to grieve for the first time in many years. The release felt good, but also churned up so many questions that he'd buried. The night was long, and no stone was left unturned—until only one question remained.

Why?

CHAPTER 25

Matt rolled over in bed and checked the time. Ten thirty in the morning. Two days had passed since the night his world had been turned upside down. He hadn't gone to class on Friday, and barely left his room at all. He wasn't planning on today being any different.

He was done. Nothing mattered anymore. Why even try when your fate was controlled by a higher power who didn't give a shit about you? And all this time he'd been convinced he was in charge of his destiny.

But now what? Even if the puppet master had plans for him, there wasn't a chance in hell he was going to comply. At the same time, though, something inside him longed to find out what the point of all this was. What use was being able to see angels and demons? No. He shook his head and rolled over, putting the pillow over his head. He wouldn't even let himself think about it.

The only option was to find a way to contact Father Devante and see about getting it removed.

His thoughts were interrupted by a light rap at his door.

"Matt!" Rob called through the door. "Open up. I really need to talk to you."

Rob had knocked a number of times since that night, and he couldn't ignore him forever. He stood up, took a deep breath, and unlocked the door.

Rob held out a sandwich and a beer. "I thought you

The Crimson Dimension

might like something to eat."

Matt's stomach growled. He hadn't eaten since lunch on the day he got infected. He grabbed the sandwich and practically inhaled it.

"Holy shit. I'm lucky you didn't take my hand off." Rob smiled. "I can make you another, if you like?"

Matt grabbed the beer and took a gulp. "Thanks, buddy. This is good. Damn, I'm hungry."

"Yeah. You've been in there for days. What's going on?"

How could he even start to answer that question? "I just had a bad couple of days." He sat on his bed and motioned to his chair for Rob. "I blew things with Victoria, and then I cut my hand open at Linda's lab." Matt turned his hand over to hide his palm. "That's all. I guess I overreacted a bit."

"You think?" Rob shook his head. "There's more to it, and you know it. Linda told us about the blood. What did you get yourself mixed up in?"

There was no avoiding it. "I got mugged after I took the pictures."

"Jesus! I knew something happened there." He pointed his finger at Matt. "Why didn't you say something?"

"I didn't want to wreck your honeymoon." Technically, he hadn't lied—yet.

"Holy shit, Matt. You should have said something." Rob cocked his head. "But why would you have the blood tested?"

"When I fought them off, I bloodied one of them up. I wanted to make sure he didn't have Hep or Aids or some kind of jungle virus."

Rob nodded. "All right. But why were you so upset on Friday?"

"Oh...that... I was pissed off about blowing things with Victoria. I jogged home thinking about it. I was just exhausted. That's all."

"If that's your story..." He stood up and scratched the back of head. "Anyway. Are you done acting like a baby?"

Matt straightened up. "What the fuck does that mean?"

"Come on. As much as you're a pain in the ass, we're bros. I can't sit here and watch you waste away. She's just a girl, for fuck's sake. Snap out of it."

Rob was right. Staying in his room wouldn't solve anything. He had to pull himself together. He couldn't hide for the rest of his life. But what was his next move? He leaned forward and rubbed his temples.

"I'm just trying to help."

Matt looked up. "I know. And you're right. This isn't like me at all. I'll figure my shit out."

Rob moved to the doorway. "Are you okay? Seriously, I mean."

"I will be. Thanks."

Rob smiled, gave Matt a salute, and left the room.

Matt stood up and walked to the window. Enough time had passed that the demons had to have given up on him, or didn't have the ability to find him. He shook his head. It didn't matter. Removing the curse was his ticket back to a normal life. He just needed the priest... Or would any priest do?

"Think."

What about the priest Victoria was working for? Perhaps the guy knew more than he'd told Victoria. It seemed a little too coincidental that one of the sculptures he was cataloging turned out to have these powers. It was worth a shot, and Matt knew where to find him.

△ △ △

Matt scanned the inside of the large church and spotted a young priest toward the front. He waved to get his attention and hurried over to meet him.

"Can I help you? Are you looking to make a confession?"

Matt laughed.

The man turned red. "Is something funny?"

"I'm sorry. It's just that we'd be here all day."

The priest smiled. "That's quite all right. You're not the first to have left it a little too long."

"Well, I'm not here to confess. I'm looking for a priest who works here, but I don't know his name. It could be you for all I know."

"Perhaps I can help?"

"A friend of mine is doing some research here as part of her studies at NYU."

"Oh, yes. I remember her. She's working with our senior pastor, Father Perry."

Matt nodded. "I'd like to speak to him."

The young priest led Matt down a short hallway and into Perry's office. After a brief introduction, he left the two alone and returned to his duties.

Father Perry was a serious looking man in his early forties. Of average height and weight, he had thinning salt-and-pepper hair and a full graying beard and mustache.

He took a long look at Matt while fidgeting with the cross hanging from his neck. "So, you're a friend of Victoria?"

"Yeah."

"What brings you here?"

Matt struggled with how to begin. "I'm here to ask you about the statues."

Perry's eyes widened. "What statues?"

"The ones in Brazil."

He shifted in his seat. "What would you like to know?"

"Well, I was the one who went to take the

photographs."

Perry's expressions were all over the place. One second he looked excited. The next he was pale and sweating like crazy. What was wrong with this guy? "Really? Do you have them here?"

Matt shook his head. "There are no pictures, but I did find the statues. Or maybe it would be more accurate to say that one of them found me."

Father Perry leaned back in the chair, a mix of emotions distorting his face. "I don't understand."

Matt paused. This could turn out to be a very bad decision, but he needed help. "This is going to sound crazy."

"I've heard it all."

"There were three statues. The one of Jesus bled. I got infected by it, and now I'm seeing strange things."

Perry almost fell out of his seat. "You have the sight?"

"The sight? So you know about this?"

Perry leaned forward, beaming. "This is amazing."

"Yeah, not the word I would use." Thank God. The priest believed him. "I need your help. Do you know how to reverse it?"

Perry startled, his eyes wide. "Reverse it?"

"Yeah. It was mistake. It wasn't meant for me."

Father Perry paused. "Why would you—"

"I told you. It was a mistake."

Perry's look of unabashed excitement faded. "I'm afraid it's not as easy as that." His eyes narrowed. "Are you one of them?"

"One of who?"

"Never mind. Let's start over. I'm afraid I didn't get your name."

"Matt."

Perry grabbed a pen and started writing. "And your last

The Crimson Dimension

name?"

"Whoa!" Why would this guy want his info? Something didn't feel right. "What's with the inquisition? My name isn't any of your business." Matt stood up. "I'd like your help, but if you won't give it, I'm outta here."

Perry almost leaped from seat. "Don't leave. You can't leave. We need to talk."

Deja vu. For the second time that week, a catholic priest was ordering him not to leave. He didn't like being told what to do by a stranger, especially under these circumstances, but this was his only option. Matt sat back down. "Can you help me or not?"

Father Perry kept looking at the door. "I think I can."

"You think, or you can? Don't fuck with me." *Please be for real.*

Parry nodded. "Yeah, but I insist on getting your last name and your phone number. I'll look into this and let you know. For now, you should go home and stay there until I call. What's your address?"

Unease prickled the skin on the back of his neck. "You know what? I'll come back tomorrow to see what you've learned."

Matt left Perry's office and started down the aisle but stopped before he'd gone more than a few steps. His paranoia was taking him away from the only person who seemed to have any answers at all. Why was he being so stupid?

If you can't trust a priest, who can you trust?

Matt headed back to the office. Just as he was about to enter, he heard Perry talking on the phone.

CHAPTER 26

Father Perry sat in his office, staring at the single word he'd jotted down on his notepad: Matt. He'd done his best to get more information, but, in truth, he was relieved he'd failed. The less he knew, the less he could divulge.

The priest was facing the biggest dilemma of his life. The choice he was about to make had the potential to either end his anguish or cause his death. The decision should've been easy. As a messenger of God's word, he was sworn to live a righteous life, abiding by God's laws and spreading the message of His glory. Unfortunately, things weren't that simple.

Mitchell Bromley's telephone call, two days ago, was foremost in Perry's mind. The demon's instructions could not be ignored. Perry was to use his connections to find the Torren Bromley's Shakath had discovered.

Father Perry hung his head in resignation. He'd been under Mitchell Bromley's thumb for three long years, and it looked like it would never end.

When the sultry Bayeth had come to his church, she'd made a confession filled with detailed sexual indiscretions. And that was just the beginning. Each time, the confessions were more vivid and more deviant.

Perry had known he was playing with fire by continuing to see her. He'd faced similar circumstances before—after all, he was still a man—but always remained in control. With Bayeth, he found himself powerless, and every word she spoke fueled the lust within him. Never finding the strength to turn her away, he soon became addicted to her arousing stories.

He found himself brushing off her non-sexual sins and lingering over her lustful deeds. When the confessions evolved into personal counseling sessions, to Perry's delight, she used the absence of the confessional's barrier to showcase her alluring body.

On the evening that changed his life forever, she'd called him at the church and asked if he could pay her a visit to console her on the death of her father. He walked right into her deception. She used her lie to invite an embrace, and he was more than happy to comply. It didn't take long before she had him past the point of no return. The hidden cameras in her bedroom recorded the entire episode, and he never saw her again.

The following day, Mitchell Bromley visited the church and asked to speak to him. He introduced himself as a local businessman with a great proposition for the church. In the privacy of Perry's office, Bromley played the video to the horrified priest. He promised it would never surface, as long as Perry agreed to launder money for him.

Father Perry's life was his priesthood. Aside from that one unforgivable act, he'd served with honor and integrity for sixteen years. He shuddered at the thought that his life's work could be ended by one gross error in judgment. But, despite the shame he would endure and his guaranteed dismissal, he could not allow the house of God to be used for evil gain.

He refused.

Mitchell Bromley rose from his seat and pointed at the crucifix hanging from the neck of the devastated priest. A ball of flame shot from Bromley's finger and hit the cross, forcing the superheated metal through his robes and against his skin. The cross-shaped brand served as a permanent reminder of who, and more appropriately, what he was dealing with.

Terrified by Bromley's overwhelming power, Perry had agreed to his role in the money laundering scheme; however, he now devoted all his free time to finding a way to get out from under the demon's thumb.

Perry's research on the Shakath had led him to the Torren, and further research suggested that one of the sacred statues might still exist. If he could find it, the holy race of the Torren might not be extinct, after all. And then he might be able to escape Bromley's control.

He'd been waiting for Victoria's findings when the good news came that Bromley had been arrested. The arrest should've ended his torment, but the FBI had somehow missed his church's involvement in Bromley's schemes. Perry considered approaching the police a number of times, but knew that if he did, the decision would be his last.

And now a Torren had just walked through his door. It seemed too good to be true, and it troubled Perry to the core. Mitchell Bromley was a shrewd and cunning creature, and it was possible, if not likely, that he knew of Victoria and the search for the statue. Perhaps, Bromley had sent Matt to him as a test of his obedience. Failure to report it could cost him his life. On the other hand, if Matt was for real, turning him in would be disastrous.

He was walking a fine line. Reporting that he'd been visited by the Torren wouldn't put Matt in any danger. Thankfully, all he had was his first name. He also didn't need to mention Victoria or the statue. If Bromley knew about her, he was already in trouble, and it wouldn't make a difference one way or the other.

He picked up the phone.

"Mr. Bromley, I have some information regarding the Torren." His voice was unsteady. "He was just in my office."

"Did you detain him?"

"No, I tried, but he refused to stay." His voice trembled.

"I told you to hold him. Did you at least get any information from him?"

"I got his first name. Matt. He wouldn't give me his last name or his address."

"Not good enough. You know more. I know you do. I want something useful. If you don't give me something more, I'll skin you alive."

Bromley's threats had a paralyzing effect on Perry. He didn't want to see that demon ever again. One time was more than enough. He let out a troubled sigh and took a few moments before continuing. "Okay. I really don't know his last name or where he lives, but I do know who can lead you to him."

"Well then, out with it."

He gave Bromley Victoria's name and read off her phone number. His mouth went dry, and a noose tightened around his neck. "Please don't harm her. She's a sweet girl who knows nothing more than his identity."

"Do I sense a hint of affection? I would've thought you'd learned your lesson."

"It's not that at all. Just don't hurt her. Get your information and leave her be. Please. I've done everything you've asked of me."

"That you have, and I look forward to your continuing service."

CHAPTER 27

Matt's heart pounded as he strained to listen to Perry's half of the exchange. The more he heard, the less guilty he felt for eavesdropping. The blood drained from his face. This Mr. Bromley was searching for him, and Victoria was now in danger. Was this the same Bromley all over the news lately? Whoever he was, he had to be connected to Zaralen.

Matt waited for the call to end, wanting to learn as much as he could.

Father Perry hung up, and let out a heart-wrenching groan.

Matt burst into the office and gripped Perry's vestment. "What did you just do, you asshole?"

Perry recoiled. "You don't understand. I had no choice."

"You fucking coward! I heard it all. You sold her out to save your skin."

"I'm sorry! You don't know what they're capable of."

"I know I'd never do that to her." He grabbed his phone and dialed her number, only to be greeted by her voicemail message. "Damnit! Damnit! Damnit!"

The beep prompted his message.

"Victoria! It's Matt. You have to get out of your place now! You're in great danger. Meet me at the café. Don't leave there without me."

He grabbed Perry's phone and forced it into his hands. "Keep trying her."

Perry nodded and dialed her number. "No answer."

"You'd better pray that she's okay."

Perry was shaking. "Yes, yes. I'm so sorry."

Matt had to do something. "I'm going to her place. Keep calling her. You have to warn her."

"I'm so sorry. I will."

It was at least an hour's train ride to her apartment. He had to get there before it was too late.

Matt sprinted out of Perry's office, down the steps to the street, and toward the nearest subway station.

CHAPTER 28

Victoria arrived home, exhausted from hosting the second day of her exhibition. She set her purse down on the entry table, hung up her coat, and fished her phone out of her purse. The display showed a number of missed calls and a few messages. She'd turned it to silent for her showing. The first message was from a number she didn't recognize and contained a few seconds of dead air. The second was from Matt.

"Victoria! It's Matt. You have to—" She pressed the delete button before the message finished and put the phone facedown beside her purse.

He had his chance, and he blew it.

After not showing up on Thursday, he hadn't even bothered to call to explain himself. Forty-eight hours had given her plenty of time to write him off. Not the kind of guy she wanted. So, what kind of guy did she want?

For starters, someone who's reliable, not moody, established, good family, clean cut...

She let out a deep breath and headed for her wine. Who was she kidding? She loved the bad-boy type. The problem was that those guys were always a source of grief, but damnit, they did it for her. Add in rugged good looks, and you had the perfect guy... You had Matt.

Victoria took a gulp of wine and sat on her couch. She barely knew the guy, so why couldn't she get him out of her head? That bastard had stood her up. No one had done that to her before, and it pissed her off. Well, two could play that game. If he wanted her, she'd make him work harder than he ever had to win her heart.

Enough about him. Her show was a huge success. She'd sold four pieces, and a collector was talking about commissioning her for a piece. Not that the money mattered, but people were actually paying top dollar for her work. The validation was overwhelming.

Victoria's phone vibrated. Probably Matt again. Let him squirm. She wanted some soothing music and a relaxing bath.

As the water filled the claw-foot tub, she poured herself another glass of merlot and turned the stereo's volume up high enough to hear it in the bathroom. After lighting a few candles, she set them on her bathroom counter and lowered herself into the steaming, inviting bubbles. Before long, she drifted off to sleep.

CHAPTER 29

Rick Lowry was a pain in the ass. To make full use of his status as a police officer, Zaralen had to play along and assume the man's life. It was killing him, especially pretending that he enjoyed Lowry's two fucking kids. Fortunately, not everything about Rick's life was bad. Zaralen didn't have to spend as much time with Lokad, and Rick's wife was wild in the sack. But best of all was the access to information.

Zaralen sat at his work computer and used the reverse phone number database to find Victoria's address. He left work, claiming he was still feeling a little shaken up, and a short time later, met Lokad in front of Victoria's apartment.

"Don't fuck this one up too." Zaralen stared his partner down. "We need the girl to lead us to the Torren."

"I'll be gentle." Lokad smiled. "For the first minute."

"Are you fucking clueless? There isn't a piece of ass in this world worth being banished over. You do exactly what I say, or I'll skin you alive."

"Now you're talking my language."

"Come on." The rap on the door went unanswered.

Zaralen knocked again. Nothing. He took his lock-picking tools out of his coat. "No noise until we're sure she's not here." The lock released, and he pushed the door open.

"She must be home," Zaralen whispered. The music, and Victoria's purse, keys, and phone on the entry table left no doubt in his mind. "Find her. I'll make sure she doesn't escape." He took out his gun.

Lokad followed suit then stepped past his partner into the apartment. After a quick scan of her living area, he searched Victoria's art studio. Once finished, he looked at Zaralen, and shrugged.

She had to be there. "Check the bathroom," Zaralen mouthed as he pointed.

Lokad stalked past Victoria's bed then paused. What was he up to now? The stupid fucker picked up a lace bra and panties, brought them to his face, and inhaled. Shit. Lokad couldn't lose focus now. The rookie still hadn't mastered his animalistic urges, and if he lost control, it could jeopardize their mission. He'd smashed his last victim's head in before he raped her, and Victoria needed to be in one piece to lead them to Matt. Zaralen pointed at the bathroom again, this time forcefully. Lokad appeared to get the message, put down the clothing, and refocused.

Lokad peered through the crack of the partly open door. He turned and smiled at Zaralen then opened the door, revealing Victoria, naked and sound asleep. Lokad set his gun on the counter and unfastened his belt.

Damn it!

Zaralen started toward his partner.

CHAPTER 30

Matt raced through the streets of Greenwich Village, stopping only when he absolutely had to catch his breath. Arriving at Victoria's apartment building, he quickly scanned the street. No one suspicious stood out, and he didn't see the feared red glow in anyone's eyes. Satisfied that he wasn't in any immediate danger, he bolted up the stairs.

He raised his hand to knock but stopped with it in midair. The door was ajar. His stomach churned. His heartbeat quickened.

Shit. I'm too late.

He threw the door open to see the back of a man, who was holding a gun. The intruder spun to face him. It was the cop Zaralen had possessed in the alley. Matt launched at him. The entry table splintered under the weight of the two men as they crashed to the floor in a heap of bodies, broken wood, and the contents of Victoria's purse. Zaralen's head hit the hardwood floor with a resounding thud, and the gun skittered amongst Victoria's belongings.

Matt scrambled over the unconscious man and grabbed his weapon.

CHAPTER 31

An explosive sound jarred Victoria from her sleep. A man stood over her with an evil grin on his face. Was she dreaming? Please God. She had to be dreaming.

Someone yelled. It wasn't a dream. She covered her nakedness and recoiled from the intruder. What the hell could she do? She was completely vulnerable. He raised his finger to his lips as if to tell her to be quiet, turned, and walked out of the bathroom.

"Don't move a fucking muscle!" a voice called from her living room. "Victoria! Are you in there? Are you all right?"

"Matt?" His voice gave her a small sense of security. Heart pounding, she scrambled out of the tub, grabbed a towel from the rack, and rushed to the doorway. When she saw Matt holding a gun, she didn't know what to think. He was obviously protecting her from the intruder, but how on earth had he gotten into her apartment? And who was the guy between them?

"So, you're the Torren," the intruder said to Matt.

What the hell did that mean? She stood just inside the doorway, using the wall as a shield.

Matt waved the gun at the man. "I know who you are. Your name is Larkat. I saw you attack that man on the street."

"It's Lokad. Don't fuck it up again." The man took a step toward Matt.

"Don't move! I'll shoot," Matt warned.

"You think that gun scares me?" Lokad asked with an undertone of amusement. "You know how this works. If you kill me, I'll just possess her."

Possess her?

"You're wrecking my plans to have some fun with that pretty little whore. After I take care of you, I'm going to make that bitch squeal. I'll show her a time she'll never forget."

Victoria's skin crawled, and she went numb with fear.

"Leave her out of this. If it's me you want, possess me and leave her alone."

"You really are a dumb fuck, aren't you? Is this the best they could come up with for a new Torren?" He took another step toward Matt. "Dmoltech will be amused. Especially when I tell him you didn't even know you're immune."

"Immune?"

Lokad froze. "Never mind. It doesn't matter."

He'd said something he shouldn't have, but what?

Matt looked just as confused as she was. He clearly didn't understand what they guy was talking about either. It really didn't matter. The only thing that was important was getting Lokad out of her place. "Matt. Do something."

Matt extended his arm like he was about to pull the trigger. That was *not* what she had in mind. "Don't shoot him!"

Matt's hand relaxed on the trigger. "What in the hell do you want with me?"

"First of all, you're gonna call your dog off Peterson."

"What? Who?"

"Peterson, the guy your Warrior's all over. Call him off."

Matt shrugged. "I don't have a fucking clue what you're talking about."

That made two of them.

Lokad pointed at Matt. "Then you're gonna come with me for a ride. My boss wants to talk to you."

"I'm guessing his name is Mitchell Bromley?"

Lokad's eyebrow arched upward. "You're not so stupid, after all. I suggest using those brains to keep her alive. After you put the gun down, we can all walk out of here in one piece."

"She's not going anywhere."

"Look here. You can hand me the gun or shoot me. I really don't give a shit. She'll either be my bitch or my new body. I'm betting you wouldn't have the heart to shoot her too. One way or another, that juicy ass is gonna be mine."

No matter how frightened she was, Victoria wasn't going to let this disgusting pig touch her. She picked up one of the candelabras on her bathroom counter. The heavy brass object, which, moments before, had served to create a relaxing ambience, was now a weapon in her hand. She threw it at Lokad as hard as she could. She missed, but the hot wax splashed across his face and into his left eye. As Lokad screamed and clawed at his face, Victoria searched for something else to throw. Her knees almost gave out when she spotted a gun on her counter. She grabbed it and spun back to face Lokad just as Matt closed the distance and delivered a solid upper cut to his jaw. Matt followed Lokad to the floor, punching him over and over again.

Blood was spraying everywhere. "Stop!" Victoria shouted. "You're going to kill him!"

Matt obeyed and, by the looks of it, not a moment too soon. Lokad lay on the floor in a pool of blood and teeth.

Matt looked up at Victoria. "Get something to tie him up with, but be careful, there's another one unconscious by the front door."

Wearing only the towel, Victoria ran to her cupboards and returned with a roll of packing tape. "What on earth is going on here?"

"It's a long story. Are you all right?" He bound Lokad's hands and feet.

"No! I'm not *all right*. Who are these guys?"

"You two are dead meat!" Lokad came to. "Let me go, you asshole! Zaralen. Where are you?"

Matt placed some tape over Lokad's mouth, shutting him up.

"Come on. Before Zaralen wakes up." He grabbed her hand and led her to the other guy.

Zaralen looked dead, except that his chest rose and fell. Thank God no one had been killed. She stared, shaking uncontrollably, as Matt tied him up. "Tell me what's going on."

"Look at his eyes." He lifted Zaralen's eyelid. "Do you see anything strange?"

"No. What am I supposed to be seeing?"

Matt exhaled. "Nothing, I guess. Never mind."

Victoria couldn't hold it together any more. Tears filled her eyes. "Matt, this is scary. Please tell me what's happening."

"Everything's okay." He rose from the floor and took her trembling body in his arms. "You're safe now." He stroked her wet hair.

Somehow, he'd known she was in danger and saved her. But how? "You still haven't explained anything."

Matt's embrace was comforting, and her breathing slowed and steadied.

"It's a long story. I found out you were in trouble and came as fast as I could. All that matters is that you're safe."

How he'd known was still a mystery, but there was no doubt that he'd saved her. The fear and tension melted away. She was safe. Victoria took his hands and looked into his eyes. "Thank you."

"No problem. I'm just glad you're okay."

He was staring at her towel-clad figure, barely covered by the white cotton. "Are you crazy?"

Matt blushed. "I'm sorry. I know it's not the time, but—"

"You're right. It's not." Men. Was there ever a time their hormones weren't at work? She had to admit that the rescue was a turn on, but Lokad's disgusting intentions completely killed any desire. "Just hold me tight." She wrapped her arms around him and squeezed.

"Lokad!" Zaralen shouted.

Victoria leaped backward.

"Where are you, you dumb fuck?" Zaralen thrashed around, trying to break his bonds.

Matt kicked him in the ribs, ending Zaralen's rant, then bent down and taped his mouth shut.

"That should do it." Matt stood back up and took Victoria's hands. "You're wet and cold," he said after a moment of awkwardness. "Let's get you dried off."

He stood guard over the captives while she headed to her bedroom and gathered her clothes. She carried them into the bathroom and dressed.

God, she was lucky. Her stomach churned. If Matt hadn't been there, things would've turned out very differently. How had he known she was danger? Matt wasn't going to avoid answering her questions anymore. She marched up to him and stared him down. "Start talking."

Matt took a step back. "I... Um..." He glanced down at the men. "We'd better not talk in front of them. We should get out of here. There might be more on the way."

Matt's warning sent a chill through her veins. She did *not* want to wait around for the next installment of this adventure. "Okay. Let's go."

After collecting the spilled contents of her purse, they closed and locked the door behind them, leaving the two thugs bound and fuming.

CHAPTER 32

Victoria rummaged through her purse while she sped away from Greenwich.

"What are you doing?" Matt asked.

"Calling the cops. What else would I be doing?" She dumped her purse on Matt's lap. "I can't find my phone. Give me yours."

"Wait. I think you should hear my story before doing that. If you still want to make the call, I'll give you my phone. I promise."

Still unable to find her phone, she had little choice but to listen. "Okay, but this better be good."

"Your priest buddy set you up."

"Father Perry? What are you talking about?"

"He told Bromley how to find you."

"Bromley?"

"The guy in the news. The one on trial."

"Matt. You're making no sense at all. What does Father Perry have to do with him?"

"Okay, I'm getting ahead of myself. Prepare yourself for one hell of a story."

Victoria sat and listened as Matt told her what had happened in Brazil. "Oh my God."

Now she understood why he'd acted so strangely when they met after the trip. Why hadn't he just told her the truth about being held up and losing his phone? The bleeding statue was a bit farfetched, but she'd have understood.

"What does any of this have to do with what just happened in my apartment? Is Bromley an art thief?"

"No."

"Then get to the point, for God's sake."

"Sorry." He exhaled. "But you need to hear the whole story or it won't make sense". He cleared his throat and quickly finished his tale.

"Okay, that's enough." She hit the brakes and pulled off to the side of the road. "I want you out of my car."

"Look at me," he said, his voice desperate. "I'm not lying. I've done a ton of shit in my life, but I've always stepped up and faced the consequences. I've been a lot of things, but never a liar." Tears welled in his eyes.

"Please. You've been full of shit ever since Brazil."

"Only so you wouldn't think I was crazy." He took her hand. "Think about what happened at your place… What that guy said… Can you explain any of that?"

He had a point. But still. She pulled her hand away. Things like that didn't happen. She sat silently, letting his story sink in. As ridiculous as everything sounded, it seemed too complicated and interconnected to be a string of lies. The hair on her neck stood up. "This is nuts. You realize that, don't you?"

Matt sighed. "I wish I was making it up, but it's really happening." He wiped away a tear that had run down his cheek. "Hey, I'm the biggest skeptic there is. You're supposed to be the one who believes in this kind of stuff."

True enough, but this went way beyond anything she'd ever considered. "This is really freaky."

"And it gets worse."

"Father Perry?" Matt's nod confirmed he was involved. "Is he connected to the men in my apartment?"

"I'm afraid so."

Father Perry had been nothing but kind to her. He'd

never said or done anything remotely concerning. "I don't understand."

Much to her shock, Matt recounted the conversation he'd overheard while visiting Father Perry.

No. There had to be another explanation. "Matt. Let's take it back to Brazil. Think really hard. Did you see Lokad and Zaralen on your trip? They could've followed you here."

"Absolutely not. I'm positive I got back to Rio alone."

"Okay. Now, be honest—no judgment. Did you do drugs while you were there, and after you got back?"

"No. I'm clean. I'll even get tested if you want me to prove it." Matt put his hand on her knee. "I know this is nuts. It took me days to come to grips, and I've lived every minute of it. I won't blame you if you don't believe. If nothing else, just trust me when I tell you that Father Perry is a dangerous man. Stay away from him."

Victoria closed her eyes, blinking back a tear. "I can't believe he's one of them."

"He's not. But he's involved."

That much of Matt's story was too clear not to believe. The demon thing was another matter. There had to be a logical explanation, although the things Lokad said supported Matt's theory. Still...no.

Whatever the truth was, Matt was mixed up in something real and the poor guy had been going through it all alone. "If I'd known that any of this would happen, I never would've asked you to go."

"It's not your fault." Matt leaned forward. "So, does this mean you believe me?"

She nodded. "I can't think of another explanation at the moment, so yeah, I guess so."

Matt flopped back in his seat, closed his eyes, and exhaled. "You don't know what that means to me." His face lit up.

"That doesn't mean we don't look for other explanations."

Matt's relieved look vanished.

Damn it. He needed her to believe him, and she owed that to him. "I do believe you. And I also wanted to thank you. You saved my life today. I'll never forget that."

Matt shrugged. "Anyone would've done the same."

That wasn't true. Father Perry, a man she'd trusted, a man she'd called a friend, had put her life in danger. Matt was special. No matter how he tried to downplay it. She leaned in and kissed his cheek.

Damn, he smelled good. She lingered, his warm breath caressing her neck. He turned his head toward her and gently kissed her.

A wave of energy coursed through her body. Heart pounding, she pulled back a couple of inches and stared into his steel blue eyes. Victoria grinned then bit her lower lip. "I knew you were trouble the moment I met you, Matt Reynolds." She gripped the hair on the back of his head and pulled him back toward her.

Victoria jumped back at the sound of car's horn, smacking her head on the rearview mirror. "What the hell?"

"Fuck them. They can drive around—"

The horn went off again.

Victoria sighed. Just as well considering everything that had happened. As much as she wanted to continue, it wasn't the right time. "He's not going to stop." Victoria flopped back in her seat and drove on before the guy behind her honked again.

"Now what?" She couldn't drive around town all night. "Any ideas?"

"Besides finding a good place to park?" He grinned.

The Crimson Dimension

"Yeah." Her face flushed. "Besides that."

Matt leaned back, and his smile faded. "Did you come across anything in your research that might explain what happened to me?"

"Nothing like that. Sorry."

"Shit. How on earth am I going to find out how to undo it?"

That was the last thing Victoria had expected to hear. "Why would you undo it? This is an amazing gift."

Matt startled. "If you'd seen what I've seen, you wouldn't be saying that. It's a curse."

Victoria shook her head. "I don't know what to think of it, but something like this doesn't just happen to people. This is big. We have a responsibility to do something."

Matt grabbed her elbow. "There's no we in this conversation."

The hell there isn't. "They're after me, the same as you." She repacked her purse. "We need to talk to the old priest in Brazil."

"I've already thought of that, but I can't afford to go."

"Well, that's no longer an issue. I'll pay for the tickets. Let's go get your passport."

Matt shook his head. "No. I've always paid my own way."

Was he kidding? Demons were trying to kill them, and he was concerned about being given a ticket? "I never paid you for the photo trip. Consider us square."

Mat tipped his head. "Fair enough, but I'm going alone."

"Not a chance." She wasn't going to be excluded.

Matt exhaled. "You really aren't making this easy."

"It's incredibly easy. You're not going without me."

Matt stared blankly down the street then nodded. "Okay, fine. But your passport is at your home, right?"

"Oh God." He was right. Two demons were tied up in her apartment. She could never go back there. Would her life ever be the same? University, her art show—was it all gone? Her heart sank. What had she gotten herself into? All she'd wanted was to be part of rediscovering some long-forgotten artifacts. To share the discovery with the rest of the world and follow in her grandpa's footsteps.

"My grandpa will know what to do. He always does." She began the sixty-mile drive north to Monroe County.

CHAPTER 33

Dmoltech snapped his cellphone shut, grabbed another cigar, and headed for his liquor cabinet.
Where the Hell are those imbeciles?

He lit the Cuban, drew in the small comfort it offered, and looked at his watch one more time. It had been over three hours since he'd called Zaralen with Father Perry's information.

Their mission was simple: capture the Torren and bring him in alive. If that proved too difficult, Dmoltech had agreed to accept his dead body as a less desirable alternative. But clearly Zaralen and Lokad had run into some trouble. He knew they hadn't been killed because he would've felt them leave his bond, but since the pair hadn't called with an update, he was left to guess their fate.

He didn't want to take his others away from stopping Peterson's testimony, but with Zaralen and Lokad not answering his calls, there was no other option. He picked up the phone again, this time to speak to Bayeth.

"Have you heard from those two fuck-ups?"

"Nope."

"Damn those two." He downed a shot of Macallan whiskey. "How are things going with you?"

"The Warrior is still protecting our friend, so I couldn't deploy my Qaton to control him, but I did attach them to one of the guards assigned to him. He's scheduled to be in the room with Peterson in a few hours. I'll make the guard talk to Peterson regarding his daughter's wellbeing."

"Perfect. As soon as you're done, get yourself and your Qaton out of there. I need you to go to Victoria's place and see what the Hell happened to Zaralen."

CHAPTER 34

Victoria drove up to a treed property, enclosed by an eight-foot stone wall. She stopped next to the security controls at a large iron gate and typed in her passcode.

This was something right out of the movies. Her grandpa must be a big deal. Matt shifted in his seat. When the gate swung open, they proceeded down the cobbled path through the woods then turned off the main access onto a service road to the back of the house.

Matt struggled to see the building through the trees, but what he could see was enormous. Victoria had said they had money, but this was crazy money. The yard lights illuminated the back of the home, giving Matt his first full view. It was a turn-of-the-century mansion, and even from the back, overwhelming.

"Wow!" Matt exclaimed. "This is where you grew up?"

"Yes," Victoria said with a smile. "Home sweet home."

She stopped beside another control pad and typed in her code. One of the four overhead doors opened, allowing her to pull into the carport.

An old man with a cane hurried to meet them.

"Grandpa!" She ran over and gave him a huge hug.

Matt followed close behind.

Victoria's grandfather took a step back and looked at Matt then back at Victoria. "Is everything okay?"

Matt looked down at his clothes. He was splattered with blood. Not a good first impression.

Victoria shook her head. "No. We're in trouble."

"What's the matter?" He raised his cane at Matt. "And who are you?"

Victoria pushed the cane down. "This is Matt. He saved me when some men broke into my apartment." She grabbed Matt's hand and pulled him toward her grandpa. "This is my grandfather, Lawrence Hallworth."

Lawrence lowered his cane and extended his hand. "Then I owe you my gratitude. Thank you for keeping my Victoria safe."

Matt shook Lawrence's hand. "Nice to meet you, sir. She's...very special."

Lawrence looked questioningly at Victoria. "Enough with the introductions. What happened? Did you call the police?"

"We're fine. Let's go inside and talk. You're not going to believe what we have to tell you."

Just like that? She was going to tell him everything? How was this going to go over?

Lawrence led them down the service hallway and through a secondary entrance into his study.

Unbelievable. Shelves filled with hundreds of books covered the walls of the circular room. A massive fireplace with an intricately carved mantle added to its grandeur. It was furnished with a matching set of six leather chairs, each accompanied by a table and lamp. An ornate oak desk with a computer completed the décor. They weren't just well off, they were filthy rich.

Matt sat in silence while Victoria explained the events that had brought them to his door, only speaking up to fill in missing details. Lawrence listened, interrupting occasionally for clarification.

As soon as Victoria finished, Matt asked, "Do you have any idea what's going on?"

Lawrence just stared at him. Then at Victoria. "You expect me to believe this?"

Matt's heart sank. Victoria had told him Lawrence would understand and know what to do. She obviously thought more of him than she should have. "Damnit." He stood up. "I'm really sorry to have wasted your time. I think I should go."

"Sit down," Lawrence ordered. "What do you think leaving accomplishes?"

Matt quickly took his seat. "I just think I've endangered her enough. I don't want to cause any more trouble."

Lawrence nodded. "I wish more than anything that you leaving would make Victoria safe, but the men clearly targeted her. She's in this as deep as you. Perhaps deeper. This demon crap is...exactly that. And you're not going anywhere until we get to the bottom of all this mess you created."

Victoria forcefully cleared her throat and stood. "It's not his fault. I'm just as much to blame as Matt. *I* sent him to Brazil. This is *my* doing. He's not going anywhere until he's safe as well."

Damn, she was gorgeous when she got worked up.

Lawrence nodded. "I suppose you're right. We owe him that much for saving you." He got up and walked to the desk. "I'll keep an open mind. Let's see if there's anything on the internet." He motioned for Victoria to sit down. "You'd better take the controls. You're so much quicker at this thing than I am."

Victoria brought up a search engine. "What key words do we have?"

"Try Torren," Matt answered. "I think that would be our best bet."

They watched in anticipation as the screen filled with results then read through the headings.

"Here's something," Victoria said. She clicked on the link. "Glossary of Christian mythology."

Matt swallowed. Hopefully, this site would provide some answers. He leaned in.

Victoria read the definition. "Torren. A trinity of two humans and an angelic warrior whose primary purpose is to prevent the Legion of the Shakath from establishing Satan's rule on earth."

Matt's face paled as sweat beaded on his forehead. He'd known there had to be more to this than just seeing things, but this was too much. "What else does it say?"

Victoria reached over and took his hand. "Gifted humans were empowered with special skills, most notably the ability to see into the Crimson Dimension, or spirit realm. They received the sight by partaking of the blood of the Savior, which flowed from statues of His image."

Matt went numb. "No. This can't be true."

"Well, I'll be," Lawrence whispered under his breath.

Victoria looked up from the screen. "Matt. This is amazing. An incredible gift."

"This is not a gift." Damn God for doing this to him. "It wasn't meant for me."

Lawrence patted Matt on the shoulder. "Sit down and take a few breaths, young man. I think we all need some time to digest this."

Matt slumped into the chair and closed his eyes. As much as he hated the news, he knew it was true. "This is a big mistake."

Lawrence cleared his throat. "You may believe it's a mistake, but I doubt it was a coincidence that the blood flowed while you were there. Matt, I think you need to consider that—"

"No. It *is* a mistake. There is no trinity. The angel is gone. And as far as powers go, other than seeing those strange things, I feel the same as I always have."

Victoria nodded. "I guess you still need to learn the full capacity of your new—"

"No." Matt grabbed the hair on the back of his head. "It can't be me. I've never been religious. I was never supposed to have the blood. Father Devante meant to take it all. He said..." Matt spun to face them. "Devante said the blood had to go to Rome. It was meant for two others."

Victoria bit her lip. "So, you might not have a partner yet?"

"No." She was missing the point. "That doesn't matter. It wasn't meant for me. I just want to be rid of it, along with those red-eyed freaks."

"Speaking of the red-eyed men," Lawrence said. "I think it's safe to assume they're the Shakath mentioned in the passage. Search this site for more details on them."

Victoria ran the query. "Shakath. A legion of demons whose primary purpose is to assist Satan in gaining world power. There are three levels or ranks, which all operate through the possession or control of humans to varying degrees. There are six of the highest level, Naygid, who each rule six Shakath, who each in turn control six lesser demons called Qaton."

"Six, six, six," Victoria commented.

"Precisely," Lawrence agreed. "The men, whose eyes appeared red to you, are likely the mid-level Shakath, since they spoke of having a boss and spewed out the imp creatures. If they work in groups of six, there are likely four more of them out there searching for you as we speak."

The news hit Matt full force, and anger welled inside him. "Bring 'em on. I've taken two of them already. I can take the others!"

Victoria threw her hands up. "Slow down a minute. A second ago, you were dead set on getting it removed, and now you want to fight them all?"

Lawrence nodded. "She's right. You're going to have to get control of your emotions if you don't want to get yourself killed."

Whatever. "I've always been able to handle myself."

Lawrence gripped his cane. "I'm not saying this for the fun of it. I don't want Victoria to get hurt because of your temper."

Matt turned to face Victoria. Her beautiful green eyes urged him to listen to her grandfather's advice.

Damnit. They were right. It was a complete fluke that neither of them had gotten killed at her place. They were in way over their heads, and he had to take a step back. "I'm sorry. The last thing I want is for anything to happen to her."

"What should we do, Grandpa? We were already thinking we should go to Brazil and talk to the priest there, but my passport is at home."

Lawrence pointed at Victoria. "You need to stay here."

"Not a chance. I'm not leaving Matt to deal with this alone."

Lawrence rolled his eyes and exhaled. He stared at Victoria for a few seconds then turned to Matt. "She's got her mother's strong will. Good luck."

That was becoming quite obvious. But it was a good thing. Matt had never liked the submissive type. Besides, on second thought, Brazil was probably the safest place for them right now. "She still needs her passport, and there are two demons tied up there."

"We'll just have to get a new one. I have contacts who can speed up the process. I'll start on it in the morning."

Victoria grabbed Matt's hand and gave him a wink. "I told you we'd figure this out. Grandpa can never say no to me."

How could she be so upbeat? This wasn't a game. They'd be looking over their shoulder constantly, never knowing if they were safe or not. And who knew what Devante would do? "Victoria." He shook his head. "This is serious."

Victoria's grin evaporated. "I know. This is how I deal with shit. I make jokes. Going to Rio *is* our best option. Devante appears to be on the good side, and he's the only lead we have. There are two demons after us here, and probably four more."

Lawrence sighed. "And if those two die in Victoria's apartment, the police will be looking for you too."

"Fuck!" Matt hadn't given the Shakaths' lives much thought. "Worse—if they're dead, the demons will be in someone else by now."

"We won't have a clue who they are. They could be anyone," Victoria said. "I'll never be able to go home."

"Maybe this will help." Matt reached into his khakis and pulled out two handguns, complete with a few extra clips. "I took this from them while you got dressed." He gripped one and took aim as if he was about to shoot. "I'll protect you."

Victoria grabbed the gun out of his hand. "I thought we just agreed that killing them would be pointless. These won't help."

"She's right." Lawrence nodded. "This is probably a spiritual fight. Maybe spells, or holy objects, or...something."

"What about the angel?" Victoria asked. "As a Torren, you're supposed to have an angelic warrior as a partner. That's your weapon. You need to figure out how to summon him."

Matt exhaled. "He screwed off when I needed him most." He wasn't about to put his trust in God again. Not ever. "I'd prefer to handle this on my own."

"Don't discount him so quickly." Lawrence looked up then shook his head. "According to this site, he's an important part of the Torren trinity. There has to be a reason he left you."

"There is no trinity. I'm in this alone." They needed to drop this bullshit.

Lawrence paused, his face reddened. "Well... Let's hope the priest has some answers. You need to find him as soon as possible." He turned his attention to Victoria. "Is there anything else on that webpage?"

"Nothing."

"Figures." Matt slammed his hand on the desk. "God sticks me with this Torren shit and doesn't think to leave a fucking playbook behind."

His outburst was met with silence.

Matt could feel Lawrence's stare. There was no question he was being judged, and coming up short. If only he'd left well enough alone and put Brazil out of his mind as Devante had urged. What a mess.

"Sir." He rubbed his temples. "I'm sorry I've endangered your granddaughter—and probably you as well. If I could undo it all, I would." He dropped his head. "I promise I'll make it right, somehow."

Lawrence nodded, and his face softened. "There's no changing the past, and you did well, considering everything. We'll figure this out together." Lawrence yawned. Well then, it's getting late and we've learned all we are going to tonight. I suggest we pack it in." He stood and grabbed his cane. "We'll work on travel arrangements in the morning."

"Good night," Victoria said and kissed Lawrence on the cheek. "We'll see you in the morning."

Matt rose from his chair and shook Lawrence's hand.

"Thanks for everything. I never thought you'd be so understanding."

"Make no mention of it." Lawrence patted Matt on the shoulder. "Victoria will have to show you to the guest room since I have trouble with the stairs."

He left them and headed down the hall.

CHAPTER 35

Zaralen managed to free his right hand. He'd been rubbing the packing tape against a piece of the broken entry table for hours. He could barely stay awake, and his cramped muscles made it difficult to move.

At this rate, it would be hours more before he was completely loose. Matt had taped him up so well that his freed hand was of little use. Another band of tape, just above his elbow, still had him hog tied. He picked up a leg of the broken table and continued the grueling task.

He froze when he heard someone try the door, followed by the familiar sound of picking tools in the lock. Moments later, Bayeth and Toal appeared. How fucking embarrassing.

"Well, what do we have here?" Bayeth mocked.

"Shut the fuck up and get me out of this damn mess."

Bayeth motioned for Toal to free him. "I assume it was the Torren who did this to you."

"Who else?" Zaralen answered as Toal helped him to his feet. The room spun, and his head felt like it was going to explode.

"Is he still acting alone?"

"His bitch is helping him, but she's not empowered." He headed to the sink to soothe his parched throat.

"Where's Lokad?" Toal asked.

"Over there." Zaralen pointed to the bound, motionless body on the floor near the bathroom.

Lokad moaned when Toal gave him a kick. "He's alive."

"No kidding." He rolled his eyes at Lokad. "If he'd died, his new cloak would've freed me by now, don't you think?"

Toal grabbed a knife from the kitchen and cut away Lokad's bindings. Lokad let out another moan and rolled over. His bloodied face was swollen and bruised from Matt's beating.

"Holy shit!" Toal laughed. "I've messed up a lot of guys over the years, but this takes the cake."

"Leave him be," Bayeth ordered. "We have more important things to deal with." She'd already dialed Dmoltech.

Shit. This was not going to go down well. He waited while she explained the situation. "Just a minute." Bayeth took the phone away and pressed the screen. "Okay. You're on speaker now."

She held the phone out to him.

Zaralen swallowed. "I can explain—"

"Shut up." Dmoltech's voice was cold, without a hint of emotion. Zaralen knew he was beyond livid. "If you don't find that punk within twenty-four hours, you're dead."

"Yes, sir." He dared not say another word.

"Bayeth?" Dmoltech called.

"Yes?" she answered.

"It looks like Perry tipped them off that we were coming. I want you to pay a visit to your old friend. He must know a lot more about Matt than he's letting on."

CHAPTER 36

Victoria watched her grandpa limp down the hall. Would this be too much for him to handle? Perhaps she shouldn't have brought Matt here, but where else could she have gone?

"Please, take his advice," she urged. "I know he's old, but he's the smartest and most resourceful person I know."

Matt nodded. "I'm amazed he even believes me."

Victoria grabbed Matt's arm. "Us." What would it take to get that through his head?

"Yeah... That's what I meant."

"Come on. I'll show you to your room."

Victoria led Matt up the stairs and pointed to the hallway on the right. "My bedroom is the second door on the left." Her face flushed. "In case you need me."

"Okay." Matt glanced between the left and right halls.

Had the innuendo gone over his head, or was he trying to be a gentleman? "Your room's in the guest wing."

"The guest wing?" He shook his head. "This place is more like a hotel than a house. I'm surprised the butler isn't showing me to my room."

"He's about ninety and only works when we have planned events now." The house had once been full of staff. Not anymore. She hated that Grandpa was completely alone here, but he insisted he didn't need the fuss. "If I call him, he could probably tuck you in by next Tuesday."

Matt laughed. "I'd much rather have you tuck me in."

There was that devious grin again. He *was* thinking

exactly what she was. Was it wrong to want him under the circumstances?

She opened his door and gave the mini-tour. "Extra pillows and blankets are in the wardrobe. Shower's in there. Hand me your clothes. I'll get them in the wash."

Matt pulled his shirt over his head.

"Oh. Uh. Not here." What a body, though. She fought the urge to throw herself at him and pointed to a closed door. "There's a bathrobe in there."

She was doing it again. Leading him on would be so cruel considering the want in his eyes. It was either going to happen or she needed to get out of here—fast.

Matt held his bunched-up clothing through the crack in the doorway. "Here you go. I can't find any towels."

She grabbed his things and headed for the door. "I'll be right back."

Victoria leaned on the washer, her pulse racing. No matter how much she wanted him, was he worth the risk of heartbreak? She wanted guarantees. Was that too much to ask? She'd created a safe life, one where she was as shielded from pain as she could get. Matt would complicate things so much. She closed her eyes. Her heart was fragile enough under normal circumstances, but this Torren situation was crazy. She had a gnawing feeling that it couldn't be reversed. What would that mean? Where would that leave her? Would he go off to become a spiritual warrior with some random guy, or...could she somehow become his partner?

She grabbed some towels and marched back to his room.

"Matt." Victoria knocked on the bathroom door.

"Almost done."

She pushed the door open. "I'll put the towels on the counter." She could see his silhouette through the fogged-up shower door. All that separated them was a pane of glass, and her indecision.

Despite the countless reasons to walk away, there was something about him she couldn't resist. She'd been fighting it from the moment they met, but it was a losing battle. It was time to let go. She slipped off her clothes, opened the shower door, and joined him.

CHAPTER 37

Matt couldn't sleep. His mind kept replaying everything that had happened since he'd met Victoria. He'd never been so happy, yet so troubled, in his life.

He propped himself up with a few pillows and looked at her, sleeping soundly beside him. She was curled up, facing him, with one hand under her pillow. The sheet only covered one leg and her hip, leaving him a breathtaking view of her body. He couldn't imagine a more perfect girl. She was stunningly beautiful and absolutely amazing in bed, but that was only half the story. He'd never met anyone who grabbed hold of life like Victoria. She was creative, focused, driven, and uncommonly honest. Something about her made him comfortable to be…himself. Matt sighed and shifted. What if the plan to have Devante cure him didn't work? Then what? There was no way he was going to be a spiritual warrior in some fucking trinity. How would he be able to be with Victoria if his mere existence put her in danger? He couldn't do that to her.

Life couldn't be that cruel. Not again. God owed him, and he was going to cash in with Devante. All he wanted was to walk away and let whoever the fuck would want that life take it over. Then they could start a normal life together.

Matt rolled back to face Victoria. Who was he kidding? A few dates and one night in bed, and he was planning their lives together. Idiot. They came from opposite ends of the spectrum, and she deserved better than the likes of him. It was time to face the facts. He'd fuck this up for sure.

But then again...

Matt reached over and gently stroked her shoulder, which caused her to shift onto her back.

The moonlight coming through the window illuminated her body. He admired her face, her breasts, her stomach, and—

Something was wrong. He turned on the bedside lamp and looked back at her body. Victoria's soft pink flesh had turned leathery and gray. Matt recoiled, slamming into the headboard. This couldn't be happening. She'd never even seen the blood, let alone come in contact with it.

"Oh God no." He shuddered. He'd infected her. "Please God...not her..." Matt was powerless to stop it, and the guilt tore at him. Anyone but her. "She doesn't deserve this. I'll do anything you want. Just leave her out of this. Please God..."

He grabbed her by the shoulders and shook her. "I'm so sorry... Victoria!"

CHAPTER 38

Father Perry sat in his living room, unmoving, still in his coat and shoes. He struggled to keep his eyes open, but his guilt drove him to continue his vigil of prayer for their safety. Perry had always thought his involvement with the half-demon wouldn't affect anyone directly. He couldn't have been more wrong.

What a coward. His fear had made him betray those who'd trusted him. Betray his God.

The knock on the door barely stirred him. He'd known they would come, and there was no escaping them. He rose from his chair and opened the door.

How fitting, he thought, when he saw Bayeth standing on the porch. *The woman who ruined my life is here to end it.*

Bayeth was accompanied by her goon, Toal, who pushed Perry backward and closed the door behind them.

"Is anyone else here?" Bayeth asked.

"I'm alone," Father Perry replied in a shaking voice.

Toal ignored Perry's answer and left the room to search the rectory for other occupants.

Bayeth motioned to his overcoat. "It looks like you're on your way out. Meeting with Matt?"

"No." Perry glanced down at his coat. "I just haven't undressed yet."

"It's one in the morning. You expect me believe you're that slow to undress?" Her voice took on a mocking tone. "If I remember correctly, the last time we met, you were very quick to take your clothes off."

"How could you be so cruel?" he asked.

She leaned in and whispered in his ear, "You made it so easy."

The last three years hadn't been unkind to Bayeth. Despite who she was and all she'd done, he still longed for her. The thought that his life was about to end, and his lusts with it, gave him some comfort.

"If you're here to kill me," he said, looking at the floor, "you already did. Go ahead and finish it."

"Who said I'm going to kill you? What if I've come for another roll in the hay?"

The statement both disgusted and aroused him. How could he still feel so drawn to her?

Toal returned to the living room. "All clear. He's alone."

Bayeth abandoned her mockery. "We're looking for Matt and the girl. Where are they?"

A spark of life returned to Perry. They hadn't found Victoria. Maybe she and Matt would escape, after all. The thought gave him some courage. The only way he could help them now was to delay their pursuers as long as possible.

"They're coming here to meet me." Father Perry's lie was the first step in his bid to redeem himself.

"Well." Bayeth nodded. She sat in a chair and lit a cigarette. "Make yourself comfortable, Toal. We have guests coming."

Toal shoved Father Perry onto the couch and sat next to him. "When they arrive, tell them the door is open and invite them in. If you warn them," Toal gripped Perry's shoulder, "you'll be worse off than dead."

The three sat for close to two hours, waiting for Matt and Victoria to arrive. Perry's assurances met with

The Crimson Dimension

increasing skepticism. His time would soon be up.

"It's pretty obvious they aren't coming," Bayeth finally announced.

She walked over to Father Perry, reached between his legs, and squeezed with all her strength. Perry retched, almost vomiting. The charade was over.

"Toal." She motioned him over. "He surprised me. I never thought he'd have the balls to disobey me. I think it's time to make him talk."

Toal grabbed him by the hair and punched his nose. The cartilage exploded in his head, blinding him. "Talk."

"Our Father, who art in heaven—" Blood sprayed off his lips as he prayed.

Toal punched him again, knocking out his front teeth.

"Hallowed be Thy name. Thy kingdom come. Thy will be done—"

Toal's repeated blows no longer mattered. Perry had lost the ability to feel them, to feel anything. He was finally free. He managed a little grin as he slipped away.

CHAPTER 39

Victoria was standing on a beach, looking out across the ocean just as the sun crested the horizon. It was the most beautiful sunrise she'd ever seen. The water warmed her feet as she waded in. Something beckoned her. She took another step.

"Victoria!" Matt's frantic screams ripped her from her dream.

A rush of adrenaline jolted her to full consciousness. Had the demons found them? She scrambled out of bed, looking for the danger. Matt was staring at her, eyes wild with fear. "I'm so sorry."

Victoria looked down and gasped. Her stomach was ashen, and the discoloration was working its way over her chest. It had to be the same thing Matt had gone through.

"Matt!" she grabbed his hand.

Fear gripped her heart and a searing pain shot through her body as she tried to resist the progression. Matt was calling to her, but she could no longer respond. The agony was too intense. Her back arched as the pain crept toward her neck.

This couldn't be right. It had been happening for a while and it hadn't hurt while she was dreaming, nor when she first awoke. Resisting was what triggered the pain.

A thousand knives stabbed her chest, and she collapsed onto the bed. No. She had to let it happen. She needed to trust that she'd okay. Battling her fears, she forced herself to surrender.

The pain vanished. In its place, a rush of comforting, warm energy flowed through her body. She was being energized, healed, empowered...bonded.

△ △ △

Victoria opened her eyes. She was hovering above Matt, who was cradling her unconscious body. He kissed her forehead while he rocked her. *Incredible*. She was becoming the second Torren—Matt's partner. A wave of mixed emotions flooded her mind. There was no turning back now. She was all in. Was she crazy? She'd known this was a possibility when they'd had unprotected sex, but she'd ignored the risk. To be completely honest, she'd hoped it would happen. This had to be the most reckless thing she'd ever done.

Victoria looked at her spiritual form. She looked the same, but felt different. Felt... No. The difference was what she didn't feel. The weight of the world had vanished. The emptiness from losing her parents was gone, and all insecurity and self-doubt had evaporated. She shut her eyes and inhaled the purest air she'd ever breathed. Time stood still. If only she could feel like this in the real world. Nothing would hold her back from achieving her dreams. Or perhaps she didn't have to leave. Maybe she could stay here forever.

But...was she ready to leave her physical life behind?

No. It wasn't her time to go. Her heart told her she had an important role to play, something only she could contribute. As a member of the trinity of the Torren, she had a duty to see this through, whatever that meant. Was it possible that she and Matt had always been destined to become Torren partners? Was that why she hadn't been able to resist him, no matter how much she'd tried?

Goose bumps covered her body as she looked down at

him. She couldn't explain it, but their bond was beyond affection. It was more powerful than she could've ever imagined. The look on Matt's face showed how much he cared for her, feared for her. She needed to let him know she was okay, but her body was completely unresponsive.

Matt continued to call to her. Tears poured down his cheeks.

It must've been awful for him to have gone through the change, fighting it, without a clue what was going on, and with no one there for him. And to have seen the demons and angel must've completely blown his mind. He deserved a lot of credit for keeping his shit together through it all.

Victoria looked away from Matt and focused on her surroundings. Was there something she should be doing in this place? Something Matt should've done if he'd known? Maybe there was a spirit to teach and guide her? She looked around, but there was nothing but light, too bright to see anything at all. There was, however, an amazing presence. Was someone, or something, watching her? Was it the warrior angel, or perhaps the Creator Himself?

"Hello? Is anyone there?"

Her voice echoed in the expanse, but there was no answer.

△ △ △

Victoria snapped back into her body. Her heart was pounding and sweat poured off her. Exhausted, she was a rag doll in Matt's arms.

"I'm so sorry." His eyes were filled with tears.

She managed to reach up and touch his face. "Thank you. I—"

"You're thanking me? Look what I've done to you."

"It's okay. I'm all right." Her assurances didn't seem to sink in. Her full strength had almost returned. "I'm so happy."

Matt's head snapped back. "You're happy?"

Victoria smiled and bit her lower lip. "Do you think I was thrilled about some random person becoming your partner?"

Matt shook his head. "Are you kidding me? Are you nuts?"

"I wanted this the moment we learned you were supposed to have a partner. Think about it. I was already involved whether we liked it or not, and somehow it just felt like the right thing to do."

Matt swallowed. "So, our night together...it was just to get the sight?"

"No!" Crap. She'd never even considered how Matt might take it. "Don't think that for a second. Sight or no sight, I wouldn't have changed a thing." There was no doubt in her mind. Fighting the urge to talk about all the possibilities ahead of them, she shot him a warm smile. He needed some to time to come to terms with what had happened.

Although they faced an unknown and dangerous future, she had no regrets. She'd already completely fallen for him, and their spiritual bond made them even closer. Her destiny had found her. "We're in this together now."

Matt paused for what seemed like forever before letting out a deep breath. "I guess I'd rather have you as my partner than Devante. You're definitely better looking."

"You're not so bad yourself." She reached over and stroked his chest.

Now what?

She'd taken a huge risk and opened herself to unknown dangers. She'd always feared that giving into her impulses could get her into trouble one day, but never imagined anything like this. But there was a new world to discover, and untold secrets to learn. The rewards had to outweigh the risks.

Victoria sighed. Everything was going to be just fine—as long as her grandpa didn't kill her when he found out.

CHAPTER 40

Morning had arrived by the time Zaralen finished searching Victoria's apartment. His hunt for information about Matt had turned up nothing. Her address book, which he'd tucked into his coat, didn't even have his listing.

It was time to go. Lokad would be fine. In his fragile state, he would soon die, allowing him to find someone in the apartment complex to possess before his time ran out.

Zaralen reached for his keys then remembered he'd been picked clean. "Damnit!"

On the off chance they'd spilled out when he was jumped, he looked amongst the debris of the broken table. A folded piece of paper caught his eye. He kneeled to pick it up.

"Bingo." Matt's address. As he was about to stand, a faint buzzing sound came from under the pile of debris. Adding to his luck, it was Victoria's phone.

"Hello?" Zaralen answered the call.

"Can I speak to Victoria Brooks?" a man asked.

"I'm sorry. She just stepped out. Can I take a message?"

"My name is Brother Stephen. An acquaintance of hers visited Father Devante in a church in Brazil. I was hoping she could put us in touch."

Zaralen smiled. Everything was coming together. "It was me. My name is Matt."

"Ahhh, we've been anxious to speak to you. Are you okay?"

"We've just been attacked. I need your help."

"Are you safe?"

"I am now, but I need to know what's going on. Tell me what happened to me. Are you like me? Do you see demons?"

"We are not like you, but we can help. My partner and I are in New York. We can come right now."

"Yes." Zaralen gave them Victoria's address. "Please hurry."

Zaralen pumped his fist. Moments ago, he'd been disgraced, but now he had Matt's address and would soon know the location of the statue. He opened Victoria's cutlery drawer, pulled out a long, sharp knife, and tucked it under Lokad's right arm.

"Hang in there, dickweed. Your new cloak's on the way."

It was the perfect time to update Dmoltech and redeem himself. But he couldn't unlock Victoria's phone, so he'd have to find another.

He turned to Lokad. "I don't know how you've hung on this long, but I need you to hold it together until the priest arrives. I'll be right back."

Zaralen found a nearby payphone.

"Do you have him?" Dmoltech asked.

"Not quite, but I have good news."

"It better be damn good."

"I have the Torren's address."

"That's it?"

"No, there's more. Two priests who know where the statue is are on their way to visit me."

"Well done! I'll send Bayeth and Toal to Matt's. You stay put."

Zaralen wanted to be the one who got to take Matt down, but dared not question Dmoltech's orders. Besides, he'd singlehandedly found Matt's whereabouts, and would soon know where the statue was. Dmoltech would have no choice but to elevate him above the rest.

△ △ △

The intercom buzzed, and Zaralen greeted the two cautious priests. "I'm so glad you're here. I'm Matt."

"Who's that?" one of the initiates asked, pointing at Lokad.

"He's the guy who attacked us. I don't think he's doing very well."

The pair exchanged uneasy glances.

"We need to make sure you are who you say."

"Okay. Sure."

"Tell us about the blood."

Zaralen remembered his brief conversation with Matt after the attack on Peterson. "The statue bled, and I got some of it in a cut in my hand."

"This is Brother Stephen. I'm Brother Marcus." He pointed at Lokad. "Is he alive?"

"He was a while ago. Let me check on him."

"Wait." Brother Stephen grabbed Zaralen's arm. "You told us you can see demons. Is he one of them?"

"No. Not him. He's just a regular guy." This couldn't be any easier. It was the perfect opportunity to free Lokad from his cloak so that he could possess one of the priests. He walked over and crouched beside his partner, keeping his back to the men. He slipped the knife out and severed Lokad's jugular.

"He's bleeding badly. Can you help him?"

Brother Marcus hurried to kneel next to Lokad. "This is bad." He tried to stop the bleeding. "Get me a towel or something."

Zaralen grabbed a shirt off Victoria's bed and tossed it

to Marcus. He crossed the room to Stephen. "I'm so glad you guys called."

Marcus threw up. This was Zaralen's cue that Lokad had possessed him. He plunged the ten-inch blade into Brother Stephen's neck. A stream of blood shot into the air when he pulled the blade free. The scent of hot blood mixed with vomit filled his nostrils and took him to the edge of climax. He drove the knife into Stephen again.

Brother Stephen dropped to his knees, grasping his neck. The blood that surged from between his fingers glistened in the sunlight coming through the window. The combination of the sight and smell was too much to handle. The fury that erupted from his core shattered his self-control. Zaralen stabbed him again, and again, until Stephen collapsed. He leapt on top of the priest, thrusting the blade repeatedly into his back long after the man's last breath.

"Zaralen!"

Lokad's voice snapped him out of his frenzied state. He drove the knife in one last time.

"Enjoying yourself, are you?" Lokad grinned, having gained full control of Marcus's body.

Zaralen looked down at the bloody mess. He'd completely lost it. He knew better than that. Especially after riding Lokad's ass over his lack of self-control. "At least I only give in when it's appropriate." He tossed the knife away. "Killing him didn't jeopardize anything. You, on the other hand, fucked everything up over the chance at a little pussy."

Lokad surveyed the bloody mess. "Bullshit, you're no better than I am."

"That's where you're wrong. I'm so much better than you'll ever be." Zaralen stood up, wiping his bloody hands on his jeans. "We've got work to do. You need to tell me everything your new cloak knows about the statue and the Torren. But first, we need to get your old cloak out of here before someone finds him."

Lokad walked back to his old cloak and studied it. "Why?"

"We don't want to leave any link to Bromley behind."

Lokad nodded. "What about what's left of the priest?"

"Who gives a fuck? His body isn't connected to us."

CHAPTER 41

Matt woke as the sun broke through the window. Somehow, they'd fallen back asleep, though he couldn't imagine how Victoria had managed it after everything that had just happened.

How could she be so accepting of him and the entire situation? And why on earth would she want to share in this curse, which she somehow thought of as a gift? She seemed a little impulsive, but he'd never thought she'd do something like this—especially after he'd described how horrific it was. He had to hand it to her for surrendering to it. Sure, she had his experience to draw from, but regardless, her bravery was incredible.

She seemed to have an inner strength Matt had never known. Not that he didn't have strength of his own. To rise above a life of abuse was no small feat. The difference between them was how naturally and effortlessly she handled herself.

Victoria shifted in her sleep. Matt reached over and stroked her hair. She mumbled something he didn't catch before her breathing returned to the slow rhythm of deep slumber.

It was unreal how fast they'd bonded. He added up the hours they'd spent together, and it totaled less than a full day. It made no sense, but their bond was much deeper than anything he'd had with Jodie, and there was no question that he'd loved her deeply.

Matt sighed. This couldn't be love. Not this quickly. Did

all Torren feel this strongly for their partners? The thought weirded him out.

He obviously wasn't going to fall asleep again, so he slipped out of bed and dressed quietly, not wanting to wake her. Famished, he searched for the kitchen and was greeted by the inviting smell of bacon. Lawrence must be an early riser.

"Morning, sir."

"Good morning. Have you seen Victoria yet?"

Matt flushed. Not only had he slept with Lawrence's granddaughter, but he'd made her a Torren. He didn't know how to answer, so he offered a half-truth.

"I'm pretty sure she's still sleeping."

"Good. At least one of us will be fully rested for the day."

Lawrence was sharing his plan to retrieve Matt's passport and take Victoria to get a new one when Matt sensed movement. He spun around to greet Victoria, but she wasn't there. Odd. It happened again, and he knew she was coming closer. She appeared with a smile in the kitchen doorway.

"I knew Matt was here." She pointed back the way she'd come, and then at Matt. "I could tell what direction you were in and how close you were. Amazing!"

"Or perhaps it was the small of bacon," Lawrence answered.

"No. For real. Matt, did you sense it too?"

Goose bumps formed on his arms. "Yes, I did."

Lawrence's glance darted from his preparations to his granddaughter then he stared at Matt. "What are you talking about?"

"Didn't Matt tell you? I received the gift last night. I became the second Torren."

"No—" Lawrence grabbed the counter for support. He

glared at Matt, his face instantly red. "You..." His whole body shook. "How?"

"Umm..." Matt flushed as he stuttered.

"You stupid ass!" Lawrence clenched his fist and took a step toward Matt.

"Grandpa!" Victoria rushed to Lawrence and grabbed his arm. "Stop it."

"And under my roof!" He shook his finger at Matt.

Victoria jumped between them. "I'm an adult. I wanted this."

Matt stepped back. Holy shit. This guy wanted to kill him. He kept his mouth shut, hoping things would calm down. That aside, everyone had completely glossed over the fact that he and Victoria could sense each other's locations. He'd known Victoria was moving, her relative speed, and in what direction. His pulse quickened. Were other abilities triggered by their union?

"Damnit, you two." Lawrence took a few deep breaths and leaned back on his cane. "Did either of you considered the consequences of your little unprotected escapade?"

Victoria placed her hand on Lawrence's for assurance. "We'll be fine. Now that it's happened, it feels so right. I've never been so sure about anything."

Lawrence sat on a stool and lowered his head. He thought for a few moments, looked up at the couple, and shook his head in resignation. "Well, there's not much we can do about it now."

Matt let out a breath. Despite the man accepting the reality of the situation, he had to think Matt was a complete fuck-up. "Sir, I'm truly sorry. I never thought—"

"Shut up and let me think for a minute."

Matt looked at Victoria. She could have broken the news a little more gently. The poor old man looked like he was having a stroke.

After a long and uncomfortable silence Lawrence finally looked up. "There goes my theory about Father Devante. But I still think you two need to get to Brazil, and as soon as possible. Even though I was wrong about the priest being your partner, you're still in danger here, and we don't have the slightest idea what powers the Shakath have."

"I agree." Victoria nodded.

"And then we can both be rid..." Matt trailed off. Even if Devante could free them, convincing Victoria was going to be a challenge. What a fucking mess. "We'll go and get my passport. And I'd like to call Rob before we leave, to let him know I'm all right. He's probably worried about me."

"Who's Rob?" Lawrence asked.

"My roommate."

Lawrence jerked upright.

"What's wrong?" Victoria asked.

"They found your apartment. Who says they haven't found Matt's?"

"Oh shit!" Matt jumped up and paced around the kitchen table. He couldn't imagine anything happening to Rob. "No. They couldn't have."

"How can you be so sure?" Lawrence asked.

"No one knows more than my first name. I refused to tell the priest anything because I didn't trust him. None of them have my last name, my address, anything."

Victoria gasped and sprinted for the bedroom.

"What are you doing?" Matt yelled behind her. He sensed her running up to the bedroom then back.

Victoria burst into the kitchen as fast as she'd left. "Matt, the paper you wrote your address down on is gone. It must've fallen out of my purse during your fight with the demons."

CHAPTER 42

Horror filled him. Rob and Kathy could be in trouble. He grabbed his cellphone. "Shit!" It was completely dead. "I need a charger. Do you have one?"

"What kind?" Victoria asked.

"Samsung."

"No. We have iPhones."

"Then we have to go. Hurry! Grab your keys."

"Wait." Lawrence pointed to the phone on the wall. "We have a landline, and my cell is in my room."

What an idiot. Matt dialed Rob as fast as his fingers would allow. "Come on, come on!" he urged as he waited for Rob to answer.

"I'm unable to come to the—"

"Fuck." He dialed Kathy.

"Hello?" Kathy said.

"Kathy, it's Matt. Is Rob with you?"

"Yes."

"Good. You and Rob have to get out of the apartment right now. Take your phones and use the back exit. There's no time to explain. Hurry!"

"What's wrong?" she asked.

"Get out now." Matt's heart was pounding so fast he could hardly breathe. "Are you at the car yet?"

"Yes, we just got off the elevator. We're getting in it now."

"Good. Start driving. I'll give you an address." He

looked at Lawrence.

Lawrence held his hand up. "You need to slow down."

"What?" Matt shrugged. "They need directions to come here."

"Let's think for a minute."

"What's there to think about?"

"Matt, he's right." Victoria put her hand on Matt's arm. "They're safe. Tell them we'll call back in a minute.

Matt raised the phone back to his mouth. "I'll call back in a minute. Just don't go home."

Lawrence nodded. "We need to consider that the demons might be staking your place out. If they are, there's no doubt Rob and Kathy will be followed."

"Well, we have to do something," Matt pleaded. "Those bastards will find them."

"I have an idea," Victoria offered. "We'll tell them to meet us somewhere secluded. Some place we can watch to see if they're being followed. If they are, we can give whoever's following them the slip."

"Okay," Matt agreed. "But we have to figure out the details fast. I have to call them back. I'm sure I've scared them shitless."

"There's a motel about fifteen miles from here," Lawrence said. "I stayed there while I had the house painted last year. The fumes were intolerable. I couldn't sleep. It took them three weeks—"

"Grandpa. You're rambling."

"Right." He tapped his finger on his temple. "The motel. It has windows in the back that face a rest stop and gas bar."

"Yeah?" What was his point? Rob and Kathy's lives were in danger.

"You can rent a room, and when they arrive, you can leave through the back window, go to the rest stop parking lot, and get into Victoria's car."

Matt liked the idea. "There's one problem. We'll never know if they were followed, and the demons might end up on our tail anyway."

"I can take a second car," Victoria suggested. "I'll watch from a safe distance to see if anyone followed."

"And what if the demons show up?" Lawrence asked.

"They'll never know I've spotted them. I'll park nearby, but not too close. Once I'm confident Matt gave them slip, I'll call him."

"Neither of us have phones," Matt reminded her. "Mine's dead, and yours was lost."

"Use mine," Lawrence offered.

"Matt can take yours, and I'll call from a payphone once I'm sure no one followed."

"I don't like the idea of leaving Victoria there. It's risky...but it sounds like the best we can do on such short notice." Lawrence handed the landline back to Matt.

Kathy answered.

"It's Matt. Are you two okay?"

"Yes. We're fine. What's going on?"

"There are some dangerous people after me. I think they found out where we live, and you don't want to be home when they come looking for me."

"This is it!" Kathy yelled. "You've gone too far this time. Are you dealing drugs or something?"

"No! I haven't done anything. I'll explain later. Where are you right now?"

"We're in the car." Her voice was cold. "We just started driving."

"Can you tell if you're being followed?"

"No, I don't think so."

"Good. Here's what I need you to do. Start driving north out of town toward Harriman State Park—"

The Crimson Dimension

After relaying Lawrence's directions, Matt hung up and expelled a huge breath. "Okay. So far so good. Let's get our butts down to the motel and set up."

Victoria ran to Lawrence's room and grabbed his cell.

Lawrence gave Matt the passcode. "Don't lose it. This is your lifeline." He patted Matt on the shoulder. "Keep me up to date and make sure neither of you confronts them. Get Rob and Kathy through the window and back here to safety."

Victoria hugged her grandpa. "Don't worry. We'll be careful."

Lawrence grabbed Matt's arm. "Don't allow your emotions to control you. Think before you act."

Matt handed one of the two guns he'd taken from Zaralen and Lokad to Victoria. "Just in case. Do you know how to use it?"

"Yes." She ejected the clip to check for bullets. "I don't love them, but Grandpa made me learn." She smiled at Lawrence. "Okay, let's go." Victoria grabbed her purse, stuffed the gun into it, and pulled out her keys. "Are yours on the hook, Grandpa?"

"Yes." He gave her a firm hug. "Be careful."

"I will. I promise." Victoria led Matt down the hall and into the garage. She activated the door openers, and as they rose, snow blew into the garage.

"You've got to be kidding," Matt said. "The roads are gonna be awful. We can't be late."

"It'll slow them down too. Don't worry. It'll be fine." She stopped at a Mercedes and directed Matt to her BMW.

"Just take it easy, and I'm sure we'll get there in plenty of time." She paused. "We don't have our coats. I'll grab 'em."

"I don't need one. I want to get going."

Victoria rolled her eyes. "All right, go ahead. I'll be

right behind you."

Matt pulled out onto the road and sped away. He could still sense Victoria, though he felt the distance between them increasing. He turned onto the highway and headed south to rescue his friends.

CHAPTER 43

"We're going on a road trip." Kathy said the words, but Rob knew it wasn't her. He was trapped in a nightmare and couldn't wake himself up.

It had all started with a knock on the door, followed by a woman and an armed man demanding to know where Matt was. After a brief interrogation, the woman took the gun from her partner, and held it to the guy's head. Rob could still hear Kathy's scream when the gun went off, spraying chunks of brain and bone all over them.

Rob had tried his best to shield her. "Please! Don't—" His stomach roiled, cutting off his plea for mercy. Something had entered him—something vile. It made no sense, but he felt it.

The unknown force was trying to take control of his body. Rob's arms moved against his will, and his muscles exploded with pain as he fought to stop it. He had to regain control. He had to save Kathy. His body went into severe convulsions, and he fell to the floor.

His earliest memories ran through his mind. His first steps, his first words. Things he'd long forgotten. His life was unfolding like a movie on fast forward. Was he dying?

No. He wouldn't let himself slip away. Kathy needed him. He fought to stop the playback, but couldn't. Shit. It was the being. It was reading his mind. A stabbing pain caused him to lose control and his memories began to play again. His fifth birthday. Rob focused on the ball glove he'd been given, freezing the picture. It worked. The creature would see no more. His memories pushed against the ball glove, harder and harder. A migraine exploded and he couldn't focus anymore. The glove faded, and his life played on. The creature was absorbing everything that was him, accessing the secrets stored in the farthest reaches of his mind.

Rob watched himself stand up and take the gun from the woman. The world had turned gray and lifeless. He heard their conversation, but it was faint. Hollow. Unable to look away, he watched himself handle the weapon with precision despite the fact he'd never touched one in his life. He raised the gun to her head and pulled the trigger. His screams were muted before they could reach his vocal cords. He prayed to God to be freed from this Hell. He begged God to let him die.

Kathy stood up beside him, wiping the sprayed blood off her face. "No matter how many times I've changed cloaks, it never gets easier." Her voice had become cold and calculated. She was trapped in the same hell as him. *No!* He pushed at the beast with everything he had left in his soul. He had to stay strong. Had to keep his sanity long enough to find her a way out.

"*Please, God,*" he begged. "*Please give me the strength.*"

CHAPTER 44

Bayeth hung up after receiving Matt's instructions. "How are we for gas?" she asked Toal.

"Full tank. Why?"

"He wants us to meet him at a motel about an hour north. I'll call Dmoltech and update him."

Surprisingly, Dmoltech was upbeat. Her announcement would only add to his good mood, but before she could share her news, Dmoltech gave her his.

"Lokad just possessed a priest from the Vatican who has information on the statue. It's the only one in existence. They don't know the exact location, but it's close to a place called Petropolis near Rio de Janeiro. Lokad and Zaralen are on their way to the airport. As soon as they find and destroy the statue, we'll be rid of the Torren once and for all."

Zaralen and his lackey were getting too much of the credit. "Did they learn anything more about Matt?"

"It appears he's still ignorant of his abilities, and his second hasn't yet risen. I think it was a complete fluke that he managed to protect Peterson. Based on Lokad's information, I don't believe Matt even knows he did it."

With Zaralen and Lokad finding the statue, and confirming that Matt was an easy target, her news had lost its punch. Nevertheless, her contributions couldn't be ignored. "I also have good news. We've possessed Matt's friends, and we're on our way to see him. Now that the location of the statue is known, I can dispatch him."

"I still want him alive. I want to see if he knows anything else."

Right. Rumor had it that Athamm and Nazkiel had handed him the last Torren on a silver platter, bound and helpless. Dmoltech was certain to use this opportunity to singlehandedly kill Matt.

"Yes, sir. We'll do our best to bring him in alive."

"Excellent. Once you deliver the Torren to me, Lucifer will surely reconsider."

"Reconsider what?"

"Oh, nothing."

Dmoltech was up to something, and she wanted in on it. Knowledge was power. "You can tell me. You know you can trust me."

"Maybe later. When will you have Matt?"

"In an hour."

"I knew I could rely on you. Be careful, and don't underestimate him."

"I won't." Bayeth hung up and turned to Toal. "Dmoltech wants him alive. This isn't going to be easy. Zaralen said the Torren saw his eyes glowing red. He'll know what we are as soon as he sees us. We'll have to act fast."

"How am I going to take him down?" Toal asked. "This body is pretty weak. I don't think I'd take anyone in a fight."

Bayeth took another look at Toal and nodded. "You might be right." She thought for a moment. "Dmoltech wants him alive, so shooting him is out of the question."

"A bullet through the knee won't kill him," Toal offered. "When he answers the door, I can put a round into his leg. I don't think he'll be much trouble after that."

Bayeth considered his idea, and although it was messy, it might work. "Are there sunglasses in the glove box?"

The Crimson Dimension

Toal took a look. "One pair. Men's."

"Okay. Wear them when you knock on the door. I'll keep my eyes hidden until he answers. Don't shoot until we're in the room."

CHAPTER 45

Victoria had bitten her lower lip so many times it was bound to start bleeding, and her heart was pounding out of her chest. She needed to calm down. If all went as planned, Rob and Kathy would soon be safe at her grandpa's. But what if the couple was followed? What if the two Shakath at her apartment were on their way? What if even more were coming? Shivers ran down her spine. Perhaps this wasn't the best plan after all. But it was too late to change it now. The plan had to work. Everything was riding on this.

A car exited the highway onto the service road which matched the description of Rob's car. Victoria squinted to make out the occupants as the car slowly approached. Small framed blonde and husky brunet. By Matt's description, it had to be Rob and Kathy. The moment of truth. Victoria turned her attention up the road to see if they were being followed. So far so good. No other cars took the exit. As Rob's car passed her, she almost vomited.

Was she that wound up? "Get a grip," she told herself. "You can do this."

She studied the exit for another minute. Still no tail. She'd worked herself up for nothing. Victoria put the car in gear, made a U-turn, and headed to meet everyone. Matt was going to be so happy that they were safe.

Victoria looked ahead and watched the couple get out of their car and walk up to Matt's door. Rob pulled a pair of sunglasses out of his pocket and put them on. Why now? It wasn't sunny out, and he would've worn them while driving—not when he was about go inside. Could they be someone else? She'd never met them so she couldn't be sure, but her gut told her something was definitely off. Victoria went numb. She stomped on the gas pedal and laid on the horn.

Kathy, or whoever she was, spun to face her just as Victoria skidded to a halt a few feet from them. She locked eyes with the woman. *Oh shit...* Her eyes glowed hauntingly red. "Oh my God!" Those weren't nerves she'd felt when they passed her. It was the sensation Matt had described. How could she have been so stupid?

Victoria screamed as the windshield exploded, showering her with glass. Her body went completely numb as the guy took aim for a second shot. This couldn't be how she was meant to go, or the time. Not now. She had to survive this.

The guy pulled the trigger but nothing happened. He frantically worked the action, trying to free the jam. This was her opportunity. Victoria tried to open the door to escape but her muscles wouldn't respond. Paralyzed, she squeezed her eyes closed and braced for the end.

There was no shot. Instead, a loud thump jolted the car. Matt appeared out of nowhere, tackling the man and slamming him against the hood. The gun skidded toward her and slipped into the wiper blade groove. Matt and the guy wrestled for position, trying to get to the weapon.

Matt had saved her from certain death, but where had the first bullet hit? Victoria forced a breath and ran her trembling hands over her face, her chest, and her arms, and they came back bloodless. Thank God. He'd missed. The car jerked again.

Matt pushed the guy and reached for the gun. His opponent was back on him in an instant, grabbing Matt's hand with both of his. No one appeared to be gaining the upper hand. "Look out!" Victoria yelled as the woman jumped on Matt's back. The trio lost their balance and crashed onto the sidewalk near the hotel door.

What the hell was the matter with her? Matt was fighting for his life and she was sitting frozen in her seat. Victoria jumped out of the car and grabbed the gun in her purse.

"Rob!" Matt yelled. "Stop it."

Oh God. It was Rob and Kathy, and they were...possessed by demons? This was insane. She raised the gun then lowered it again. "I can't." They were Matt's friends. She reached for her mace and raced to Matt. The men still had a death lock on each other's hands, and Kathy was pounding on the back of Matt's head with her all her might. Victoria pushed Kathy back and unloaded the mace in her face. Kathy reeled and fell backward onto the ground.

Matt and Rob stumbled through the open doorway into the room, still fighting to gain control of Rob's gun. The pair grappled and slammed each other around, knocking over an end table and shattering a lamp.

Victoria slammed herself into Rob, sending all three to the floor. The gun slipped from the men's grasp and slid under the bed.

With the gun no longer the focus, Matt quickly got the upper hand. He flipped Rob over and pinned his face to the floor. Matt frantically scanned the room. "Grab the phone cord!"

Victoria jumped between the beds where the phone sat on the nightstand. *Shit*. Kathy was gone. Victoria yanked the cord from the wall and tossed it to Matt. "I'm going after her." She raced out of the room to find Kathy leaning on the hood of Rob's car, coughing and struggling to

The Crimson Dimension

breathe. Thank God she hadn't gone anywhere. Victoria grabbed her and tried to force her back into the room.

Kathy spun away and ran blindly down the sidewalk. "Help! Help! I'm being kidnapped!" She stumbled off the sidewalk and faceplanted on the parking lot.

This was beyond messed up. People were running to help Kathy, and Victoria couldn't risk going after her. What was she supposed to do now? Victoria ran back to Matt, who was tying Rob's hands behind his back. "We're in big trouble. Kathy's screaming for help. We have to get out of here!"

Matt's face said it all. He was devastated. "We need Kathy..."

"I'm sorry. She ran off before I could get her."

"Don't give up," Matt urged. "Pop the trunk. We're not leaving without them."

Matt hauled Rob to his feet and pushed him out of the room and into the trunk. He slammed the lid. "Where did she go?"

Victoria pointed at Kathy, who had a crowd forming around her. "Murderer!" Kathy yelled, pointing at Matt.

"Oh my God!" Victoria exclaimed. "This is crazy!"

Matt made a move for the car then stopped. "We have to get Kathy and get the hell out of here."

He took a few steps in Kathy's direction.

"No!" Victoria stopped him. "Leave her," she urged. "We've got to go! We're going to get arrested."

"I can't! We can't leave her." Two men started for Matt. "Fuck!"

Matt grabbed Victoria's hand and rushed her into the room. "Lock the door behind me and get out through the window! Keys are under the floor mat. I'll take Rob and catch up."

"Matt." Victoria tried to get his attention. "Matt!"

"What?"

"We're going to figure—"

"Not now." He pushed her toward the window. "Go!"

He grabbed Rob's gun and burst out the door. "Everyone back off!"

Victoria paused outside the window and watched Matt get into her grandpa's car. Thank God. She ran to her car and sped away.

CHAPTER 46

The adrenaline rush of the fight had long since run its course. Matt spent the drive back to Lawrence's struggling to come to grips with Rob and Kathy's possession. If only he'd taken a minute to think about all the possibilities rather than just assume everyone was safe. His friends had probably been possessed while he was getting laid. Could he have been more selfish? He slammed his hand against the steering wheel. "Damnit!" His hands shook so hard he could barely steer.

How the hell were they going to get out of this mess? And he'd lost Kathy, or whoever she was now, and Rob... The demons had gotten Rob. Tears welled in his eyes.

Unable to focus, he had to pull over. He leaned his head on the steering wheel and closed his eyes. The demon started shouting and kicking again. "Shut the fuck up, you bastard. You took my friend. I'm going to kill you!"

Images of the demon jumping into the cop's body ran though his mind. One of those things was in Rob. How the hell was going to get it out? An exorcism? Fuck. This wasn't some stupid movie.

He had to do something, and sitting here sure as hell wasn't doing anyone any good. He had to keep his shit together and work this through. First thing was to return to Lawrence's and make sure Victoria was safe. Then, they had to get to Devante for some answers. He wiped the tears from eyes, turned back onto the road, and drove on.

Seeing Victoria filled him with relief. She ran over to

meet him as he got out of the car and threw herself into his arms.

"Thank God you're okay." She held on tight.

Grief gripped his soul, and the tears came again. "Rob... I don't know what to do..."

"I can't imagine what you're feeling." She stroked his head. "We'll figure something out. I promise."

"What do I do?" Matt pointed at the trunk. "It's Rob in there, but it isn't." Matt slammed his fist into the car. "It's all my fault."

"Don't be so hard on yourself." Lawrence had caught up with Victoria. "It's not your fault. Place the blame on the Shakath, where it belongs."

"Fuck!" Matt took a deep breath and looked up at the sky. "Why did you do this to me?"

"Hey." Victoria took his hand. "We have Rob in our care. We'll keep him safe until we can find a way to free him."

"You don't understand," Matt replied. "The demons probably know every detail of my life now. They won't stop at this. If I don't surrender to them, they'll go after everyone I know."

"We won't let that happen," Victoria said. "There has to be a way to free him. Remember who we are. We're partnered with the warrior angel. Surely he can help us."

"Then where is he?"

"Try to remember what happened the last time you saw him," Lawrence said.

"He just stood there while those little imps, or Qaton, or whatever they're called, went after Peterson. He didn't start fighting them until I yelled at him."

"You commanded him!" Lawrence's face lit up. "What exactly did you say?"

"I don't know. I think I called him a name or something

and told him to go protect the guy."

"I've got it!" Victoria clapped her hands. "Do you remember what the guy in my apartment said to you?"

"He wanted me to go with him. What does that have to do with anything?"

"He told you to call your dog off Roger Peterson. It made no sense at the time—"

Matt's pulse quickened, and a spark of hope ignited. The angel was probably sticking with Peterson until ordered otherwise. "You're brilliant!" He gave her a huge smile. "Warrior!" he called out. "Or whatever your name is... We need you back here."

"Well?" Lawrence asked. "Did it appear?"

"No." His face turned red. "I feel like a complete idiot."

Lawrence tapped his finger to his chin. "You said that he appeared and vanished a number of times. Can you think of why?"

"He only hung around while I could see one of the demons. When I lost sight, he took off."

"If that's the case," Victoria said, "maybe your command worked. The Warrior might've left Peterson, but we won't know until we see the demon in Rob."

Matt took the keys out of his pocket and put his thumb on the trunk button. He paused. There was no way to know what was about to happen. Would the Warrior appear? If it did, what would it do?

"Listen up, angel." He looked around the yard. "Rob is my best friend. If you kill him, I'll... I'll..." What the hell could he do? "Just please don't hurt him."

He faced the trunk and popped the latch.

Rob's body lay in the trunk, lifeless. Fear paralyzed Matt. Had he been in there too long? Had he suffocated? As he bent down to check for a pulse, Rob jolted upright and hit Matt in the side of the head with a tire iron.

Matt staggered backward. Fortunately, Rob hadn't been able to take much of a swing. Though it hurt like hell, Matt was okay. He grabbed the cold steel and yanked with everything he had. The tire iron flew out of Rob's hand, causing Matt to tumble backward into the snow. "Fuck!" he yelled.

Rob scrambled out of the trunk, kicked Matt in the ribs, and ran west to the tree line.

Victoria rushed to Matt and helped him to his feet. "Are you all right?"

"Yeah." Trying his best to ignore the pain, he took up the chase.

"Matt!" Victoria called to him as he ran across the lawn and into the woods. "The angel! It's here!"

Matt looked over his shoulder to see the Warrior gliding at his side. "It's about time! Now let's get that fucker!"

Everything went black. Matt hit the ground hard, his head spinning. He opened his eyes to see Rob standing over him with a piece of wood. He gathered his wits in time to roll out of the way of Rob's second strike, which missed by mere inches. Matt rolled again then struggled to his feet. This wasn't going to be easy. How was he supposed to fight his best friend without severely injuring him—or getting killed?

"Don't do this!" Matt said. "I don't want to hurt you."

The demon ignored the warning and ran straight at him, swinging the wood as he approached. Matt spun to avoid the strike and managed to trip him. He launched himself on top of Rob's body, and they tumbled to the ground.

"What are you waiting for?" he yelled to the Warrior. "Wipe the demon out like you did to those imps!"

The angel didn't move. It just stood there with its

flaming sword in hand, apparently waiting for Matt to do something.

"What?" Matt pleaded. "What am I supposed to do?" Subduing Rob's body had been the easy part, but now he desperately needed the Warrior's help. This was new ground. Could Rob even be saved?

The angel stood ready but continued to do nothing.

"Kill it!" he shouted. "Remove it. Save Rob!"

Nothing worked. Why wouldn't it help him?

Matt looked up and screamed, "Don't do this to me. Not again. Haven't I paid enough?" Was this the ultimate punishment? Did he have to kill his own friend to survive? "No!"

Rob thrashed around, trying to break free. "Let me go!" he hollered from beneath Matt's weight. "Get off me!"

"I'm sorry, Rob." He hoped Rob could somehow hear him.

He wouldn't allow himself to lose hope.

"Think." Matt tightened his grip. Back in the alley, when the cops had shot the possessed man, his soul had risen from the body. That meant Rob was in there. How in the hell could he get him out? "I know you're in there. If you can hear me at all—if you have any control—do something to show me."

An odd feeling enveloped Matt, familiar yet foreign at the same time. He struggled to focus on the sensation, but every time he did, his thoughts went back to Rob. He should've been able to place the feeling, and frustration crawled through him. Then it hit him. The reason thoughts of Rob kept flooding his mind was because the feeling *was* Rob. His despair washed away, and hope filled him. "Rob! I can feel you. I know you're there. Stay strong."

He'd somehow connected with Rob's spirit. The connection was foggy and kept slipping away, but Matt fought to keep the link intact.

"Help me, Matt," Rob cried out. "Help!"

"Yes!" This was Rob's true voice. It was very faint, and seemed to come from a great distance. "Rob! Hold on!"

There was something keeping him from reaching his friend, as if a physical membrane separated them. With every shred of his energy, he forced himself through it.

Matt gasped and snapped his eyes shut. The cold bit his skin worse than the time he'd broken through the ice of the Contoocook River as a child. He held his breath and forced his eyes open to try to orient himself. Everything was a blur, but he wasn't submerged. With his air running out, he had to risk a breath. Matt's lungs filled with the purest, most invigorating air he'd ever breathed.

The trees, which moments before had stood vivid against the snow, faded into the background. Nothing looked real. Everything had taken on a holographic quality, except that he was staring directly into the face of the vilest thing he'd ever seen. The demon's glare radiated pure hatred. Despite the clarity of the demon, Matt's own hands appeared blurred. No. He was actually seeing two separate images, his body and spirit. Holy shit.

"Matt." Rob's plea stole his attention.

Matt looked up to the angel for help. It too had become incredibly vibrant, but the damn thing still just stood there, as useless as ever. Why had he expected anything else?

"Rob! I'm here." He searched for his friend's spirit.

To his amazement, the demon's face faded to reveal Rob's.

"There you are!" Matt shouted. "I see you." He was going to get this son of a bitch out of Rob or die trying.

A sickening stench hit Matt, and he watched in desperation as Rob's eyes reddened and the demon's face reappeared. "No! Don't go."

The demon struck him in the jaw, causing Matt to see stars. How in the hell had he done that? Matt had Rob's hands firmly pinned to the ground. Matt's head snapped back from another blow, this time from the left. The fucker was incredibly strong. He couldn't take many more. He had to do something.

The demon took another swing, but Matt let go of Rob and managed to deflect the strike. When he did, Rob's hand caught him in the chin.

Shit. His opponent was fighting him on two different battlefields. The demon was using Rob's flesh to fight in the physical realm, while his much stronger demonic form battled in the spiritual realm. While Matt concentrated on holding Rob, the demon was free to strike at him in the spirit realm.

Two can play that game. It took all Matt's concentration, but he managed to use his physical hands to hold Rob, and his spiritual ones to defend against the demon's assault. The bastard was incredibly fast, and the punches never weakened, no matter how many times it swung at him. It took all he had to keep from being knocked out. There was no way he'd be able to switch to the offence.

"Help!" he called to the Warrior. Still no response.

"Victoria?" Maybe she could help.

There was no answer. She likely couldn't hear him in this place.

When he concentrated on the faded surroundings, his consciousness snapped back into the physical realm.

"Matt!" Victoria was standing in front of him, screaming his name. The demon struck him again. He'd left his spirit vulnerable. What in the hell was he supposed to do?

"Oh my God, it's going to kill you!" Victoria screamed. "Tell me what to do."

"Hold Rob!" He couldn't afford another strike. He plunged back in.

Victoria positioned herself above Rob's head and helped pin his hands to the ground.

Matt focused his thoughts on the spiritual fight, giving him a much-needed edge. He deflected another swing then drove his fist down into the black, featureless face.

A flash of light to Matt's left caught his attention. Fearing the appearance of another demon, he spun to defend himself. To his relief, Victoria materialized beside him. Her spiritual form was even more beautiful than her physical one.

"Grab his arm!"

"Hold on," Victoria answered.

Something was different. Her words were amazingly clear, as if he'd thought rather than heard them.

Victoria rushed in and grabbed the demon's arm, keeping him from hitting Matt's spirit form.

Fueled by fear, anger, and frustration, Matt pounded on the demon until it went limp. Thankfully, Rob appeared unscathed, even though he was occupying the same space as the demon.

"Rob!" he shouted for his friend once again. Rob's face appeared while the demon's faded. "I've got you, buddy. Hold on while I get you out of here." He took hold of Rob to pull his soul away from his captor. He heaved backward, drawing Rob partly out of his body.

"No!" Victoria's words resonated in his mind. *"I think you'll kill him if you rip his spirit out."*

Matt froze. What in the hell was he doing? He'd almost killed his friend. He released Rob's soul, and it snapped back into his body. He focused his energy on the demon until it materialized once again. Matt grabbed it by the neck and pulled its oily, faceless head away from Rob's. This was it. He pivoted into a headlock and yanked with every shred of energy he had left. Matt and the demon flew backward, clear of Rob and Victoria.

The instant the demon was separated from Rob's body, the Warrior came to life. He raised his sword above his head and marched toward the demon with laser focus. At that moment, Matt understood the role of man and angel in the trinity. The angel couldn't act against the demonic beings unless they were separated from the humans they possessed. The sword would likely kill anything it touched. Matt's purpose was clear. He was the device to divide spirit from flesh.

Matt let go of the demon as the Warrior arrived and stepped back to allow it a clear swing. As the sword sped along its arc, the demon leaped off the ground and sprinted back toward Rob. The Warrior launched after him.

"Victoria!" Neither he nor the angel could catch up in time.

Positioned between the demon and Rob, Victoria lunged forward and drove herself into the approaching demon. The force of the impact sent her flying backward like a rag doll run over by a freight train. She hit the ground hard, but so did the demon. He'd missed his mark. The Warrior swung the flaming two-handed sword, and severed the creature's head.

The sound of the sword slicing through demonic flesh was one Matt would never forget. It was the sound of victory, and revenge. The demon erupted into flames and disintegrated before his eyes.

Matt ran to Victoria's side. "Are you all right?" She was groggy, but conscious. He started to laugh. "We did it!"

Matt turned to the Warrior, but it was gone. "Thank you," he called out into the empty woods.

CHAPTER 47

Dmoltech paced his office, waiting for Bayeth's call. Despite the difficulties along the way, everything had turned out according to plan. Peterson was no longer a threat, the statue would soon be destroyed, and Matt was probably being bound and gagged this very moment.

Once he extinguished the Torren, he would summon Lucifer and boast of his accomplishments. Surely, his extraordinary tale would give Lucifer cause to reconsider the decision to pass him over. After all, he was, without doubt, the most qualified for the presidential position during their reign over mankind.

His cellphone rang, ending his daydream. "Hello," he answered, smiling in anticipation of the good news.

"It's me," Bayeth announced.

Dmoltech was still unfamiliar with her new voice. He would miss her former cloak, having enjoyed the pleasures of her exquisite body many times. Hopefully, she'd picked something comparable. "Verify," he demanded.

"Six, three, seven, four, two, nine."

"Is it finished?" he asked.

"Big problems. They captured Toal."

His heart skipped a beat. "What?"

"We were ambushed at the motel. If I hadn't attracted attention, they would've had me too."

"Fucking, bloody Hell! Where are you? I'll send Zaralen and Lokad to help round him up." This was getting very personal. Dmoltech would enjoy staring Matt in the eye while he took his last breath.

"At some shithole upstate motel. I don't have the exact location with me. It's in the car, and there are fucking pigs swarming the place. I've been here an hour answering their asinine questions. It was almost impossible to find some privacy in order to call you."

"Damnit!" he yelled. "Now what do we do?"

Before Bayeth could answer, an undeniable, stabbing pain rocked Dmoltech. One of his bonds was severed. He'd lost another Shakath to the depths of Hell.

"Fuck!" He slammed his hand down on his desk.

"Master?"

He searched his bonds and confirmed his hunch: it was Toal. At least it was him rather than one of the others. Toal was only useful because of his choice of large and dominating cloaks. His position could be filled by whatever demon the roll of dice produced as his replacement, if Lucifer ever granted him another. No, the real problem was that the Torren must be developing. For all he knew, Matt's second had emerged.

"Are you there?" Bayeth prompted again.

"Your fucking gorilla just got banished."

Bayeth didn't respond.

"No more games!" His victory was slipping through his hands. "I want him bound and lying at my feet at any cost."

"It will be my pleasure."

Dmoltech couldn't trust in any of his remaining Shakath, not even Bayeth. He needed to take full control of every move going forward. "What have you told the cops?"

"I told them I was abducted by a complete stranger and managed to escape. Nothing more."

"I think it's time to come clean with them."

"I don't understand."

"Listen carefully. I want you to tell them that Matt, Victoria, and your husband killed the old cloaks back at your apartment. You came home and caught them in the act. They tied you up and took you there, but you managed to escape. Say you were conflicted about exposing your husband, but have now come to your senses."

"Genius."

"I know," he said as if he didn't love hearing the compliment. "If the cops haven't found them by the time Zaralen and Lokad leave for Rio, I'll keep Zaralen back to help. Lokad should be able to find and destroy the statue on his own."

"What do I do now?"

"Cooperate with the police. I'll be in touch."

CHAPTER 48

Rob was shivering. He forced his eyes open to find himself lying in a snow-covered forest. Where was he? How had he gotten here? He could barely recall his own name. All he knew was that he'd freeze to death if he didn't get out of the cold.

Laughter? He turned his head in the direction of the sound. A young man cradled a woman in his arms.

He looked familiar, someone Rob should've known. Rob's hair stood on end. Somehow, he knew this man was dangerous. He had to escape. Rob struggled to get up, but his muscles were jelly. Shit.

Then, like a tidal wave, the memory of Toal's possession flooded back. He braced himself for the nausea to return, but it didn't come. Something was different. Everything he was seeing was crystal clear. The foggy view through Toal's eyes was gone. Rob wriggled his fingers. Yes! He'd decided to move his fingers, and they'd worked. Above all, the sickening presence of the demon was gone.

Overcome with happiness, he sobbed.

The couple rushed toward him. Rob's heart pounded as they approached. Could one of them be Toal? Would the demon possess him again? Rob couldn't go through it a second time...but there was no escape. His muscles still wouldn't respond enough to get up and run.

"Stay back." He could barely lift his arms in defence.

"Don't be afraid." The woman knelt beside him and cradled his head. "You're safe now."

Her sympathetic gaze and caring tone could surely not be Bayeth's. Rob exhaled and melted into her supporting arms. The guy was still a concern. "Who are you?" Rob knew him, but from where? His name began to form. "Matt?"

"Yeah?"

"What happened?"

Matt had a ridiculous grin. "Buddy, are you okay?"

Rob took a few breaths, his strength returning. "Uh huh."

Matt started laughing.

"What's so funny?" the lady asked.

"That was fucking unbelievable!" Matt exclaimed as he jumped to his feet. "Did you see that? Holy shit! I thought for a minute that the bastard had me. But when you held Rob and jumped in to help me, man, did I ever kick his ass!" He raised his arms in the air and shouted.

The woman laughed along with him. "And the angel!" She joined in on the celebration. "He was amazing! I knew he would come through."

As the two carried on, Rob's memories fully returned. He closed his eyes and welcomed them home as they filled his consciousness. Matt had saved him...somehow. Kathy— Oh my God! Where was she? Did the demons still have her? His eyes shot open, and he looked to Matt for the answer.

"Victoria!" A man called from nearby.

"We're over here!" She had to be the girl Matt was involved with.

Matt and Victoria ran off to greet an old man who'd arrived at the edge of the small clearing. "What's all the yelling about? Are you two all right?"

"Couldn't be better!" Victoria announced.

"What happened?" The man's gaze was full of

suspicion.

"Matt pulled the demon out, and the angel killed it. It was amazing! I wish you could've seen it."

The old guy's eyes lit up. "How did you manage that?"

"We crossed over into the spirit realm and fought the demon in there. Matt yanked it out, and the angel cut its head off."

"Yeah. That bugger was just waiting for me to pull the demon away from Rob. He must not be able to do his thing when they're inside someone."

"Extraordinary...but don't you think we should attend to Rob? He looks a bit out of sorts."

That was an understatement. Their conversation made little sense, but they were missing the most important thing. "Where's Kathy?" he interrupted. "Have you freed her yet?"

His question brought complete silence. They all looked at Rob.

"She's—" Matt looked down at the ground. "She got away."

"She what?" Rob mustered the strength to stand. "Which way did she run?"

"She's not here," the old man replied.

"I can see that." What a stupid thing to say. "And who in the hell are you?"

"Lawrence, Victoria's grandfather." He reached out and placed his hand on Rob's arm. "I understand that you're upset but try to stay calm."

"We lost her at the motel." Matt lowered his gaze. "We tried..."

Rob ripped his arm away from Lawrence. "Then let's go get her. What are we waiting for?"

Matt took a step toward him. "You don't understand, Rob. It's not that easy."

"No! *You* don't understand. We have to find her now. She's possessed by one of those demons. You have to set her free!"

"She was screaming that I kidnapped her. There was a crowd. I'm sure the cops are all over the place looking for us by now. We can't go back there."

Rob wasn't interested in hearing excuses. He wanted her back, at any cost. "We can't leave her with that thing for another second. We have to go. Now!"

"Rob—"

"Shut your mouth! I'm not done! You don't know what it feels like to have one of those *things* in your body, to feel the pain and be helpless to do anything about it. Kathy's still being tortured. We have to find her and set her free now!"

Matt grabbed his arm. "You have to calm down, Rob. We need a plan."

Victoria nodded. "We can't go back. Believe me, we tried to save her, but it's not Kathy right now."

They just weren't getting it. "She's still in there!" Rob paced frantically. "And since when have you ever needed a plan? You're just being a fucking coward. I'll go myself. Give me your keys." He rushed Matt.

Matt shoved Rob, knocking him back a few steps. "Jesus! Get a hold of yourself. That demon is dangerous. Even if you find her, there's nothing you can do about it."

"Don't you dare call her a demon!" Rob pushed Matt back. "Kathy needs our help!"

"We have to make a plan. We can't just rush—"

"You pussy!" He took a swing at his friend.

Matt launched himself at Rob, knocking him to the ground.

Victoria jumped between them. "Stop it!" she shouted. "This is wrong."

"You ungrateful bastard!" Matt pointed an accusing finger. "How about, 'Hey, Matt. Thanks for saving my fucking life.' Would that be so hard?"

"We wouldn't be in this fucking mess in the first place if it weren't for you! Both of you." He pointed at Victoria. "I heard the demons talking. I know about the statue. You guys are responsible for Kathy, and you'd better figure out how to save her."

CHAPTER 49

Zaralen arrived at the precinct an hour before his shift began. He did his best to act interested in his co-worker's mundane lives and how the Knicks had played last night then sat at one of the computers and logged onto the investigation database. The file on the Hoboken apartment double murder was already taking shape.

Matt and Rob's specifics were posted, along with photos of the two. He printed them off. There wasn't much on Victoria, just an artist's sketch and her first name. He'd have to make an anonymous tip by payphone, providing her full name and address.

Bayeth had played her part to perfection. There was no doubt in the lead investigator's notes that Matt, Rob, and Victoria had killed Bayeth and Toal's former cloaks. The motive was simple. The three had discovered they were being scammed and retaliated against the con artists. The report noted that the dead pair had previously been arrested for conning a foreign investor out of four million dollars. Those charges had been dropped because the victim had changed his story and returned home to Greece.

Zaralen continued to scroll through the report. The investigator wasn't sure what the dead pair had to gain from Matt and his friends, but that was insignificant. The bodies and a credible eyewitness were enough evidence for an arrest warrant. Once behind bars, Matt was as good as dead.

The Crimson Dimension

Where was the pair hiding? Nothing came up for Matt on the New York license database, but Victoria's name got a few hits. He selected the Victoria Brooks residing in the Henderson Block in Greenwich. Bingo. Her last address was in Monroe County, a short distance from where Bayeth and Toal had fucked up catching Matt. This could be it. He ran the address, and the screen returned a sole driver's license belonging to a Lawrence Hallworth.

"Shit." Zaralen moved the mouse over the logout button. Wait. Hallworth had been living there for fifteen years. Victoria and Hallworth had lived there at the same time, as recently as last year. "Jackpot!" They were connected.

"What?" his partner, Officer Karen McKinney, asked.

Zaralen startled. "What the fuck? Do you mind?"

"Settle down. You're sure acting weird lately. Is everything okay between you and Deb?"

"None of your business."

"See. That's what I mean. Lighten up." She grabbed Rob's picture off the printer. "Why the hell are you looking at that murder? That's Jersey's problem."

He wasn't going to be able to keep McKinney in the dark, and would need her cooperation to make any progress. He pointed at the picture of Matt. "This is the guy in the alley. The night I got sick." He hoped he wasn't saying too much. The last thing he wanted was for the police to make connections between their former cloaks.

"Holy shit, you're right." She tapped the picture. "Nice work. But it's still not our problem. Pass that on to Jersey Homicide."

"I have a hunch about where they might be hiding, but I don't want to bother Homicide if it turns out to be nothing. I just need to pay someone a visit to confirm my hunch. If it pans out, I'll pass the info on."

"Yeah, right," she answered. "You're looking for a promotion, and you think this might do it." She rubbed her chin. "Fine. Let's go. There's no way I'm going to miss out on the glory."

"It's a little outside our area," he warned.

Karen cocked her head. "New Jersey?"

"No. Monroe County."

Karen laughed. "Well, at least it's in our state. I'm still in. Let's go."

CHAPTER 50

Matt kissed Victoria. "Good morning."

"Hey." She yawned. "Did you sleep?"

"Not at all." His mind wouldn't stop racing. "Why?"

Rob's accusations haunted him. Everything was his fault. "We have to get Kathy back."

Victoria sat up and took Matt's hand. "I know." She leaned in and kissed him. "We're halfway there. We saved Rob, and we'll get her too."

If only it were that easy. It was pure luck that Rob had fallen right into their hands. Rob's account of his possession had given them some insight into how the Shakath operated, and how dangerous they were. Bayeth would suspect they were hunting her, and the entire state was looking for them now that they were fugitives. Even if they managed to find her, there were no guarantees that anyone, including Kathy, would come out alive.

"We're running blind here." Matt got up and paced.

"I know." Victoria sat there, twirling her hair with her fingers.

What he wouldn't give to be free from all this insanity. Free to spend time together like normal people. Why did any of this have to happen? Then again, he wouldn't have been here beside her if it hadn't. Would he do it all over again, knowing where it would lead him?

"Earth to Matt."

Her voice pulled him out of his daydream. "What is it?"

"About running blind..." She smiled, apparently amused that he'd checked out. "During my transformation, before the light overtook me, I was searching for help. Something or someone was there, but I couldn't find it. I think we should look again."

"How do you propose we do that?"

"We crossed over into the spirit world during the fight to free Rob. We need to go back in there. We might find answers."

Why hadn't he thought of that? He stopped pacing and nodded. Probably because his transformation was one of the most painful, terrifying experiences of his life, and he hadn't exactly had time to enjoy the scenery while he fought for Rob's freedom. Victoria was onto something, and it was the best idea either of them had come up with. "You rock."

He took her hand, lay down on the bed beside her, and concentrated on the other side of the veil. The room faded, replaced by the bright expanse.

"This is amazing. I feel so free," Victoria said.

"Me too," Matt answered.

"Matt!" Her voice quivered.

"What is it?"

"Something's strange. I never spoke a word. I think you can hear my thoughts in here. Watch my mouth. Am I talking?"

"No, you're not. But I can hear you!" This was unbelievable. What else could they do in here? *"Say something else."* Matt projected his thought.

"I feel it again. That presence. Can you?"

He couldn't. Matt forced himself to clear his mind and let this place truly take him in. He closed his eyes and concentrated on his most peaceful memory.

A slight tug almost pulled their hands apart, but Matt

tightened his grip.

"Matt. Open your eyes." Victoria sounded worried.

Was he dreaming? They were standing on the banks of the Contoocook River, except that it was more vivid and beautiful than he remembered.

"Where are we?"

Matt's heart was pounding. Was this a vision or were they really here? *"This is my secret fishing hole. The one I told you about. I imagined being here."*

Matt stared out across the water. This was real. He was sure of it. And the more he immersed himself in this world, the more real it became.

"The presence I felt isn't here. We should go back."

Matt knew they were supposed to be searching for a way to help Kathy, but the landscape was too incredible to ignore. He turned to Victoria. *"A few more minutes won't—"* Goose bumps covered his arms. God, she was beautiful. Her clothing had changed. She wore a simple white flowing dress that fit her perfectly. Matt swallowed. How could he have lucked out on a girl like this?

"You were saying?" Her smile said she'd busted him gawking, but it didn't seem she could hear his musings, just as he also couldn't hear the thoughts that must be running through her mind.

"I... I was just hoping we could spend a few more minutes here. I'd love to share this place with you."

Victoria nodded. *"I would like that."*

Matt took her hand and led her down a small trail to the water's edge, where the river slowed and formed a large azure pool. No words or thoughts were exchanged. He stood with his arm around her, taking it all in. All sense of the outside world had vanished. Nothing else mattered but the two of them. Matt looked down, gently pressed his lips against Victoria's ear, and whispered, "You have no idea what this means to me. Thank you."

Victoria slowly turned her head toward Matt, until her lips met his.

He stared into her eyes with a mixture of disbelief and amazement. The physical and emotional connection was magnified a hundredfold in this place. He'd never felt so fulfilled by a simple kiss. Victoria's sigh revealed she'd felt it too.

"That was incredible!" Victoria stroked his cheek with her fingers.

The feeling had yet to subside. *"I have no words. I...I—"*

"You don't need to." Victoria twirled her hair with her finger. *"I want to try something. I want you to see me, all my strengths and weaknesses. Will you let me share myself with you?"*

Matt paused. If this was possible, she was willing to share the core of her being with him. No secrets. Was he ready for this? He looked into her eyes, and then at the ground. No. This was too much to offer. He couldn't even be fully truthful with himself regarding his own life. How could he be trusted with hers?

"Victoria. I can't tell you how much that means to me but—"

"Please don't say no. I need to do this. I can't explain it, but I think you know we should."

Matt closed his eyes. She was remarkable, and he had the opportunity to know her deeper than any person on earth would ever know another. If he went here, he could never allow himself to fail her. He couldn't let fear hold him back.

He nodded.

Victoria opened her memories to Matt.

Her childhood was wonderful. She'd been a priority in

every decision her parents made, and they'd provided her every opportunity to pursue her dreams. Sure, the money had helped, but it paled in comparison to the love and support they'd given her at every step of her life. The empty pit in his stomach grew. If only...

The pure agony of her parents' deaths tore at Matt's soul. Matt had had his share of pain and heartache, but he'd never suffered loss to that degree. Losing Jodie was the worst he'd experienced, but there was no comparison. It must've been even worse considering how wonderful her life had been up to that point. Matt had only known neglect and abuse and had learned early in life to harden himself against heartbreak.

It was amazing how such different journeys converged on the same path. She'd also spent the balance of her life avoiding connections, walking away from those she'd gotten close to, even engaging in meaningless sexual relationships to try to fill the void. His heart broke for her. The amazing thing was that she'd never lost her spark or sense of adventure. She always pressed on, always pushed herself to rise above.

Matt laughed when he relived their date through her perspective. He'd been an idiot to think he was in control. Thank God that, despite his blundering attempts to get into her pants, she'd seen right through him and known in her heart that he was actually a good guy, and possibly worth the risk of heartache.

Matt was overcome. She saw potential in him that he couldn't. Despite his imperfections, she had faith in the man he was, and would become.

"*My turn,*" she urged.

A knot formed in his gut. *Here goes nothing*.

It was easy to let her see his happy memories, but he couldn't let the wall down to expose the darkness.

"*What's wrong?*" she asked.
"*You can't go there.*"
Victoria slowly nodded. "*When you're ready, I'll be here.*"

△ △ △

Matt snapped out of the Crimson Dimension. Her love and acceptance were driving him to open up, and he was losing his ability to guard his past. He felt too strongly about her to hurt her, but it was inevitable. "Victoria," he returned to speaking aloud. "I think this was a big mistake."

"I know." She smiled. "We didn't search for answers at all. Let's go back in."

"That's not what I meant."

She cocked her head. "What do you mean?"

"I'm not sure I'll ever be able to let you go there… I've lived a pretty fucked-up life."

"You're a good man. I know it."

"You might change your mind."

She took his hand. "I'm not going to judge you. I just want to know everything about you."

"But there's so much I haven't dealt with myself yet."

"I let you see all of me, and as you saw, I have a lot of issues of my own."

She wasn't going to let this go, and the more he argued, the more annoyed she looked. The worst she'd done was sleep around a bit. That was the least of his faults. "This is different."

"You're so bull-headed, it's driving me crazy! What could be so horrible that you can't let me see it?"

Matt started trembling. "I can't face the pain."

Victoria's face softened. "Maybe I can help you through it. Trust me. It will be okay."

"Maybe I don't want to go through it." She needed to drop it. Why wouldn't she understand that he wasn't ready?

"I bared my soul to you, Matt. What could be so bad?"

"My dad!" he shouted. Tears welled in his eyes. "There! Are you happy now?"

"Oh, Matt." Victoria wrapped her arms around him.

Now that the dam was breached, he could no longer hold back his emotions. His tears turned to sobs, and he collapsed onto the bed. Unable to find the words, he nodded. "Okay." He returned to the Crimson Dimension and opened himself for her to see his deepest, darkest secrets.

△ △ △

Victoria swallowed. Had she pushed too hard? No. Matt needed this just as much as she wanted it. He was never going to see his full potential until he broke through. She vowed to give him all the love and support he needed to get there.

Matt's childhood unfolded for her like a movie. A lonely, unloved child, he'd done his best to find his way on his own. Time after time, he sat neglected as his parents argued, drank, and shot up. How could anyone care so little about their child? She reached for Matt's hand.

Things only got worse. Victoria cringed when Matt's father hit him for spilling his milk at the dinner table. He'd only been five, for God's sake. That was the first time he'd been hit. The abuse only increased as he got older.

Victoria paused. Maybe Matt was right. Perhaps his past was best left there. He'd warned her that she wouldn't like what she saw...and she'd told him to trust her. She couldn't turn back now.

Thankfully, it wasn't all bad. Once he was old enough,

he'd sneak off to his secret getaway along the river. Now she understood the significance of that little patch of grass. He was safe there. A place to dream. A place to cry where no one would see.

Things changed once Matt met Jodie. The two of them were inseparable, and they were happy together. She was Matt's first, and it was truly something special. Jealousy welled within her, but she pushed it down. How could she allow those feelings to take away from one of Matt's only fond memories? Besides, this had all happened many years ago, and they'd since gone their separate ways.

Victoria panicked. He'd gotten Jodie pregnant? Where was his child? Matt had never even hinted that he was a father. Victoria searched Matt for the answers. Then it hit her like a punch in the gut. The guilt and shame Matt carried from the abortion was so real that Victoria could literally feel its residue.

Matt's nightmare continued, yet he found a way to endure the constant barrage of insults his father dished out regularly. Unable to bottle up all the anger, Matt got into fights, shoplifted, and vandalized property. He even allowed himself to get caught, because the attention, even for the wrong reasons, was better than nothing at all. His life bottomed out when he began taking the same path as his father, turning to alcohol and drugs for an escape. Victoria's heart broke.

Then, like divine intervention, the McLeods entered his life. Against all odds, Matt's determination to succeed drove him to clean up his act, and the change was remarkable. His drive and resilience were remarkable, given everything he'd endured. Finally, his memory brought her to his graduation.

When he'd started high school, no one had thought he'd had it in him to graduate, and his miraculous turnaround hadn't gone unnoticed. To his amazement, his name was called out as the recipient of the Bennington High School Award for Outstanding Improvement. He stood on the stage, humbled, as his fellow students, the faculty, and all the parents gave him a standing ovation. He scanned the audience to find his parents. They hadn't bothered to come.

Matt walked home, feeling on top of the world yet completely alone. As he approached his house, he could already hear their drunken argument.

"Where have you been?" his father hollered when he stepped inside.

"At school. It was my graduation. Remember?"

"I'm sorry." His mother rushed to his side. "You know I wanted to come, but I had to work." She pointed to Matt's award. "What's that?"

As if it mattered. "It's nothing."

"Oh, Mike!" She took it from Matt's hands. "He won an award." She read the engraving. "Outstanding Improvement."

"Gimme that." His dad grabbed it.

"Give it back!" Matt demanded.

"So, now he's a big man," he mocked. "He graduates from school, and now he's a bigshot. Pride cometh before a fall. A damn plaque doesn't make you a man. That's something you'll never be. You're nothing but a little pussy."

Matt's deep desire for his father's approval was so obvious. How could that monster not show him one ounce of love?

Victoria trembled as the cruel man smashed the award on the coffee table. Matt's sorrow turned to rage. He launched at his father and unleashed every last shred of his anger, frustration, and grief.

Matt packed his bags and never stepped foot through that door again.

"Now do you understand why I didn't want you to see that?" he asked.

Victoria wiped the tears that had run down her cheek. *"I don't know what to say. I'm so sorry for you."*

"I don't need anyone to feel sorry for me."

"That's not what I meant." She didn't know how to express what she was feeling. *"I just want you to know that I love you."*

△ △ △

An enormous weight lifted off Matt's shoulders. He'd allowed her to see everything, and she accepted him.

"I love you too."

CHAPTER 51

Zaralen leaned his forehead against the steering wheel and sighed. "Are you sure this is it?"

Karen studied the printout one more time. "Yeah. It's the same address I looked at the last time you asked."

He didn't need her damn sarcasm. Zaralen reached out through the window and pressed the button. So much for the element of surprise. This place was a mini Fort Knox with security cameras, an iron gate, and the intercom system.

"Hello?" an old man answered. Likely Hallworth. "May I help you, Officer?"

"I'm looking for Lawrence Hallworth."

"Yes, this is he."

"I'd like to ask you a few questions, sir."

"Regarding?"

"Victoria Brooks. Are you related?"

"I'm sure you already know she's my granddaughter. Is there a problem?"

"We believe she has some information that will help us with an investigation we're conducting. Is she here?"

"No, she isn't. I'm sorry you've wasted your time."

This whole fucking charade was a waste of time. He needed to keep his cool. He was close. He could taste it. "Have you seen or talked to her recently?"

"I haven't gone out in days, and no one has been to visit."

He'd avoided the question. He must've at least spoken

to her. "Still. We'd like to come up and ask you about a few things."

"I don't know anything, and I have work to do. If I hear from her, I'll get her to call you. What's your contact information?"

Zaralen shook his head in frustration. Turning to Karen, he whispered, "That pecker isn't going to open the gate without a warrant."

"Doesn't look like it, but I know she's in there."

"How are you so sure?" Zaralen asked.

"He said he hasn't been out for days, but there're multiple tire tracks in the snow."

"I knew it." Matt was in there and probably slipping out on some back road while the old fucker bought time. Zaralen backed the police cruiser away from the gate, put it in drive, and slammed his foot down on the accelerator.

"What do you think you're doing?" Karen yelled.

"Hold on!" he answered as the car exploded through the iron gates, sending them flying into the trees.

Seconds later, Zaralen was pounding on the door.

Karen was at his side, demanding that he stop. "What are you doing? Have you gone nuts? We're gonna get canned!"

Zaralen pulled his pistol and fired a couple of rounds into the latch then kicked the door open.

"Oh my God!" Karen yelled. "That's it. I'm radioing dispatch." She brought her hand up to her shoulder mic, but before she could push the button, Zaralen pistol whipped her, sending her unconscious to the ground. He removed her gun from its holster and fired three rounds into her head.

"Fucking bitch." He kicked her limp body. "God, I hated you."

Zaralen changed clips while he scanned the front

entryway. A jolt of adrenaline shot right through him. The Warrior, sword raised, stood twenty feet away. He'd fucked up. He was completely vulnerable. All it would take was one of them shooting him. He'd never avoid the Warrior before he could enter a new cloak.

"I know you're here, Matt!" he shouted into the house. He had to wrap this up fast. "You can't hide from me. If you don't show yourself, I'll kill every fucking person I find."

"They aren't here." Lawrence stepped out from behind a doorway. He was older and frailer than the exchange on the intercom had suggested. "I'd like to propose a truce. Give us Kathy back, and Matt will promise never to interfere with you or your group."

Hallworth was a fool to think he had any bargaining power. Or, was he buying time for Matt to escape or possibly get a clean shot at him.? Zaralen closed the gap to Hallworth and used him a shield. "Come out now. Unarmed, or the old man is toast! You have five seconds. One..."

Finally, Matt and Victoria appeared, hands raised above their heads.

"Where's your friend?" Matt could've figured out how to free Toal's cloak, or the guy might've died with Toal. Not knowing was a huge risk.

"Who?" Matt asked.

"Don't fuck with me!" He pressed the gun against Lawrence's forehead. "Your buddy."

Victoria waved her hands frantically. "Please don't shoot! Rob's dead. It's just us."

She seemed to be telling the truth. Even if she wasn't, they all looked scared as shit, which meant they didn't understand their advantage. He could end this whole shit show with three quick shots, but Dmoltech's instructions had been very clear. Matt was to be delivered alive. He could shoot the other two, but Matt would run, and he was fast. No. He needed to use Matt's friends as leverage to get him cuffed and in the cruiser.

"Okay, I promise I won't kill your grandpa as long as you all cooperate. I only want Matt. The rest of you can go free."

Zaralen backed Lawrence over to Karen's body. He took her handcuffs and grabbed his pair. "You two." He pointed the gun at Matt and Victoria. "Lie on the floor face-down." He handed the cuffs to Lawrence. "Put these on them."

"You said you only wanted Matt," Lawrence objected.

"Shut up! I need to make sure Matt is safely loaded up. Once he's in the car, I'll let her go."

Lawrence nodded, struggled to his knees, and cuffed them.

Zaralen let out a breath. "Everyone outside."

Lawrence helped Matt and Victoria to their feet, and the trio headed out the door.

"Don't worry." Lawrence turned to Victoria. "I won't let him harm you."

Fat chance, old man. You're dead as soon as they're locked in the cruiser. "You two." He motioned to Matt and Victoria. "Get in the car."

Zaralen shoved them into the backseat, and with his prisoners secured, turned his attention to Lawrence. "You surprised me. I figured you were smarter than this. You realize you're a dead man." He raised his weapon.

"You've mixed up the guns," Lawrence said.

"What?".

"I know what you're intending to do. You're going to kill me, place your partner's gun in my hand, and make me fire off a shot to produce powder burns. Then you'll claim I shot her."

"Not bad, old man, but you aren't going to stall me any longer."

"You're not listening. You mixed them up. You're pointing her gun at me right now. The ballistic evidence will show that she killed me. How are you going to explain that?"

Zaralen looked at the gun. It was the same model as the one holstered at his side. He mentally replayed his actions to figure out which weapon he was holding. Wait. What did it matter? He was sick of playing this role and planned to change anyw— Movement caught his eye. Too late. Lawrence's cane caught him right between the legs.

Zaralen gasped and folded over in agony. Another explosion of pain as the cane crushed his hand. Zaralen screamed, and the gun hit the ground between them.

He had to get it back before Lawrence swung again. Before he could, a huge weight landed on his back, and he crashed to the ground.

Zaralen lunged forward, and just managed to get the tips of his fingers on the weapon before Lawrence knocked it away with his cane. He had to regain control. Everything was riding on this. Zaralen rolled and twisted, sending the person on his back sprawling sideways. It was Rob.

This was disastrous. Matt must've figured out how to separate Rob from Toal for the Warrior's blade. If Zaralen didn't end this fight, he was dead meat. Getting to his feet, he faced Rob, who was coming at him again. Zaralen drove his fist as hard as he could into Rob's face. His broken hand stung so badly that he almost passed out. Thankfully, Rob staggered.

He spun to face Lawrence. "You're dead!"

"Don't move!" Lawrence had retrieved the gun and was pointing it at Zaralen.

He obeyed, but only to get his bearings. His hand was a mess, and the pain was unbearable. He needed a new plan, and fast.

"Grab his keys," Lawrence told Rob.

Zaralen's options were limited. Forcing Lawrence to shoot him was the worst option by far. The Warrior would send him to Hell if it was a fatal shot. Thankfully, none of them had figured that out yet. Matt would separate him if he surrendered so that was off the table too. Zaralen had no choice. He had to gamble. "You really think you can come out of this on top?"

Rob paused.

Zaralen started laughing. "Go ahead and shoot me. I'll just possess one of you stupid shitheads. There's—"

Zaralen's vision went black, and he hit the ground hard. The echo of the pistol rang in his ears. Shit. Blood poured from the right side of his chest.

"Hurry and get those keys," Lawrence repeated. "Matt and Victoria need to be freed before he dies."

Zaralen was losing consciousness. He couldn't stop Rob from going through his pockets.

"I got them," Rob yelled. He ran to the car.

This couldn't be the end. Hell was not an option. Zaralen reached out and grabbed Lawrence's foot as he tried to join Rob. Lawrence toppled over, giving him the only chance he would get. Zaralen clambered on top of Lawrence and hung on desperately. The instant, terrifying pull told him his cloak was deceased.

The Warrior raised his sword, took a few steps in Zaralen's direction, and swung.

The blade stopped inches from making contact. He'd done it. Zaralen had made it into the safety of Lawrence's body.

"No!" Victoria had reached her grandpa. She turned to

Matt. "It's got Grandpa."

Matt ran in behind her. "I'm coming."

Zaralen fought for full control of Lawrence. It couldn't come soon enough. He raised the gun, which Lawrence had just used on him, and shot at Victoria. His aim was off. She turned and ran back to Matt and Rob.

He wouldn't miss again. The possession complete, he struggled to his knees to get a better position. The old man's body slowed him.

The trio sped off in the cruiser before he could take another shot.

CHAPTER 52

"We can't leave him there!" Victoria screamed. "Rob. You have to turn around."

"No," Matt objected. "We can't. He'll shoot us."

"Oh God." Victoria's world collapsed around her. She slumped over in the back of the cruiser. This couldn't be happening. He was her rock, the only constant in her life. "We have to go back! We have to find a way."

Matt grabbed her hand. "How? He has guns. How are we going to get him down without getting killed, or killing him?"

Tears flowed down her face. "We can't just leave him there!"

"Hey." Rob looked back over his shoulder. "I know exactly how you're feeling. Kathy's out there somewhere. I'd risk everything to free her too, but Matt's right. It's too dangerous."

"Shit." Matt kicked the seat. "Let's think this through."

"There has to be a way." Victoria leaned on Matt, tears erupting. This was completely insane. People were dying, and it had to end—but how? "This isn't who I am. I can't do this anymore." She'd willingly become a spiritual warrior, committed herself to a life of combat, chaos, and death. If she could've taken it all back, she would've. "This is all so wrong. I've made a terrible mistake. I'm not meant to kill. I create."

"Hang in there." Matt squeezed her shoulder. "We'll

figure things out. I promise."

That was a pretty big promise, considering they'd been constantly on the run since this whole thing started. Was it possible to turn it around? How could she get Grandpa back? She closed her eyes and buried her head in Matt's chest.

Lawrence's voice rang out over the police radio. "My name is Lawrence Hallworth. I'm afraid to say that my granddaughter, Victoria Brooks, along with Matt Reynolds and Rob McLeod just killed two of your officers and stole their car."

Hearing the demon speak through her grandpa paralyzed her. Yet, it was comforting to know he was still alive. She had to stay strong, for him.

"Oh no!" Matt threw his head back. "We're in major shit. We need to dump this car right now."

"The rest stop is up ahead," Victoria said. "There's an abandoned farmhouse just before it. We can ditch the cruiser there."

Rob pulled into the farmyard and drove past the dilapidated house. A weathered, run-down barn, leaning from years of wind and rot, provided the perfect hideaway for the squad car. The snow would soon cover the tire tracks, making its discovery nearly impossible.

"What do we do now?" Rob asked as he and Matt forced the barn door closed. "We obviously can't just sit around here."

"We need money and a car. Do you guys have any cash?"

"I don't have my purse," Victoria realized. And with no coat, she was already shaking from the cold.

Rob pulled his wallet out. "I've got a few bucks on me and my bank card."

"Me too," Matt added. "We're gonna have to withdraw

everything in one shot. I'm sure they'll trace us whenever we use our cards."

The rest stop was partly hidden behind a stand of trees across the field. The three fugitives sprinted to the edge of the bush, just behind the diner.

"I'll try and figure out a ride." He handed his card to Victoria. "My PIN is fifty-two eighty-six."

Victoria and Rob left Matt crouched behind the trees and hurried into the diner. Victoria emptied Matt's account then watched for trouble while Rob did the same.

"This will have to do," Rob said as he handed his stash to her. "Twenty-three hundred isn't peanuts, but it won't get us very far."

She wished she had her purse. "I could only get two forty from Matt. We'd better get back."

Matt was waiting for them, sitting in a beat-up old truck with a mischievous grin on his face. "Hurry up. We've got to get out of here."

"Did you steal this?" Victoria hesitated.

"Are kidding me?" Matt motioned for her to get in. "We're wanted for murder. Stealing this piece of shit is the least of our worries. And dump your phones. They'll be tracking them for sure."

CHAPTER 53

The midday sun shone like a guiding light above the skyscrapers of New York City. What better place to hide than in the middle of over eight million faces?

As soon as they could, they abandoned the stolen truck and took a cab the rest of the way into the heart of the city. When Matt was satisfied they'd put enough distance between themselves and the truck, he instructed the cabbie to take them to the nearest shopping center.

"What are we doing here?" Rob asked. "I thought we were going to find a hotel room."

"We need to buy some clothes. The cops know what we're wearing, and we need coats."

"I agree," Victoria said. "But we can't stop there. We need complete makeovers. The cops probably got a picture of me from Grandpa's, and Kathy probably gave them one of you two."

"It's not her. Stop using her name," Rob objected.

"What else am I supposed to call her?" She glared at Rob. "You're not the only one dealing with this, you know!"

"Enough!" Matt wasn't in the mood for arguing semantics. They had more important things to worry about—like how they could get a hotel without a credit card or identification. "We need to get busy. Let's split up and meet back in an hour. Get yourselves a hat, glasses, hair dye, and new clothes. Make sure they're warm. God only knows where we'll be sleeping."

Victoria divided the cash between them. "We need to

blend in so make sure nothing is bright or flashy. I know the stores are full of Halloween costumes, but don't waste our money buying fake mustaches or noses or anything stupid like that."

"I'm not an idiot." Rob glared at Victoria. "Listen to your own advice. No one's going to rent a room to us if we look like trouble."

Matt wandered off, leaving the two to their argument. He would give anything to be back in Rio, being scolded by Kathy for his and Rob's incessant debates. And this time, he never would've left.

Shopping completed, they needed a place to hide out. When he and Rob had first visited New York, looking for an apartment, they'd stayed in the cheapest hotel they could find. They'd soon discovered that the sleazy dump served as the area's rendezvous for prostitutes and their johns. Cash only. No questions asked. Perfect. "Let's go. I know a cheap place where we can stay."

"You've got to be kidding?" Rob protested when they arrived. "Not this dump."

Victoria grimaced. "I agree with Rob. It's disgusting."

"Oh, so *now* you two are agreeing with each other." He threw his hands up in surrender. "Fine. I'm open to suggestions."

None were offered.

"How much for a room with two beds?" Matt asked the seedy looking man behind the desk.

"I normally charge by the hour." He grinned.

"How much?" he repeated.

"Seventy-five."

He counted the money out then motioned for Rob and Victoria to follow. They'd hung back while Matt made the arrangements.

The guy closed his outstretched hand around the key.

The Crimson Dimension

"You didn't say there was three of you."

"What's the difference to you?"

"Twenty-five dollars."

"Damn crook," Matt muttered under his breath. A good portion of their money was already spent, but with no other options available, he set the money down on the counter.

"What do we do now?" Rob asked after he flopped down on one of the sagging double beds.

"We lie low for a few days until things calm down and figure out how to get Kathy and Lawrence back."

That got Rob and Victoria's attention. They were looking to him to figure this out, but he had nothing. He was drowning. The only person who might be able to help was sitting in a little church in Brazil, five thousand miles away.

"Do you have any ideas?" Rob asked.

"Not yet." Still, he'd gotten everyone into this mess, and he was sure as hell going to find a way out.

"Let's see what the damage is." Victoria sighed as she turned on the old fifteen-inch television.

As expected, their photos were being shown on all the local channels. Rob and Victoria froze when Kathy and Lawrence appeared onscreen, making heartfelt pleas for them to turn themselves over to the authorities. Seeing the anguish on their faces was too much. Matt shut the TV off.

"What are you doing?" Rob reached for the remote.

"Watching that bullshit isn't doing anybody any good."

"It's just so surreal," Victoria said. "They look so normal onscreen." She wiped away a tear. "Their eyes look normal. They sound normal. No one in the world would doubt their stories."

"Yeah. Even if we manage to get them back, I don't know if we'll ever be able to clear our names."

"What do you mean *if?*" Rob spun to Matt.

Bad choice of words, but he hated making promises he might not be able to keep. "Grab a box of hair dye. We'll never be able to help them if we're sitting in jail."

Matt dyed his sandy mess jet-black and slicked it back with half a tube of gel. Thick sweat pants and a three-quarter-length hooded parka completed his ensemble.

Rob lightened his hair, and went with baggy jeans, a down coat, and a ball cap. Not bad at all. Even Matt wouldn't recognize him in a crowd.

"Holy shit." Matt's heart skipped a beat. Victoria was stunning as a platinum blonde. She wore jeans and a hoodie under a full-length black coat, which ended just above a pair of black boots.

Not wanting anything left in the room that could identify them, Matt gathered up the dye packages and stuffed them into a bag with their old clothes. "I'll dump all this and get us something to eat."

Three subs and a case of Bud in hand, Matt stopped by the television behind the check-in counter. The live update now linked them to the murder of two Catholic priests. The newscaster described how Father Michael Perry was bludgeoned to death hours after a visit from Matt. Additionally, Father Marcus Sophronia, visiting New York from the Vatican, had been brutally murdered in Victoria's apartment.

In complete shock, he set the subs and beer down on the counter and continued watching. The cruiser had been recovered, thanks to its GPS tracking device, and the stolen truck had also been found. Interviews from Bennington relayed his era of juvenile delinquency, and he cringed at a shot of his drunken father yelling at reporters as he slammed the door in their faces. A ten-thousand-dollar reward had been offered for a tip resulting in an arrest.

"Those three are dead meat," the clerk commented. "You don't kill cops and get away with it. And to top it off, they kill a couple of priests. That's the death penalty, for sure."

"Yeah. They'll get theirs." He stuffed his trembling hands into his pocket.

"Hey, aren't you the guy who just booked? I thought your hair was," he paused, "lighter." He looked back at the television.

Their cover had been blown. There was no doubt the guy had identified him and was about to try to collect on the reward. He bounded up the stairs.

"Get your coats on! We've been made."

They raced down the back stairwell and into the alley. Approaching sirens echoed in the night as they descended into the labyrinth of the subway system. Maybe New Jersey would be safer.

They found another hotel with the same "no questions asked" policy. Matt checked in alone, and Victoria and Rob joined him once the clerk went back to his office.

Exhausted, he plopped on the edge of the bed. They'd been going nonstop since the fight with Zaralen nearly eighteen hours earlier.

Victoria sat next to him and took his hand. "We made it."

"For now. But we can't keep running forever."

"We'll think of something."

Rob was asleep the second his head hit the pillow. Victoria and Matt weren't so fortunate.

"Whatever happens," Victoria said, "I'm glad I'm in this with you." She stroked his hair until he drifted off.

CHAPTER 54

Ignoring the cold, Dmoltech stood on the steps of the cathedral to address the crowd of journalists and supporters. That morning, Roger Peterson had announced that he'd made a terrible mistake. Bromley wasn't laundering money through the charities, but had rather donated millions of dollars anonymously to their causes. All charges had been dropped. He looked out at the damn humans. They'd thought they had him, but they were wrong. No one could stop him.

"Thank you all for coming," Dmoltech began. "I've called this press conference to set the record straight on a few important matters. First, I must commend the NYPD and the FBI for their dedication in serving the fine state of New York. Their work will continue to protect us from those who truly take advantage of the generosity of our wonderful nation. I hold no ill will toward them for their error in implicating me. Everyone makes mistakes, and they deserve forgiveness. Let's hear it for the boys in blue, shall we?"

The audience joined him in applauding.

"Secondly, I hope that none of the charities will suffer as a result of this fiasco. Those organizations provide a tremendous service to our community. I know that donations have dropped off dramatically over the last few months, and their ability to help those in need has been hampered. I urge all New Yorkers to dig deep into their pockets to get these fine organizations back on their feet.

The Crimson Dimension

I've done my best to stay out of the limelight with my donations, but since my support of these charities is now public, I'd like to challenge everyone to give by matching dollar for dollar all donations received during the next month."

This time, there was no need to prompt them for their applause.

He raised his hands, motioning for silence, though he wanted nothing of the sort. Bromley was back, larger than life, and had been restored from pariah to prince. His donation challenge was brilliant. He could start moving the backlog of dirty money again, and Joe Public would now double it.

"Lastly," he said after the applause finally subsided, "as many of you know, my nightclub, The Cathedral, hosts the best two-day Halloween party in New York. Friday night will remain open to the public, but Saturday will now become a private event. I am proud to announce the first annual Halloween Charity Ball. I realize it's very short notice, but I already have confirmation from dozens of celebrities, politicians, and the who's-who of our business community. I promise that this private function will be a night to remember. I encourage all the invitees to attend and give their support to these worthwhile charities."

After fielding a barrage of questions, he retreated into the club.

Dmoltech grinned as he headed for his office. Restoring his kingdom was the first step in his bid to regain Lucifer's favor. He'd pulled it off with panache, despite the overwhelming urge to condemn the police and announce a multi-million-dollar lawsuit against them. No one could argue that he lacked diplomacy and control, not even the Prince of Darkness. The show of political savvy was, in his opinion, rather presidential.

Even if his legal victory failed to impress Lucifer, destroying the last of the statues would guarantee his reinstatement.

With the knowledge gleaned through his Shakaths' cloaks, he'd learned that the statue was guarded by a single elderly priest, and that Victoria had become Matt's second. With the couple running from the law, no one could stand in his way.

The one question that remained was which Shakath he would send to Brazil. So much had changed. Most noticeable was the absence of Radok and Toal, who were both burning in Hell. Bayeth, Zaralen, Athamm, and Lokad were all that remained.

Bayeth was doing a wonderful job portraying the devastated wife of Rob McLeod, while Zaralen was playing a similar role as Lawrence Hallworth the Third. Although they were the most competent of his Shakath, sending them would rouse suspicions.

Athamm was equally problematic. Not only was he still Dmoltech's prime suspect in killing Nazkiel, he had to keep his distance from him until everything settled down. Although the DA had dropped Bromley's charges, the FBI would still be watching him, and it wouldn't help his comeback in the least if they found out he was in contact with the head of the New York mafia.

That left Lokad, still residing in Father Marcus, as the only one available to travel to Brazil. Lokad's lack of experience was a concern, but the job was relatively simple. Dmoltech grinned. The destruction of the blood source would occur around the same time he was hosting his charity ball. October the twenty-eighth would go down in history as the date the mighty Dmoltech put an end to the Torren forever.

That left one last detail—ridding himself of the

annoyance of Matt and his little bitch. Granted, they'd managed to kill Toal and figure out how to use their Warrior, but they were still no match for Dmoltech's power. Killing them would be easy, and one more feather in his cap. Patience was the key. They would come to him, as the Torren always did, drawn like a moth to a flame. He looked forward to the encounter.

Back in his office, he sat down in the soft leather chair and lit a cigar. He leaned back, placed his feet on his desk, and wondered if the president of the United States used business cards.

CHAPTER 55

Matt opened his eyes to the sounds of the squeaky shower faucet. Rob was out of bed and had also woken Victoria. "What time is it?" he asked her.

"Almost noon." She sat up and rubbed her eyes.

Matt's stomach growled. He hadn't eaten since grabbing a chocolate bar during their shopping trip the day before. Remembering their abandoned dinner, he hoped the three submarine sandwiches and case of beer had given the hotel clerk severe indigestion.

"We need some food." He announced as Rob opened the bathroom door. The steam from the shower spilled out into the room. "And I could use a shower too."

"Yeah. You stink." It was good to see Rob still had his sense of humor. It was hard to image what he must be feeling. "I'll go grab us some food. I saw a McDonalds a few blocks away when we arrived."

"Okay." Victoria smiled. "I'd like a bagel and a coffee. Two and Two please."

"Egg McMuffin and black coffee for me." Matt handed Rob a twenty. "Be careful, buddy."

"I'll be fine." Rob pulled on his coat and grabbed the ball cap. "I'll be back in fifteen, tops."

Matt counted the rest of the money. What would they do once it ran out? You'd think God might at least be interested in keeping his Torren alive. Still, considering everything that had happened, it was miracle they weren't all dead. His hand shook as he put the cash back in his

The Crimson Dimension

wallet. Was it a miracle? Matt shook his head. No. It was a lot of quick thinking, and some dumb luck, that was all. He'd get them through this; they just needed to have a little...faith.

The hair on the back of his neck stood on end. That word resonated through his soul. A warm assurance radiated in his mind. He looked up at the sky through the window. Their last conversation hadn't gone too well, but... *Here goes nothing.*

"I still don't understand what you did to me, or why, but that's not the point right now. This isn't about me. My friends need my help, and they could sure use yours too. All I'm asking is..." He ran his hand through his hair. *"I don't know what I'm asking for exactly. Whatever. I hope you're listening..."*

Shit. Like that was going to get results.

He walked over to Victoria and gave her a kiss. "Wanna join me in the shower before Rob gets back?"

CHAPTER 56

Rob took forever, but the food totally hit the spot. If only there was more of it. "Okay. Let's figure out how to rescue Lawrence and Kathy."

"Now we're talking." Rob perked up. "We could call her cell and plan a meeting."

Matt rolled his eyes. Rob just wasn't getting it. "Are you kidding? There'll either be fifty cops or a bullet waiting for us."

"Well," Rob rubbed his head, clearly distraught, "what do we do then?"

"I'm lost as well," Victoria admitted. "Any ideas?"

Matt looked back and forth between Victoria and Rob's despondent faces, and his anger welled again. "I can only see one option," he announced. "I'm going after Bromley."

"Are you serious?" Rob asked with a mixture of hope and concern in his voice.

"Do I sound like I'm joking?" Did he have any other choice?

"Not a chance!" Victoria's angry scowl burned through him. "You're talking about facing their leader...a Naygid or whatever the hell the site called him. We know nothing about him. This is suicide. Besides, how is confronting him going to get Grandpa and Kathy back?"

"He can't be that different from the others. We've learned from them, and we've handled them pretty easily. I can cross over just like I did with Rob. Once I have him, I'll threaten to kill him unless he releases them." The plan was nuts, but the words kept spilling out. "When Kathy and your grandpa are safe, I'll have the Warrior kick his ass all the way to Hell."

Rob jumped up and paced around the room. "I want Kathy back more than anything, but I don't think it's a good idea. One thing I learned during my possession was that Dmoltech scared the shit out of the Shakath."

"Dmoltech?"

"That's Bromley's real name. He has a lot of power over them."

"What power?"

"I only know what I saw and heard while I was controlled. I never saw Dmoltech, so I have no idea what he can do."

"Look." Matt rubbed his chin. "The way I see it is that I've been given these powers to fight them. Why would I not be given enough to finish the job?"

"That's a huge gamble, Matt," Victoria said. "We shouldn't put faith in things we haven't tested."

There was that word again. "Faith..." Was he using it as a copout because he wanted to act without a sound plan, or was there something real? He'd never felt so sure without any idea why.

He turned back to Rob. "Do you want to save Kathy or not?"

"Of course I do, but aren't you listening?" Rob plopped back down on the bed and rested his head in his hands. "You do this all the time. You make rash decisions and never consider the consequences."

"I've heard this all before, Rob."

"I know! So why don't you ever change? Dmoltech is more powerful than the others. Victoria's right." He motioned to her and nodded. "You're going to get yourself killed, and then we'll never free Kathy and Lawrence."

Rob's face turned red. "If you're too stupid to care about your own life, that's fine, but remember you might get them killed in the process."

"I'll get them back. I know it." He had to.

"Even if you save them, the demons will hunt us down afterward. They easily found me and Kathy and they know a ton more about us now. They'll kill anyone who gets in their way, including our families and friends."

"That's exactly why I have to go after him. They'll never leave us alone until every last one of them is rotting in Hell."

Victoria shook her head. "There has to a better way." Her pleading eyes locked on Matt. "We could contact Bromley and try to bargain with him."

"And lose my advantage? We've got the element of surprise. It's never going to get better than this."

"I just thought we could—"

"No," Matt snapped. "You don't make deals with the devil."

Victoria leaned in, her look challenging. "Then what?"

"I meet him head on."

Victoria threw her hands in the air. "Why am I even talking to you?"

"Rob?" Matt grabbed him by the shoulders and stared directly in his eyes. "For Kathy."

Rob finally nodded. "I agree. But not without a solid plan."

"Excellent. I need you to tell me everything you learned from the demons. What can you remember that might help me find Bromley?"

Rob looked up and thought for a few moments. "I don't know much, but finding Dmoltech will be the easy part. He owns The Cathedral and has his office there."

"Are you fucking kidding me? Why didn't you tell me

sooner?"

"I didn't want you running over there half-cocked. He's dangerous."

Enough of all the mixed messages. Rob and Victoria were constantly whining about freeing Kathy and Lawrence, yet they opposed every idea to do something about it. What else was Rob holding out on? Matt grabbed a chair and positioned it to look directly into Rob's guilty eyes. "Rob. It's time to act. I understand it's life and death, but you're not helping me by trying to protect me. I need everything you know. No holding back. What can Dmoltech do?"

"I don't know."

Matt rolled his eyes. "Come on! You said you could see what was going on while you were possessed. Tell me."

"I already told you everything I know."

Damn it. He wished there was more info on Bromley. "So, we know he has a few extra powers, and that he owns The Cathedral. Good enough for me. I'll go tonight when the club is open and slip in."

"You stupid ass!" Victoria launched at Matt, pushing him backward onto the bed. "This has got to be the dumbest idea I've ever heard. Has nothing we just talked about registered in your thick skull? You're going to get us all killed."

"No one's dying, other than that son of a bitch." Matt rolled to his side and got up. "Rob agrees." He looked to him for support.

Rob deflated. "She's right."

"Come on... We're not going to save them sitting in this damn room."

"And we can't get ourselves killed by running over there like idiots! We need to start over." Victoria offered her hand to Matt.

Her warm touch sent a wave of calm though his mind and body. No. He pulled his hand away and ran it through his hair. The day was wearing on and they were wasting precious time. They'd gone over the same shit for hours and hadn't gotten anywhere. How many scenarios were they going to run through until Victoria and Rob would finally understand that facing Dmoltech was their only option? Why wouldn't they just trust him?

"I need some air." Matt stomped to the door and threw it open.

The butt of a gun hit him solidly in the forehead. The room spun and he went down hard.

CHAPTER 57

Rob's stomach was in knots. He'd fucked up big time. It was only a fifteen second call from the payphone outside McDonalds. He'd just needed to hear her voice, to let her know to hold on until they found a way to save her.

The next minute played out in slow motion. Men rushed into the room, pointing guns and yelling for them to put their hands up. Victoria screamed while one of them picked her up and slammed her face-first into the floor. Matt was out cold. They were already zip-tying his hands behind his back.

"Turn around. Hands where I can see them."

There was no point resisting. Regardless, they kicked his feet out from under him before binding his hands.

"Get them on the bed," one of the men ordered the others. None of them were uniformed. Perhaps the undercover operation had nothing to do with his call? Not that it mattered anymore.

Rob was forced to sit next to Victoria, with Matt lying to her left. Matt let out a groan. Thank God he was alive.

"I'm sorry," Rob whispered to Victoria.

"For what?" she answered with a puzzled look on her face. "You didn't—" Her focus shot to the door, just as a man in a suit walked into the room. "Rob... That man is a demon."

CHAPTER 58

Victoria had felt him coming before his red eyes confirmed her suspicion. The demons had found them. But how? Feeling a sensation to her left, she turned to see the Warrior, sword in hand, ready to strike. If only it could take the initiative.

What was she supposed to do? Matt was out cold, and there were men with guns aimed at them. It would be pointless to leave her body to fight the demon. She would be shot dead the moment she tried.

"Good work, boys." The man sat on a chair. "The woman and the cold-cocked bastard are to be kept alive. If any of them tries anything, shoot that one." He pointed at Rob.

"We won't give you any trouble," Victoria assured him, as she stared at Rob.

Rob, looking terrified, nodded in agreement.

Victoria looked down and sighed. There had to be a way out of this mess. She studied the demon, praying for some inspiration. Wait. They were being kept alive, and there had to be a reason for it. *Think.* Nothing came to mind, but whatever it was, it gave her some time. Matt had to wake up now. She needed him to help figure this out.

They sat there for what felt like an eternity. Matt had opened his eyes a few times but only briefly. He was in bad shape. "Please let me help him," she begged. "You said you wanted him alive. He could die lying there."

The man took a good look at Matt and nodded. "Get

some ice," he ordered one of his henchmen.

It took an hour before Matt finally started to come around. Still largely unresponsive, he needed more time to fully recover. Thankfully, the waiting continued.

Eventually, the man's phone rang.

"You here?" He paused. "Great. Wait in the van." He put the phone back in his pocket and opened the door to the black of night. They'd been there all day.

"Load them up. I want the girl and the sack of shit in the back. Put the guy in the middle seat behind the driver."

This wasn't good. Their options, whatever they were, were quickly running out.

"Where are you taking me?" Matt asked as they dragged him out. Moving him appeared to have snapped him back into reality.

"Shut up." He gave Matt a push.

"Take it easy," Victoria objected.

One of the men jammed a gun into her shoulder. "You walking, or do we have to hurt you?"

"I'll walk." Victoria stepped into the van and sat beside Matt, who was looking around frantically. "Stay calm. They'll shoot Rob if you try anything."

Rob collapsed as he approached the van. "Kathy!" he sobbed.

Victoria spun to look at the driver. Kathy was staring at Rob with no emotion whatsoever. Poor Rob. His heart had to be ripped to shreds. What if her grandpa was waiting at their destination? Would she be able to hold herself together?

"Load him up before we attract any attention," Bayeth barked at the men.

They buckled Rob into the seat behind her and slammed the van door shut. The other demon opened the front passenger door. "That's a wrap, boys. We'll take it from here." He hopped in and shut the door.

"Kathy," Rob continued. "Stay strong." He kicked the back of Bayeth's seat. "Let her go, you bitch. Let her go or we'll kill you."

"Matt. Are you with it?" Victoria whispered while Rob had Bayeth's attention.

"Yeah. My head is killing me, but I'll be okay."

Rob continued his rant, cursing Bayeth and trying his best to assure Kathy that everything was going to be okay.

The van jerked forward. Matt was ten steps behind, and time was no longer on their side. "Cross over. We can talk in there."

"What in the hell happened?" Matt appeared fully alert.

"No time for the full story. They found us. They want us alive. They're using Rob for insurance that we cooperate. It looks like we're about to meet Bromley... Dmoltech."

Matt nodded. *"I don't like the odds. Two of them plus Dmoltech. We need to do something before we get there."*

"I agree. I have an idea."

Matt nodded. *"What?"*

"We can't do anything to Kathy. We can't risk hurting her for Rob's sake, and the fact that she's driving."

"Get to the point," Matt urged.

"On three, we grab the demon in the guy, and pull him out."

"Works for me. One, two, three."

As hoped, the demon was caught completely off guard. As soon as its ugly head cleared the back of the headrest, the Warrior struck.

"Fuck!" Bayeth slammed on the brakes. She spun around and pressed a gun into Rob's face. "If I feel anything at all, he's dead."

"Don't shoot!" Matt yelled.

The plan had worked, but Bayeth was beyond pissed. Victoria needed to calm her down before she killed Rob. "We won't touch you. I promise. Perhaps we can make a—"

The man in the front seat started to scream. He must've regained control of his body and was coming unglued. Bayeth turned and fired the gun. His head practically exploded, spaying chunks of his brains all over the window.

"No!" This was all her fault. It was her plan and now an innocent man was dead. "We won't do anything. Please. No more killing."

"That's completely up to you." Bayeth's voice was eerily calm, considering everything that had just happened. She unfastened Rob's seatbelt. "Lie between the front seats with your face to the floor. Slowly."

The gun remained against his head the entire time. Bayeth put the van back in gear and drove off. "The remainder of this trip is going to go without incident, or Rob dies."

CHAPTER 59

Matt and Victoria walked ahead of Rob as they climbed the stairs from the back entrance to The Cathedral. There was nothing else they could do. Bayeth still had the gun against Rob's head.

They were ordered to stop in front of a steel door. Bayeth entered a code on a keypad, and it slid open. They walked into an office, where Bromley was seated at his desk.

"Look at his eyes," Victoria whispered.

Matt was already staring at them. Rather than the red glow of the Shakath, Bromley's were completely black. It was like staring at two black holes.

"We finally meet." Bromley rose and motioned to his couch. "Have a seat."

"We'd prefer to stand." Matt checked if the Warrior had appeared and was relieved to see him next to Victoria. "Besides, that would be a little tough with these." He turned and displayed his bound wrists.

"My apologies." Bromley turned to Bayeth. "That's no way to treat my guests."

"Sorry, sir." She pulled a small blade from her leather boot and cut the bindings.

Matt exchanged glances with Victoria. Bromley's confidence clearly had her rattled.

"That's better." Bromley smiled. "May I offer you and your second a drink? Perhaps a smoke?" He took a cigar for himself and lit it.

"No thanks." Damnit. Lawrence had obviously told him about Victoria's transformation. He likely knew everything. "I see you've brought your Warrior as well. I assume we are to battle?"

Matt's mouth went dry. They were in deep shit.

Bromley drew on the cigar. "Cat got your tongues?"

"We're not here to fight," Matt replied, trying to sound unshaken. "We'd like to make a deal."

"Really?" Bromley chuckled. "You want your friends back."

"Yes," Victoria answered. "Unharmed and demon-free."

"And what could you two possibly have that I want?"

"The location of the statue?" Had either of them told Lawrence the exact spot?

He laughed again. "I know where it is. Or I should say, where it was. One of my Shakath is probably smashing it to pieces as we speak. I learned that it was near Petropolis days ago. And when the old man was possessed, his mind revealed its exact location."

"Of course you know about that one. There's another, and there are more of us." Victoria recovered beautifully.

"Bullshit." Bromley was unfazed by the attempt.

Matt wasn't ready to abandon the plan. What else could he possibly do when Bromley held all the cards? Matt took a step toward Dmoltech, reached up, and pulled the Cuban from his mouth. "Maybe I will have one after all." He had to look like he was still in control. "You have no idea who you're facing." He exhaled a cloud of cigar smoke into the demon's face.

Bromley's sidesplitting laughter filled the room. "You're funny! And bold. I like those qualities. You would've made a good Shakath." He took his cigar back from Matt.

Matt had hoped to unnerve Bromley, but he hadn't even come close. He retreated to Rob and Victoria, who were still standing near the door. "Run!" He spun to open the door and was horrified to see a keypad in place of a handle. "Shit."

"You weren't thinking of leaving so soon, were you? We still have business to attend to." Bromley was now sitting behind his desk, feet up on the table.

"We were hoping to make a deal." Maybe he could still salvage the situation.

Bromley shrugged. "You already said that. What's to deal?"

"If you release our friends, we'll promise to leave you alone to do whatever it is you do."

He raised an eyebrow. "You'll trade the fate of the world for a dying old man and that guy's bitch?" He pointed to Rob.

"Fate of the world?" Victoria asked.

"We're not here to run nightclubs and snort coke, although it *has* been fun."

"Look," Matt began. "I don't care about whatever you're up to. I care about my friends. You're a businessman. You make deals. We could make a deal. Let them go and we won't bother you anymore. They're innocent. Please. It's the right thing to do.

"You're mistaken if you're expecting sympathy from me. You've inconvenienced me, you've overestimated your abilities, and it's going to cost you dearly. Bayeth," Bromley ordered, "once the battle begins, I don't want you interfering at all. They are mine and mine alone. Is that clear?"

"Yes, sir. What about Rob?"

"Kill him."

The impact of the bullet tearing through Rob's chest

echoed through the room. Matt stood terrified as his friend's t-shirt turned from white to red. Rob's left leg buckled, and he toppled over onto the floor. Matt went numb as the room spun around him. He grabbed Victoria for support. Rage ignited in his soul, and he turned to face Bromley. "You bastard!" Matt clenched his fists. "You didn't have to do that!" He fought back the tears. "You're a dead man."

Bromley ignored Matt's threat, lifted his arm, and pointed his index finger at Victoria. A fiery sphere materialized in front of his outstretched hand. The orange and red globe, which looked like a softball made of molten lava, crackled and hissed as it accelerated across the room toward her. The Warrior leaped in front of her and deflected it with his sword. The ball of fire exploded on the floor, causing the carpet to burst into flames. Another one followed, almost getting through.

He wasn't going to lose her too.

"You fucking bastard." He turned to Bromley, eyes locked on his target.

His war cry resonated above the sound of the explosions as he sprinted toward the demon.

Dmoltech fired the burning spheres at Victoria until Matt was almost on top of him then turned his attack on Matt.

The fireball struck Matt in the chest as he leaped over the desk. It burned right through his clothing and continued until it hit bone. The force of the impact knocked Matt aside, and he collapsed on the floor at Dmoltech's feet. His body went numb as he beat at the flames, trying to extinguish them.

Victoria cried out in horror.

Dmoltech turned his attention back to her. "There's only one Warrior between the two of you, and I can play this game all day."

Thick smoke from the spreading fires reached the smoke detector and triggered the alarm.

"And now it's your turn, you stupid bitch. The Warrior can fight your spiritual battles for you, but he's useless against a bullet."

Matt grabbed at Dmoltech's leg but couldn't stop him from reaching into his desk drawer and pulling out a gun.

While Matt struggled to get to his feet, the shock of his injury yielded to pain. He dropped back to his knees. His body shook uncontrollably and no matter how hard he willed it, he couldn't stand. Couldn't do anything to help her. The outer edges of his vision turned black. He fought to regain focus, but the room slowly faded away. Rob was dead, he was lost, and Victoria would soon be joining them. He'd given everything he had, but it wasn't enough.

Matt surrendered. *Help me, God.* His body went limp as he slipped into unconsciousness.

Matt jolted upright. Cold water from the sprinkler system poured down on him. He drove his foot into Bromley's shin just as the gun went off. The bullet lodged in the steel door, inches from Victoria's head.

Matt kicked again, this time into the side of Bromley's knee. The sound of popping cartilage, accompanied by the man's scream, announced that Bromley was going down. Matt jumped on top of him, slamming his head repeatedly into the floor.

"Say goodbye, motherfucker!" Matt crossed over into the Crimson Dimension. "Victoria! Come hold him down."

Dmoltech sprang out of Bromley's body and landed on his feet beside them. Matt spun to face him.

The Naygid, commander of the Shakath, stood up, clearing the ten-foot ceiling by mere inches. Like the Warrior, he had a powerful body and massive wings;

however, his skin was blackened and charred and his wings leathery and worn. Regardless of Dmoltech's weathered exterior, there was no question that he and the Warrior were of the same breed. And there was no denying the power he possessed.

Dmoltech now stood between Matt and Victoria. Matt waited for the angel's flaming sword to take the monster's head, but the strike never came. The Warrior remained with Victoria, protecting her from the demon's resumed volley of fireballs.

Matt's spirit left his injured body on the floor and sprinted toward Dmoltech. Three translucent, tentacle-like appendages protruded from Dmoltech's back. Two appeared to go on forever before disappearing from sight, but the third was connected to Kathy. There were three more, apparently severed, oozing a black, oily liquid. Perhaps a weakness. Matt lunged forward and grabbed them.

Dmoltech let out a shriek and arched his back. His leathery wings snapped together. The force knocked Matt backward onto the floor.

Matt got to his feet as the demon fired a series of fireballs at him. He twisted and rolled out of the way just in time. A sickening stench of scorched flesh and brain tissue filled Matt's nostrils as the fireballs struck the unconscious Mitchell Bromley in the forehead. The top of Bromley's head was gone. Matt shuddered. It could've been him lying there.

As he'd hoped, his attack had taken Dmoltech's attention away from Victoria and the Warrior. The angel was free to engage. Dmoltech spun and deflected his sword with a powerful explosion, sending the weapon clattering to the floor. The two beings launched at each other, locked grips, and fought for the upper hand.

Victoria ran to Matt's body. "Are you okay?"

"Yeah," he panted. He fought to remain conscious as the spiritual battle raged around him.

The angel and the demon battled each other with fevered intensity. Fireballs exploded throughout the room as Dmoltech tried to hit the Warrior, and, finally, the demon's efforts paid off. The angel was losing ground. Without his sword, he could only defend, and if they didn't help him, the fight would soon be over.

"*Get him his sword*," Matt told Victoria as she joined him through the veil.

Despite the pain, he ignored his body's message to quit, and leaped back into the mix. It was all Matt could do to remain conscious, but he hoped he could slow Dmoltech enough to give the Warrior a chance until Victoria retrieved the sword.

Materializing out of the hazy background, Victoria appeared with the flaming sword in hand. She ran toward the battle and thrust it through the charred, leathery skin of Dmoltech's back. Dmoltech let out a bloodcurdling cry and reeled backward, knocking Victoria across the room.

Matt lunged for the sword and pulled it from Dmoltech's back. The edge caught two of the tentacles, slicing them clean off. They exploded in a flash of lightning, and Kathy collapsed. Dmoltech screamed and launched away from Matt, toward the Warrior.

Without the sword, the Warrior suffered another fiery blast. He staggered backward and fell to the floor.

"You're mine!" Dmoltech formed another fireball, undoubtedly the last the angel could take.

Matt ran toward Dmoltech and swung the sword with all his might.

The blade struck demonic flesh and sliced right into his bony neck. Dmoltech's grotesque head hit the ground with a thud.

Time stood still while Matt raised the sword and waited, unsure if Dmoltech's decapitation was indeed victory, or if, perhaps, two more heads were about to sprout from his oozing neck.

"I think we did it," Victoria said as she reached his side.

Matt kept his eyes focused on Dmoltech while the remaining tentacle turned to dust, and millions of tiny flames ignited and danced over Dmoltech's charred skin. They consumed his head and body within seconds. Nothing remained.

The Warrior, panting, burnt, and bloodied, strode to Matt and reached out for his sword. He vanished the moment he closed his hand around the grip.

The deafening alarm, the sprinkler's spray, and the raging fire demanded Matt's attention. He returned to the physical realm. The full pain of his injury rushed back. Thick black smoke had replaced most of the breathable air.

"Victoria!" Matt rushed to her and grabbed her hand.

"Let's get out of here." She was coughing hard.

"Hang on." Matt ran to Rob. Knowing it was futile, he still tried to wake him up. "Come on, Rob. You have to be alive." He shook his lifeless body.

Matt started chest compressions. Blood bubbled out of the bullet hole with every thrust. He looked to Victoria for help. Her expression told him what he didn't want to hear.

She put her hand on Matt's back. "Matt. I'm sorry, but he's gone. Kathy is too. I can't find a pulse."

"Maybe if we just—"

"Matt." She gripped his arm. "We have to go. There's nothing we can do for them."

CHAPTER 60

The morning sun had just crested when they got back to their hotel. It was a dangerous move, but they had nowhere else to go. After satisfying themselves that their hotel wasn't being watched, they slipped into the safety of their room.

Matt looked horrible. His blood-soaked shirt and bruised cheek paled in comparison to his empty eyes. It was hard to imagine how he felt, knowing that he blamed himself for Rob and Kathy's deaths. A tear ran down her face. Had her grandpa suffered the same fate? Had Dmoltech's death killed everyone bonded to him?

Matt had shut off. Her attempts to comfort him were met with silence and he barely even winced while she cleaned his wounds.

"We need to get out of here." Those were the first words he'd spoken since leaving The Cathedral. "Why don't you grab a quick shower while I keep watch."

Victoria stepped into the hot shower. The water felt wonderful as it flowed through her hair and cascaded over her body. Gray sooty water spiraled down the drain until it eventually cleared. If only their problems could be taken care of that easily.

She wrapped a towel around her body, left the bathroom, and sat on the bed.

Matt sat beside her and stroked her hair. "Let's get you dressed. We've got to go."

"In a minute. You need to shower as well." She peeled

off his shirt and took another look at the burn. "Wow." It looked a little better than before her shower. "It's stopped bleeding." Did they perhaps have some healing powers? Matt's hand had healed soon after he'd first been transformed. Time would tell, but regardless, he needed some antibiotic cream before it got infected.

"Try to rest while I shower," Matt said. "It might be a long time before we have a bed again." Matt finished undressing and stepped under the streaming water.

Victoria walked over to the window and stared between the curtains. Her grandpa had to be out there, somewhere. He couldn't be gone. She collapsed onto the bed as tears poured down her face. What would she do without him? He'd been her rock since her parents died.

"Hey, hey." Matt was done and back at her side. "We'll be okay."

"I need to find out what happened to Grandpa."

"There's a good chance he survived. We won't give up until we know."

Victoria wiped the tears from eyes. She had to stay strong. "He's the only family I—" Her hands started to shake. "What day is it today?"

"Wednesday. Why?"

"Please no... I can't lose him today of all days."

"Why? I don't understand."

The tears came again. "Today is the day my parents died."

Matt grabbed Victoria and hugged her. "Even God can't be that cruel. He's got to be alive."

Victoria managed a weak nod.

"Hey." Matt patted her hands. "Grab your stuff. We need to get as far away from this town as we can."

Victoria's heart sank. Matt was right, but they would never find her grandpa if they left New York. She would likely never find out if he was safe, or even alive. She couldn't bear being unable to say goodbye at least. She wiped more tears from eyes and grabbed her coat. "Promise me we'll find Grandpa."

"Of course," Matt replied. "We just need some time to regroup and let things calm down. We'll figure out how to find him and make sure he's okay."

Matt's logic was weak, but he had to be right. God wouldn't let her lose her grandpa on the anniversary of her parents' passing. No matter what, she would never give up hope.

"I'm ready." She nodded and gave Matt a determined smile. "As soon as I visit my parents' graves."

CHAPTER 61

Victoria paused at the entrance to Brooklyn's Green-Wood Cemetery. It always amazed her that the towering structure was referred to as a gate. Calling it that was like calling the Mona Lisa a finger painting. Walking through the spectacular Gothic Revival style arches, crowned by their intricately carved pinnacled gables, made her feel like she was entering a portal into the eighteen hundreds. The four sculptured panels, depicting the themes of death and resurrection, had always offered her the promise that she would be reunited with her mother and father someday.

They made their way along the winding roads, past trees, sculptures, monuments, and mausoleums, to her parents' resting place. The cold wind bit her hands as she carried small bouquet of flowers.

"It's just over there," she said, pointing away from the road toward a snow-covered pond. "They're close to that mausoleum."

"Take all the time you need. I'll wait here." Matt slouched down on a nearby bench.

Victoria left the plowed asphalt and walked the last fifty yards to her parents' plot through the ankle-deep snow. Hers were the only footprints blemishing the perfect white landscape. Spotting their headstones, she finished her trek.

Her heart almost stopped when a figure appeared from behind the nearby mausoleum. There was no mistaking her grandfather's familiar silhouette as, cane in hand, he closed the gap between them. Her heart stopped. She'd walked right into a trap. Victoria scanned the area for more red eyes. Wait. She spun back to her grandpa. His tired brown eyes stared lovingly at her.

"Grandpa!" she shouted as she ran to meet him. She threw her arms around him. "Are you okay?" The demon was gone. Her stomach was calm.

"Other than a few bumps and bruises. I hoped you would come today. You know I wouldn't miss it for the world."

"I was so worried about you." Tears of joy streamed down her face. "I was afraid you were dead."

"Quite the opposite. Last night, I was hit by a force and a blinding light that knocked me off my feet. When I regained my wits, the demon was gone."

Matt slid to a halt beside them. "Thank God you're alive! We were so worried that you... I don't get it, but I'm so happy to see you."

Victoria replayed the series of events. "I don't know if your cord was cut off or the one that dissolved after Dmoltech died... Perhaps—" Victoria stopped talking. Matt had cut Kathy's cord. The last thing he needed was another reason to blame himself for everything.

Lawrence, looking puzzled, turned to Matt and placed a hand on his shoulder. "I'm so sorry, Matt. I heard they found Rob at The Cathedral last night. It's been all over the news this morning. You and Kathy have my deepest sympathy."

Matt shook his head. "Kathy was with him. We lost her too."

"No, they rescued her from the fire. She's in hospital in a coma."

"That's incredible," Victoria hugged him. "She's alive!"

Matt took a huge breath, his expression impossible to read. "Is she going to make it?"

"That's what they say. And I suspect that she was freed like I was."

"That's fantastic," Victoria said. Things weren't as bleak as they'd first seemed. She took Matt's hand. "Rob would be grateful to know you saved her. He wanted that more than anything."

"Yeah." Matt nodded. "If only we could've saved him too."

Nothing she could say would lessen his grief. She knew that all too well. Only time would help. "I'm so sorry." She kissed his cheek.

"Yeah, well... I don't want to rush you, but we really shouldn't be here longer than we have to." He motioned back to the bench. "I'll head up and give you two a minute."

"Thank you, Matt," Lawrence said. "You look exhausted. My car's just over there." He handed him the keys and pointed to the roadway.

Victoria turned and stared at the granite monument. *In loving memory of Timothy and Elizabeth Brooks. Beloved by all who knew them.* The words were so empty. They didn't even come close to expressing what her parents had meant to her.

"I miss them."

"Me too." His embrace warmed her heart. "Now let's get out of the cold, shall we?"

Victoria held Lawrence's hand as they made their way back to the car. Things were going to be fine. Deep down, she knew it. "I'm driving, old man." She smiled. "I can walk faster than you drive."

Matt jumped out and helped Lawrence into the car. "So now what?"

"We have to get you two out of the country."

Matt nodded. "Where will we go?"

"Rio, of course. It makes the most sense. You need to speak to the priest."

Victoria hopped into the driver's seat. "What about Kathy?"

"I'll see to it that she receives the proper care."

"Thank you," Matt said. There was a hint of hope in his eyes.

Victoria smiled. She'd come full circle, having started with plans to visit the church. Now she would see the statue with her own eyes— "Wait. Dmoltech sent a Shakath there to destroy the statue."

"Shit." Matt slammed his hand on the back of the front seat.

Lawrence turned to Matt. "Maybe you killed Dmoltech before the demon got there."

Matt nodded. "Yeah. Let's hope so." He looked out the window for a moment. "There's only one way to find out. But how are we going to get there? We'll never get through airport security."

"Don't worry about that." Lawrence smiled. "I know a few people who can get us there completely under the radar."

Victoria couldn't believe her ears. "Grandpa?"

"Come now." He was blushing. "Do you think I could've acquired my collection playing strictly by the rules?"

CHAPTER 62

The road narrowed and became increasingly rough as Matt and Victoria made their way to Father Devante's church. He turned the rented jeep onto the narrow trail that wound through the jungle on the last leg of the journey.

Lawrence had stayed behind at the private estate he'd rented for their stay. It was amazing how easy it had been for them to leave the States and enter Rio without being caught. Apparently, anything was possible with the right connections and enough money.

Memories of the life-altering day flooded his mind as they drew closer to their destination. Had the Shakath found the church? Was Father Devante okay?

"It's just up ahead." He recognized the spot where he'd been accosted by the priest and his men. "This is where it all started."

"Don't worry. Whatever we find, we'll be okay."

It had been three weeks to the day since Matt had set his eyes on the statue. So much had happened in such a short time. He'd changed from a self-proclaimed atheist struggling to find his place into...into... He still wasn't sure. He'd never thought he'd say it, but God was real, and He cared, at least a little, about the human race. Nevertheless, there were a lot of issues they still had to work out.

Rob's death was by far the hardest thing to deal with, although it was also the force that drove him to keep going. There was no time for sorrow. Matt funneled his emotions into something more productive. Anger. There were five more groups of Shakath out there. They would all pay with their lives.

Victoria balanced him. She was everything, literally his soulmate. He'd never felt so loved and accepted in his life. It was hard to imagine how two diametrically opposed yet equally powerful emotions could live inside him. They needed to be kept separate. One could never taint the other.

The car rounded the last bend in the road, and the village opened up before them.

"Oh my God!" Matt hit the brakes hard. He shut the motor off, jumped out, and walked the rest of the distance to the church. His eyes were fixed on the charred remains of the brick exterior. The roof was gone, and the bells that had hung in the towers had fallen from their perches. A gaping hole was all that was left of the magnificent stained-glass window. When he reached the entrance and looked in, there was nothing but ash and rubble. On its side, broken into four pieces, lay the blackened marble image of Christ.

Matt grabbed a piece of a burned pew and hurled it across the sanctuary. His war cry surprised him as much as it obviously did Victoria. She stood there, mouth wide open.

"Matt. Are you all right?" She looked deeply concerned, almost afraid. "There's nothing else we could've done." She placed a comforting hand on his shoulder. "We did our best."

"It wasn't enough."

Victoria walked over to the fallen statue. "This was the statue?" Her voice trembled.

Matt nodded.

She picked up a piece and ran her finger along the

detailing. "Rob said this was the last one, hidden from them for decades."

"Yeah." Matt picked up a piece of the rock and hurled it. "That makes us the last of the Torren."

The ensuing silence was broken when a man appeared in a doorway at the opposite end of the sanctuary. "Who's there? What do you want?"

There was no mistaking Father Devante's thickly accented English. Matt rushed through the maze of debris separating them.

"*¡Dios santo!*" Devante exclaimed. "You are alive! My prayers have been answered."

Thank God he welcomed them. Devante would've had every right to hate Matt for what he'd done. He took Devante's outstretched hand and shook it enthusiastically.

"I imagine you have a story to tell."

"We sure do." Matt began as Victoria joined him. "I'd first like to introduce you to Victoria."

"Welcome to what is left of my church." He looked both pleased and distressed. "May I assume that you also have the gift?"

"I'm honored to meet you," Victoria answered. "And yes, I have it too. We came seeking your help."

He gave Victoria a warm smile. "Then all is not lost."

Matt looked back at the broken statue. How could Devante be so optimistic with everything in ruins?

"We must leave for the Vatican without delay," Father Devante announced. "His Holiness will be most pleased to receive you."

The End

ABOUT THE AUTHOR

Drawing inspiration from the remote landscapes and the isolated environments of Alberta Canada, author **D.A. VandenBrink** writes stories of speculative fiction. The thrilling plots and sub-plots of characters with intriguing and conflicting agendas helped create the series *The Crimson Dimension*. He is known for his passion for supernatural thrillers, horror, and the paranormal.